A FATHER FOR CHRISTMAS

LYNN STORY

I0641425

To Larry with love

CHAPTER ONE

The chilly October air hit Sherry in the face as she stepped outside ushering her son Wyatt to the car.

"Zip up your coat."

Wyatt whined. "Mom, I'm just walking to the car."

She sighed indulgently, "yes, I know sweetie." They were already behind schedule, she hoped she could drop him off at Seaboard middle school and still beat the traffic downtown to work.

She tried to keep her voice light and cheery.

"I just don't want you to catch a cold and be sick for the holidays."

"Who cares?" He mumbled as he climbed into the back seat.

The holidays were hard without her husband. It'd been four years since the accident that claimed his life and left Wyatt injured. For her son, the holidays were especially difficult. Not only did he feel the loss of his father more deeply, but because of the brain injury he suffered in the accident, the holidays, especially Christmas, could be sensory overload. She struggled to make it enjoyable for him.

The drive to school was short, and Wyatt could have walked the distance, but it was on her way to work, so dropping him off was easy and it gave her a few more minutes in her day with him. Not that they were sharing much quality time together this morning. She maneuvered the minivan into the drop offline, narrowly avoiding a school bus pulling away from the curb. Glancing in the rearview mirror, she saw Wyatt frown.

"Everything alright?"

Removing his headphones, he looked at her.

"I said, is everything alright?" she repeated.

"I guess so." He was watching a group of kids that had just gotten off the bus. "You can stop here."

She inched up a little further so the next car could slide in behind her. She had barely stopped when Wyatt opened the door to get out.

"Have a good day," she called out quickly. Wyatt's reply was closing the van door. She watched him go, hoping the older kids were going to be nice to him as the car behind her honked its horn. She waved and then pulled away to drive downtown to work at Port City Industries.

Port City Industries was the largest employer in Gates Point, the downtown office alone had nearly two-hundred fifty employees. Most of the companies' employees in Gates Point worked in the shipyard along the river, building and rehabbing Navy ships and submarines.

In addition to the Port City employees in the downtown office there were several companies that leased space in the building, and it seemed like they were all trying to pull into the underground parking garage at the same time this morning. Sherry checked the time. It was seven forty-five. Drumming her fingers impatiently on the steering wheel she waited for her turn to go through the gate. She had a reserved spot, so she wasn't worried about finding a place to park, but the elevators would be crowded, and she would probably have to endure several stops on her way to the twenty-fifth floor.

Finally, alone in the elevator and her patience worn thin, her mind was preoccupied with the things she needed to do today.

She was worrying about Wyatt at school and didn't see Kay Dandridge, CEO and Owner of Port City Industries, as they almost collided.

"Whoa!" Kay's voice snapped Sherry back to the present.

"Sorry, Kay."

"You, okay?"

"Yeah, just a little pre-occupied this morning." Sherry noticed Kay was holding a small stack of files. "Where are you going with those?"

"I came in early and was organizing my office. I thought I'd save you some work and file these."

Sherry hurried to her desk to set her purse and coffee down. "Oh, no you don't."

"Why not?"

"Because I have a system and I don't want you messing with it."

Kay feigned surprise. "Why do you think I would mess with your system?"

"No one touches the files until I have reviewed them." She took the files and glanced over them briefly before placing them on her desk.

Kay looked at her long-time personal assistant. "That seems a bit unnecessary."

"Really? Okay, can you tell me if those files are also available digitally?"

Kay blinked. "I have no idea."

"Exactly! I will get to them this morning." Sherry said, removing her coat.

"Okay, okay." Kay laughed.

"And just for future reference, that goes for any other documents coming out of your office." Sherry glared at Kay while trying to hide a smile. She loved working for Kay, and she was grateful that their relationship was one that she could send her boss packing back into her office without fear of reprisal.

"Yes, ma'am." Kay turned back to her office, leaving the door open.

Sherry sighed at the stack of files. Those were not part of her list of things to do today, and she needed to think seriously about what to do for Wyatt for Christmas. She knew he was working on a wish list, but he didn't have the same enthusiasm for it the way he used to. He was too old for Santa, although she tried to keep the spirit alive. She put her things away and went into Kay's office to make coffee, only to find Kay had beat her to it. "What gives?"

"What?" Kay was the picture of innocence.

"First you are trying to do the filing and now you've made your own coffee? Something is rotten in Denmark."

"You are far too young to be that cynical. Besides, I told you I came in early."

Sherry placed her hands on her hips. "Why?"

"Why what?"

"Why did you come in early?"

"Oh, I don't know." She shrugged, "Ethan is working a big case, and he was up early, and I didn't feel like sitting around the house alone."

Sherry shook her head as she walked back towards the open office door, intent on returning to her desk. "You need a hobby and working extra hours, isn't it."

"You're just mad because I touched the files." Kay teased.

"I'm not mad, but I seriously do have a system."

"I totally believe you." Kay shook her head in amusement. "Not to change the subject, but how's Wyatt?"

Sherry sighed involuntarily. "I'm not sure. He says he's okay."

"I'm sure he would tell you if something was wrong." Kay tried to be comforting.

"I'm not so sure anymore. He's getting older. He'll be a teenager in a year and a half, and he is already starting to act like one."

"What do you mean?"

"He is brooding most of the time. He hardly ever takes those damn headphones off. When I ask if everything is alright, he just mumbles that it is and puts the headphones back on. I tell you Kay; I don't think I like where this is going."

"Wyatt's a good kid. He isn't having trouble at school, is he?"

"None that any of his teachers have called me about. But this morning I caught him looking at some kids that had gotten off the bus and he didn't look happy to see them."

"Did you ask him about them?"

"Of course."

"What did he say?"

"That everything was fine."

Kay got up and came over to Sherry. "Why don't you sit down for a minute, the phones and the files can wait."

Sherry was reluctant but sat down in a guest chair while Kay poured her a cup of coffee.

"I honestly don't know what to do."

"What do you mean?" Kay asked.

"I mean, I am trying to make things as normal for him as possible and the harder I try, the less normal things seem. Especially, the holidays."

"Is he still seeing a counselor?"

"Yes."

"Are you?"

"No, I don't have time."

Kay frowned, "Yes, you do. The company pays for it, and you can make an appointment during work hours."

Sherry shook her head, "I can't do that."

"Why not?"

"Because I'm not a slacker. I will not let my work suffer so I can go tell someone my problems. Problems, they cannot solve for me, so it is a waste of time."

Kay could see Sherry was getting agitated. "Okay, you don't have to go, but you need to take care of yourself so you can take care of your boy."

"Just when am I supposed to do that? He has after school stuff like soccer."

Kay didn't want to upset her, so she put a hand on Sherry's arm, "I don't have all the answers either, but just promise me you'll take care of you."

Sherry smiled, "I promise."

"Okay then. Let's get to work."

"You got it." Sherry returned to her desk and tackled the files on her desk.

James Ian "Mac" McIntyre, Naval Criminal Investigative Service Director, sat staring at his computer screen. He had been reviewing case files for two hours and he was tired of staring at the monitor. He leaned back and rubbed his eyes.

"Excuse me, director?"

"What is it, Trina?"

Trina Williams, his administrative assistant, was standing at his door. I'm going to leave for the day. "Do you need anything?"

"A vacation."

She smiled, "Yes, sir."

"Have a good night, Trina."

Mac leaned back in his chair. A vacation was something he had rarely taken. Minimizing the screen, he opened his email and took a deep breath while typing out a message to his boss, telling him he was going to take a few days off. Then he sent a second one to Trina and Gary Monroe his assistant director letting them know he would be out of the office and out of reach for a few days. He then he shut down his computer collected his badge, gun and cell phone from his desk drawer and headed home. He was cooking a burger when his cell phone buzzed with an incoming call.

"McIntyre, here."

"Are you serious? You're taking a few days off?" The Secretary of the Navy's gruff voice barked over the phone.

"That a problem, sir?"

"No, I was just making sure I read your email correctly."

Mac smiled, "Yes, sir."

"Where are you going?"

"I have no idea, fishing probably."

"Well, just have a good time. See you in a few days."

Mac clicked off.

He had put little thought into where he would go or what he would do. He stared at his phone, then sent a text to Kay Dandridge before he lost his nerve. They hadn't talked in several months and as far as he knew, she was still in love with FBI Special Agent Ethan Craddock, but he didn't know where else to go or who else to call. It was a sad commentary on his social life. His boss, who was Kay's grandfather, had introduced them to each other a couple of years ago. They had dated very briefly, and she had opened his eyes and heart to the possibility of having a relationship again. But, as luck would have it, just about the time he thought a relationship with Kay was something he could do, she reconnected with a long-lost love and just as easily as she walked into his life; she walked out. In fairness, they had kept in touch, but it wasn't the same. Mac wasn't sure if he could be friends with her now that he knew he could love again.

It was an hour later before he received a response from Kay.

"Can't wait to see you, call me the minute you get to town."

He smiled to himself, well at least she was still talking to him. He packed a bag and closed his house. Leaving late at night meant traffic should be light. He rolled down the windows to let the cool night air keep him alert while driving.

The drive to Gates Point proved to be relaxing. Arriving just before midnight, he found a hotel downtown and checked in for four days.

Once settled in his room Mac sent Kay another text. "In town."

"Breakfast tomorrow?"

"Where?"

"Stacks, it's near my office. Think you can find it?"

"Yes."

"See you at 7am?"

"See you then." Mac smiled to himself. He knew he was playing with fire. Kay was deeply in love with Ethan and had been for years. But for now, he was going to focus on the fact that he would see Kay again. He stared out his hotel window thinking of how he and Ethan Craddock were friends and that Kay's grandfather could kill his career if Mac did anything to hurt his beloved granddaughter. It was a risk he was willing to take. He had no intention of causing problems for Kay in her relationship with Ethan, but he was still drawn to her for reasons that he couldn't explain even to himself.

"Did you read this note the school counselor sent home?" Sherry asked as Wyatt stood in the kitchen drinking milk with the refrigerator door open.

"No, they said it was for you."

"Close the door and sit down, please."

"Tell me what is going on at school? I don't want to hear it from a teacher."

He said down and shrugged.

"Are the classes too hard?"

"No, I'm not stupid!"

"No one ever said you were stupid. Why would you think a thing like that?"

"Because..."

Sherry was growing concerned by the minute. "Because why?"

"The classes are boring; they are for dumb kids."

"Okay, first you know better than to call people dumb or stupid."

Wyatt kicked his foot against the table leg. "Whatever."

"I've had enough of your attitude lately, young man. If you have an issue at school, I need to know about it. I can't fix it if I don't know what the problem is." She waited a moment to give him a chance to answer. When he didn't, she ploughed on, "Are you having problems with bullies at school?"

"You want to know what the problem is?" He shouted.

"Yes, I do." She said calmly, trying to keep her own anger in check. It was times like these she missed her husband.

"I'm tired of everyone treating me like I can't do something. These classes are boring, and I'm not stupid. I don't need to be in special classes. There is nothing wrong with my brain. And yes, kids tease me at school. They tease all of us that are in the special classes and I'm tired of it."

"Okay, that's good. I didn't know any of that. So, I can talk to the teachers and see about getting you into different classes, ones that you will enjoy. Does that sound okay with you?"

She watched as her son relaxed a bit and stopped kicking the table leg. He made eye contact with her. "You can do that?"

"Of course I can."

"Okay, cool."

Sherry smiled. "Now go start on your homework if you have any and I'll start on dinner."

"How about I cook dinner and you do my homework." Wyatt laughed.

"Nice try, kid." Sherry laughed, shooing him out of the kitchen.

She leaned against the counter and sighed. Well, that was done. She congratulated herself on a minor victory. Parenting was hard enough. Being a single mom was something else entirely. Her heart squeezed at the thought of her late husband.

She had moved through her grieving, but sometimes she missed having a partner; someone to help her with these moments. She often wondered if she had been there, things may have turned out differently. Maybe she could have seen the on-coming car in time, or if she had been driving at least Wyatt would still have his father right now. Sherry looked towards Wyatt's bedroom door, now closed. She knew he hadn't told her everything and she would have to call and schedule a meeting with the school counselor. She needed to get to the bottom of things and maybe even have Wyatt retested. If he wasn't learning anything in the classes, she would have him moved and the sooner the better.

She pushed the thoughts aside as she pulled chicken from the refrigerator and put it in the air fryer, then chopped vegetables for a salad. She had bought a small pie for them to have for dessert tonight.

Wyatt emerged from his room just as she was putting dinner on the table. "Is that pie I smell?"

"Yes, we will have pie for dessert tonight if that is okay with you."

"Awesome!" He sat down at the table.

When she joined him, "Okay, you know the rules, what is one positive thing that happened to you today?"

Wyatt thought for a moment, "I didn't get beat up today for being a nerd, I didn't get into trouble, and I scored a goal at soccer practice."

Sherry smiled, "Fair enough."

"What about you mom, what was your positive thing today?"

"I prevented a disaster in the file room." She smiled, handing him a plate of salad and chicken.

"Really? What happened? Did the files blow up or something?"

"No, why would you think the files would blow up?"

"You said, disaster."

"Well, that's true I did, but no. Ms. Dandridge got to work early this morning and she almost filed some documents on her own before letting me check them."

"That doesn't sound so bad. Why can't she file them? She owns the company, right?"

"Yes, that is true, but I oversee the records room and I have a system. Ms. Dandridge doesn't know the system and she could have messed things up if she had gone into the file room without help."

"Wow, sounds like you boss Ms. Dandridge around just like you do to me."

"I don't boss anyone around, eat your dinner." She said, smiling.

"Bossy."

Sherry laughed. He was such a smart kid and with that came a sharp wit that she sometimes wished he didn't have. She got up to take the pie out of the oven.

When Wyatt finished his dinner, he announced he was ready for dessert.

"You want it now and not later while watching TV?" she teased.

"Now, please. It smells great."

"Do you want ice cream with it?"

His eyes got big, "Yes ma'am."

Sherry gave him a piece of apple pie with vanilla ice cream.

"Don't eat it too fast and give yourself a headache."

"I know I'm not a little kid."

It made Sherry sad to admit he was right. "You're right, I apologize."

She served herself pie and ice cream and joined him at the table.

"Listen son, I don't want us to have secrets, okay. So, you tell me anytime you are having a problem at school, and I will make sure it is taken care of, okay?"

"Yes ma'am."

"Thank you."

"Will you tell me if you are having a problem at work?"

"Do you want me to?"

"If we don't keep secrets."

"Yes, you're right. Okay, it's a deal. I'll tell you if there is a problem at work."

Wyatt smiled; he had his father's smile. "I'll do the dishes." He offered.

"I'll help you."

CHAPTER TWO

"Kay, do you mind if I'm a little late tomorrow? I need to talk to the school counselor."

Looking up from her desk, Kay asked, "is everything alright?"

"I'm not sure. Wyatt is struggling with his classes. He says they are boring, and that people treat him like he is dumb. I think I am going to have him tested again and maybe see about getting him out of the developmental classes."

"Okay, sure, take all the time you need."

The next morning, Sherry parked in a visitor spot when she dropped Wyatt off for school. The idea of being in 'regular' classes excited Wyatt, and she hoped it would work out for him. But ultimately, she would have to do what was best for him, even if he didn't like it. She took a deep breath and entered the administration office.

A stern looking middle-aged woman looked up as she entered, "May I help you?"

"Yes, I have an appointment with Ms. Johnson."

"Just a moment, please." The woman picked up the phone and spoke briefly. "Right this way."

Sherry gave her a friendly smile and followed her back to an office. The woman stood to next to a door with a nameplate announcing Ms. Johnson's office.

"Excuse me," Sherry said when the middled-aged woman behind the desk didn't look up immediately.

"Oh, hello." Ms. Johnson stood and greeted Sherry, "Please come in and have a seat."

"Thank you," Sherry felt nervous. They had met once previously, and Sherry had been impressed by her in the past. She seemed to have a sincere interest in Wyatt's success. Sherry hoped today would be the same.

"So, you wanted to talk about Wyatt's classes." Ms. Johnson, asked.

"Yes, Wyatt feels like the classes are not challenging him enough, that they are too easy, and he is getting bored. I wanted to talk with you to see if that is the same impression his teachers have and if we could consider moving him into other more challenging classes."

"I see," Ms. Johnson drew her attention to her computer, "let me check his progress and evaluations." Her fingers darted over the keyboard. "Yes, well, his grades and test scores seem to show that he is comprehending the information and scoring high on all his tests, but socially, he is behind most of the other children."

"Could that be because he can't relate to the other kids in his class and will be more successful in a classroom with kids on the same intellectual level?"

"Possibly." She paused and tapped on the keyboard again. "I see you are a single parent."

Sherry bristled, "That's right."

"And Wyatt is an only child."

"Yes."

"Perhaps he needs more social interaction."

"I'm sorry, what does that have to do with his academic success?"

"We like to think they are connected; studies have shown that....,"

Sherry raised her hand to cut her off. "You're telling me you will not put my son in a class where he will be challenged and will learn because you don't think he has enough friends?" Sherry's anger was rising in her chest.

"I'm saying that we need to consider all aspects of Wyatt's life, not just the academic piece."

"Yes, but it is the academic piece that is causing the problem right now and is affecting his social life at school."

"How do you mean?"

"He is being picked on for being in these classes. How is that helping?"

"Ms. Davis, you had him placed in those classes."

"Yes, based on test scores for academic placement. Maybe we need to retest him."

"I'm sorry we can't do that until the end of the semester."

"So, you are just going to let my son languish in classes where he isn't learning anything and is hurting his self-esteem?" Sherry stood up, incensed.

"I'm afraid that is our only option at the moment."

"I see. Thank you for your time." Sherry turned and showed herself out. She was so angry by the time she got her car, her hands were shaking. She closed her eyes and took a deep breath before driving to work.

Mac rose early, showered, and dressed before leaving to meet Kay at the diner. It was six fifty when the waitress pointed him to an empty booth. He was sipping black coffee when Kay walked exactly at seven. He stood to greet her as she approached the booth.

"Kay." his voice catching a little in his throat when he said her name.

"Mac, it is so good to see you." She leaned in and kissed him, "you're looking wonderful."

"You, too." That had sounded smoother in his head when he rehearsed this moment over and over in his mind. "Please." he pointed to the seat across from him.

Kay had barely sat down when the waitress appeared. "Coffee?"

"Please." Kay nodded, then turned her attention back to Mac.

"You are looking well. I trust Grandpa isn't working you too hard."

Mac chuckled, "What do you think?"

"You must handle it well." She laughed, knowing her grandfather didn't think it was possible to work too hard.

The waitress returned with fresh coffee for them both, saving Mac for the moment.

Kay stirred sugar and cream into her cup. "What brings you to Gates Point? Are you working on a case?"

Mac needed to regroup and collect his thoughts. This was moving so fast, and he was losing track of the words he wanted to say. He shook his head and swallowed the hot dark liquid, hoping he didn't sound like an idiot. "No, I took a couple of days off and I couldn't think of where else to go."

The cup Kay was holding froze halfway to her gorgeous red lips. Mac thought she must have put a little color on them this morning. Kay wasn't one to wear a lot of makeup, but her lips were a deep shade of red. "What do you mean, you took a few days off? That doesn't sound like you."

"I took a couple of days, that's all."

"Are you okay? I mean, you're not sick or something, are you?"

Mac chuckled, "No I'm not sick, well sick and tired of the job maybe, but otherwise healthy."

Kay eyed him suspiciously. She didn't believe he was telling her everything, but she also knew not to push him.

"So, you took some time off and you came to Gates Point on your way to where?"

"Nowhere, I came to see you."

Kay leaned back and blinked, "Mac, you know Ethan and I...."

He held up his hand to stop her. "Yes, yes, you and Ethan. I know, and I wouldn't do anything to cause you any difficulty in your relationship. But you're still my friend or at least I thought so."

Kay smiled, "Of course we are friends."

"I thought I'd say hello to my friend while I was in town."

"It really has been a long time since you took a vacation, hasn't it?"

"Yes, why?"

"Because most people go to the islands or the mountains someplace to have fun. You drive three hours to meet me for coffee."

Mac would have laughed if he wasn't true. He felt like the conversation was going in an emotional direction he would rather avoid. He looked around the diner.

"Where's Eddie? It isn't like him to let you out of his sight like this."

Kay took a deep breath, "Eddie retired, said he wanted to spend more time with the grandkids."

"Good for him." Mac took a sip of coffee. "So, who's your new security detail?"

"I don't have one. I didn't replace Eddie.

It was Mac's turn to stare. "What? You don't have anyone guarding you? No one driving you to and from work?"

"No, and it feels so liberating, not to be babysat all the time." She lifted her chin slightly in defiance of what Mac was about to say.

"Are you crazy? Does Ethan know about this?"

"Yes, he knows."

"Is he happy about it?"

"I wouldn't say happy, exactly." Kay hedged. In fact, Ethan was not happy about it, and she was pretty sure he was having her followed to and from work, but by whom she had no idea.

"So no, he isn't happy, well I'll give him credit for that. Why haven't you replaced Eddie?"

"I just told you I don't like being followed around like some wayward toddler."

"Kay," Mac leaned forward and lowered his voice, "I realize you don't like it, but Eddie wasn't a professional. If you had proper security, you'd never know they were there. You can't not have a detail. You are the owner and CEO of the states' largest defense contractor, you need security."

"I won't be forced to live my life in fear."

Mac leaned back and studied her. God, she was stubborn.

"Look, I know more than anyone why a good security division is important. Almost all top executives have some sort of personal security."

"Yeah, and a lot of those people are worth a lot more money than me and have an over inflated sense of self-importance."

"That may be true, but you were kidnapped and nearly killed, twice in the past. That should speak for itself."

Kay just stared at him. He wasn't wrong, and that just made her that much more irritated. "You sound like Ethan."

"Good, then maybe you'll listen to one of us."

"I doubt it." Kay laughed.

"Does your grandfather know about this?" Judging by the look on her face, he could tell that she hadn't told her grandfather. "You know," Mac started, a plan forming in his mind as he talked. "He worries about you."

"You wouldn't dare!" Kay was already on to his tactic. "I swear Mac, if you tell my grandfather about this, I'll..."

He grinned at her, "You'll what?"

"I'll think of something. I thought you said you were my friend." She pouted.

"I am, and friends look out for each other."

Kay was silent for a few moments while sipping her coffee and watching Mac over the rim of her mug when she had a brilliant idea. "Mac, you said earlier you are tired of your job."

"Yes, that's right."

"Then why don't you retire?"

"What the hell would I do in retirement?" he laughed.

A smile spread across her face, "You could come work for me as my head of security and put your money where your mouth is."

Mac just stared at her for a moment. Damn, she was good, too good. He had left himself wide open.

"I'm not sure I'm ready to retire," was all he could think of to say.

"Bullshit." Kay laughed. "Listen," she checked her watch, "I have to run. But why don't you come by the office later this morning and look around and give me an honest security assessment."

He nodded, "Okay, fair enough."

Kay stood up and stepped over to his side of the table. She kissed him lightly on the cheek. "See ya soon."

Mac stared after her for a long moment. Well, one thing he was sure of, things were never dull around Kay.

Sherry was still angry when she sat down at her desk. She struggled to get logged into her computer, having to retype her password three times before she got it right. Then she spilled the contents of her purse while putting it in her desk drawer.

"Dammit!" She muttered, reaching down to pick up the items.

"Everything okay?"

Sherry jumped, "Oh!"

"Sherry, are you okay?"

"No!"

Kay looked surprised at Sherry's state of mind this morning. "Come into my office when you get your things together."

Sherry sighed. She closed the drawer, giving up on re-organizing her purse and sat for a moment with her head in her hands. This day was going from bad to worse. Her stomach was in knots when she stepped into Kay's office and closed the door.

Kay watched as Sherry took a seat in front of her desk, wringing her hands.

"Kay, I apologize for snapping at you like that. It was uncalled for and unprofessional."

Kay blinked. "You think I called you in here because you snapped at me?"

Sherry looked around the room, "Well, yes."

"I asked you to come in here because you are clearly upset about something, and I want you to tell me what I can do to help."

Sherry stared at Kay for a moment. "What?"

"We all have bad days. If you snap at me because I ask a dumb question, I probably deserve it. I don't care about that. What I care about is that I know you went to see Wyatt's school counselor today; and now you are more upset than I think I have seen you in a long time. So, tell me what is going on."

Sherry sighed and sank back in the chair. She didn't want to burden Kay with her problems; they were hers to fix, not Kay's. But it was also tempting to vent to someone about the guidance counselor and her attitude towards Wyatt's problems.

"Kay, I appreciate it, but I need to solve my own problems."

"Okay, but do you want to talk about it? It might help you find the path forward."

Sherry smiled a little. "Okay." Kay was persistent.

"Wyatt told me that his classes are boring, and that people treat him like he is dumb. He is getting teased by some of the other kids. So, I went to talk to his counselor to see how he is doing academically and maybe get him into more challenging classes."

"Sounds reasonable. What did they say?"

"They said no." Sherry was almost in tears. She was so angry.

"Why? Are his test scores not high enough?"

"No, that is just it. His grades say he should be in more advanced classes, but the school will not allow him to move because of his social skills. They started asking if I was married and if Wyatt was an only child, like I'm a terrible parent or something." Sherry couldn't stop the hot tears that were not racing down her cheeks.

Kay got up and came around the desk to put her arm around Sherry. "You are a wonderful parent. If you weren't, you wouldn't be so upset right now."

"What am I going to do?"

"Will they not even consider allowing Wyatt to change classes?"

"Not until next semester." Sherry sniffled.

"Okay, how long until this semester ends?"

"The end of December."

Kay nodded and sat down in the chair next to Sherry. "So that is two months. Do you think he can hold on until January?"

"Probably, I haven't talked to him about it yet."

"Talk to Wyatt, see if he can hang in there and in the meantime, maybe see if the school will let him take some online classes on his laptop if his work in the classroom is complete. Something more challenging for him."

Sherry nodded. She had been too angry to consider the options. "That's a good idea."

"Listen, I have to run to a meeting. You stay in here and take all the time you need to pull yourself together. If you need to take the rest of the day off to get this straightened out, go ahead. I can manage for a day, and I promise to stay out of the file room." Kay smiled, trying to lighten the mood a little.

Sherry nodded, "Thank you."

She sat there for a moment after Kay left, thinking about what she had said. Two more months wasn't that long and with the

Thanksgiving, Christmas, and teacher work days there weren't that many school days left. Sherry took a tissue from the box on Kay's desk and dried her eyes. She needed to fish her mascara out of the bottom of her desk drawer. She was sure her makeup needed attention, and her face always got puffy when she cried.

"Excuse me." A deep male voice startled her.

She spun around to see a man standing in Kay's open doorway.

"Can I help you?" she demanded.

"I was looking for Kay...."

"She's in a meeting. Can I help you with something?" She managed. His ice-blue eyes were completely distracting, his salt and pepper hair cut short was enough to make her swoon and the way he filled out his jeans was just plain sinful.

"Well, I don't know. Maybe I should come back another time." He stood, studying her. "Do you mind if I ask, are you okay?"

"What?" Sherry looked at him confused for a moment, then remember the lack of mascara and the puffy eyes. Damn. Just typical for today, on top of everything else, a gorgeous man walks in the office, and she stood there looking a fright.

He took a step into the room, and she realized how tall he was. He had to be six foot two inches, with broad shoulders. She imagined the muscles that were hiding under the shirt and jacket. "You look upset. Is there anything I can do?"

"Oh," she touched her face, and felt the heat rising in her cheeks, "uh, no thank you. I'll be fine. I'm sorry. What did you say your name was?" She walked past him back out to her desk, trying to regain her composure.

"My name is James McIntyre, but my friends call me Mac."

She made a pretense of looking at Kay's calendar. "Did you have an appointment with Kay?"

"No, but when I spoke with her over coffee this morning, she asked me to stop by and give her a security assessment."

Kay had mentioned nothing about an early morning meeting, a man called Mac, or a security assessment. "I'm sorry she didn't mention anything about you stopping by. You're welcome to wait for her if you like." She indicated the guest chairs and sofa. He looked at her with disappointment but nodded and took a seat.

She felt like she should be suspicious of this man and his story, but she wasn't. In fact, she was glad he was there.

CHAPTER THREE

I t was clear that Kay's assistant was upset. He wondered if Kay had done or said something to her to make her this distraught. He wanted to ask her if he could help, but he got the distinct feeling she would not open up to him and tell him her problems. And he didn't blame her. She didn't know him and being a friend of Kay's might not help if Kay caused her tears. He sat quietly and watched as she organized something in a drawer then, focused on her computer. He admired how she pulled herself together and answered a few phone calls until Kay returned.

"Mac! I'm so sorry to keep you waiting."

"No problem, we didn't exactly set a time and I know you're busy." He leaned down for Kay to plant a light kiss on his cheek. His eyes drifted upward to see the assistant watching them. Or rather, watching him.

"Come on in." Kay stepped towards her office. "Have you met Sherry?"

Sherry's head jerked up at the sound of her name.Mac smiled, "Only briefly."

"Sherry, this is Mac, my friend I told you about from D.C." Kay gave Sherry a knowing look. But Sherry clearly didn't remember their prior conversation, so Kay tried again. "Mac, works for NCIS." Kay smiled and then walked into her office while the information sunk into Sherry's head.

Sherry's eyes widened. It had been nearly two years since Kay had met Mac on a trip to visit her grandfather in D.C. Kay had come back and told Sherry about going on a date with the good looking and mysterious Mac. He had captivated Sherry before she had ever met him. But everything changed for Kay when she returned home and reconnected with Ethan Craddock her long-lost love. Sherry had even advised Kay if she had to choose between the two men to choose Mac. Kay had only given Sherry an indulgent smile. As mysterious and gorgeous as Mac was, Kay's heart belonged to Ethan. Sherry admonished herself, she should have recognized the name when he introduced himself, but she was so upset that the name hadn't registered. That was twice this morning she managed to embarrass herself and that was before they were properly introduced. Sherry got up and rushed to the ladies' room to repair her makeup. When she returned, Mac was still in Kay's office and the door was open. She took a deep breath and stepped inside. "Excuse me, does anyone need coffee? I just remembered I forgot to make it this morning."

Mac turned to face her. "Coffee would be great."

Kay hid a smile. She knew Sherry was using the coffee as an excuse and she had seen Mac drink three cups at the diner. Surely, he didn't need any more caffeine. But she kept her mouth shut and watched as Mac's eyes followed Sherry's every move.

Kay continued her conversation, "As I was saying, we have this building, the yard down on the riverfront, and then two facilities in other states. So, each location has handled security independently. Eddie handled this building and contract uniformed guards handled the yard."

Mac tore his eyes away from Sherry to refocus on Kay. "Who's handling the building now?"

"We have a private security company in the building at night after hours."

Mac frowned and shook his head in frustration.

"I seriously don't understand you sometimes."

"Who does?" Sherry mumbled.

"Did you say something?" Kay asked, accepting the coffee.

"Nope." Sherry shook her head and offered a cup of coffee to Mac. He took it and gave her a quick wink, having heard what she said.

"Sure." Kay drew out the word.

"Leave her alone, haven't you upset her enough for one day." Mac scolded.

Sherry froze and looked at Kay. Kay looked from Sherry to Mac in horror. "What are you talking about?"

"She looked upset when I arrived and...."

"And you assumed I had upset her?"

Mac, suddenly regretting his words, looked from Kay to Sherry, who was clearly mortified. "Well, yes."

"I didn't upset her." Kay looked at Sherry for confirmation.

Embarrassed that her personal life was now the topic of discussion, Sherry stammered, "No, it wasn't Kay's fault. I was upset when I got to work." Her cheeks were burning red hot, and she couldn't get out of the office fast enough.

Kay scowled at Mac. "Nice job. I hope you're better at security."

He looked sheepish. "I'm sorry."

Kay got up and closed the door. "She had a rough morning."

"Obviously."

"What kind of person do you think I am that I would make Sherry as sweet as she is, cry?"

"I don't think you are a bad person, but I don't know her, and she was pretty upset when I got here. I thought maybe you had fired her or something."

"Wow."

Mac gave Kay an apologetic look. "Sorry."

"Sherry is a wonderful person, I couldn't run this company without her, but she is having a rough time with her son right now."

"Is he in trouble?"

"No, he is struggling with school and the school doesn't seem to want to help. Sherry is a single mom, and her son has struggled since his dad was killed in a car accident."

"That is rough."

"Yeah, it is, but Sherry is strong, and she manages very well on her own. I think today she was more upset out of frustration than anything else. She is got to be completely mortified that you saw her like that, not to mention, bringing it up in conversation."

"Maybe I should apologize to her."

"I would let it go." Kay advised. "Okay, why don't we take a tour of the building, and you can give me some initial thoughts."

She got up and opened the door. "Sherry, is the rest of my day free?"

Sherry tapped the keys on her keyboard. "Yes, amazingly enough."

"Thank you, Mac is going to tour the building and give us a security assessment."

"Good, we need it."

Mac smiled from behind Kay.

"Why?" Kay asked, surprised.

"Well, let's see, we've had a couple of terrible corporate attorneys, so background checks might be a good idea, anyone can just walk in here and frankly, I would think you'd be a little more cautious about that. I mean, I understand why you kept Eddie on, but honestly, if we had some proper security, do you think anyone would have made an attempt on your life?" Sherry paused and looked thoughtful, "When was that again, a year ago? Two?"

Kay put her hands up in surrender. "Okay, so why are you just telling me this now?"

Sherry shrugged, "You never asked."

"Since when has that ever stopped you?"

"You'd be surprised." Sherry smiled.

Mac snickered.

"Oh, so you two are in cahoots already? I see." Kay turned to look at Mac.

He held up his hands, playing innocent.

After Kay left, taking Mac on a tour of the building, Sherry finally had a moment to calm down from the events of the morning. She decided she wouldn't say anything to Wyatt just yet, unless he asked her. She decided she would make an appeal to the principal of the school and if that didn't work, she would look into finding a different school for Wyatt. The only trouble was, they would either have to move to a different school district or she would have to find a private school for him. A private school would be expensive, and she would probably have to sell the house and find some place less expensive to live in order to afford the tuition. But she had to do something. She looked up the phone number to the school principal and left a message. Having done all she could do at the moment about Wyatt's school, she focused on work. The mail arrived, and she began opening the various letters and invitations that Kay got on a weekly basis. She found her mind kept drifting back to Mac and those intensely blue eyes. She could see how Kay had been attracted to him when they first met. Who wouldn't be? But it wasn't just the gorgeous eyes or his chiseled good looks; it was he exuded a calmness. His body was still. He didn't fidget or bounce his foot when waiting for Kay. Was it confidence? He wasn't cocky and he seemed somewhat introverted. He didn't feel the need to make idle conversation, which she appreciated, especially since she had embarrassed herself earlier.

She shook her head. Sherry didn't have time to be thinking about Mac or any other man. She had to take care of Wyatt and focus on her job or Kay was going to fire her, as Mac had assumed earlier.

It was lunchtime before Kay and Mac returned to the office. They paused as Sherry watched nonchalantly from her desk.

"Mac, thanks for stopping by. Are you going to be in town a few more days?"

"At least until Sunday."

"Why don't you come have dinner with Ethan and I before you leave?"

"I'd love to, if you think Ethan has the time."

"I'll call him. I'm sure we can work something out with his schedule."

Mac nodded.

Kay kissed his cheek, "I'll text you and let you know."

"Okay." Mac looked past Kay to Sherry and caught her eye, "It was nice meeting you."

Sherry smiled. She wasn't sure what to say, so she gave him a small wave.

"I'll see ya, Kay."

He strode towards the elevator. The doors opened and just before they closed, he gave Sherry a small smile and nodded. Kay had turned back towards her office and missed the slight gesture, but Sherry didn't, and her heart leapt into her throat.

Kay leaned against the doorframe to her office and look over at Sherry.

"You okay?"

"Yeah, I'm fine. It's been a hell of a morning though."

"Yes, it has."

"Are you really going to get Mac to work here?"

"I was thinking about it. Why?"

"You sure that is a good idea?"

"Why wouldn't it be?"

"Because you two have history."

Kay waved her hand dismissively. "That is in the past and we have both moved on."

"You sure about that?"

"Of course."

"Have you told Ethan about your plan?"

"No, I just thought of it today when I met Mac at the diner for coffee."

Sherry nodded. "Uh huh."

"What? I can have friends that are male; it is purely platonic."

"Now."

"Yes, now."

Sherry shook her head. "Okay, I believe you if you say so."

"You don't think I should hire him?"

"I didn't say that. I just asked if you were sure, you two were over."

"It's been two years, and he knows I'm in love with Ethan."

"What about Mac? Does he have a girlfriend?"

"Not that I am aware of, but he wasn't much into relationships when I met him, because of the long hours and nature of his job."

"I see." Sherry shuffled some papers on her desk.

Kay gave her a devious grin. "Are you that concerned about my relationship with Mac or are you more interested in his availability?"

"Oh, please!" But she could feel her cheeks burning, "Like I have time for a relationship." She said a little too quickly.

"Yeah, I see your point." Kay gave her a look that said she wasn't buying it.

"Here's your mail."

"Sherry, seriously, are you okay?"

"Yeah, I'm sorry about this morning. I was just so mad. I called and left a message for the principal and if that doesn't work then I'll just find Wyatt a new school."

"Do you think that is a good idea?"

"I don't know. I want what is best for him."

"I know you do, but stability is important too."

"But not if he is being held back or being bullied."

"I don't disagree. But talk to Wyatt before you decide. He is a bright kid and I'm sure he will tell you what he needs, then you can weigh your options."

"You're right, of course."

"And tell me if I can help."

"I'm going to take lunch now if that is, okay?"

"Of course."

Sherry nodded. She was determined to handle this on her own. But there was no arguing with Kay. She picked up her purse and the paperback she kept in her desk drawer and walked down the block to a small park. It was popular at lunchtime, and she was lucky to find an empty bench in the sun. The weather was sporadic this time of year. It could be seventy degrees one day and fifty degrees the next. She pulled out a small box of carrot sticks and her book and tried to forget the world for a few minutes. Her lunch break was the only time during the day she had to herself. She had some quiet time after Wyatt went to bed, but she was usually too tired to enjoy it. Opening the book, she let herself be swept away to another time and place.

She was so absorbed in the story she wasn't paying any attention to the people or the surrounding noises. It was only when a shadow crossed the pages of her book that she tore her eyes away and looked up. A silhouette of a man stood in front of her. The angle of the sun prevented her from being able to see his face. She put her hand up to shield her eyes.

"Can I help you?"

The man moved to the side enough for her to make out Mac's features.

"Hi, sorry I didn't mean to startle you."

"Oh, hi. What are you doing here?"

"I was walking around the building to get a feel for various access points that might need to be more secure. I was on my way over there," he nodded to a restaurant, "for lunch when I saw you sitting here alone."

She turned to see the Chinese restaurant behind her. She knew they delivered to the building, but she had never been inside. "I hear they have good food."

"May I?" He pointed to the bench.

"Oh, yes, please." She scooted over to make sure he had enough room to sit down.

"Do you think it is safe to sit out here alone?"

Sherry looked around the park. "Well, I never thought about it until now, so thanks."

Mac followed her gaze around the park. "I'm just saying you should always know your surroundings."

"That can be said for anywhere."

"You're right." He nodded. "Why don't you let me buy you lunch?"

"Oh, I couldn't. Besides, I only get an hour and that is half over-with already."

"If you want to go to lunch, I will let Kay know you're with me."

Sherry sat staring at him. The idea of having lunch with an adult was something she craved. But she felt guilty at the same time.

She looked over at him. "Do people always do what you tell them to do?"

"Yes." He gave her a smile.

"And you think Kay is one of those people?"

"Let's find out." He pulled his cell phone from his pocket and punched in the number. He waited, "Kay, it's Mac."

Sherry watched with fascination.

"Listen, I ran into Sherry out here in the park and I'm going to take her to lunch. You mind if she is a little late coming back?" He waited while Kay spoke.

Sherry would have given anything to hear what Kay was saying.

"Perfect, see you later." He slid the phone back into his pocket. "Do you like Chinese?"

Sherry stared at him blankly for a moment, "Yes, I like Chinese."

"Great." He stood up and offered her his hand. She took it gingerly and joined him as they strolled across the park to the restaurant.

Mac held a chair out for her.

"Thank you," she said quietly, uncomfortable with the new attention.

The server brought them water while they looked over the menus.

"What's your favorite?" Mac asked, looking over the top of his menu.

"General Tso's." she smiled.

"A woman after my own heart."

When the server returned, Mac ordered them both General Tso with rice.

"So," Sherry said, wringing her hands in her lap, "what brings you to Gates Point?"

"Fishing."

"Have you caught much yet?"

"No, haven't even seen the water."

"Kind of hard to catch fish, that way." She laughed.

"Well, I text a message to Kay to say hello, and we had breakfast. That is when she came up with the idea to have me give her some security advice."

Sherry sipped her water.

"You know she won't stop there. She has an obsessive need to fix things."

"Like what?"

"Like people mostly. When she sees a problem. She is not happy to sit by and let someone work it out themselves, she must step in and solve it for them. It is always with the purest of intentions. Rarely does the person she is helping even realize what is happening. She likes to keep things quiet if she can. "

"I'm guessing that is thanks to you."

Sherry shrugged, "Sometimes."

Mac pegged her with a stare, "listen, I want to say something about this morning."

Sherry slumped, embarrassment washing over her yet again. "God, you don't have to bring that up."

"I feel like I owe you an apology."

"No, you don't. It was just a terrible morning and bad timing."

"I don't want to pry, but if there is anything I can do, I'd be happy to do it."

Sherry gave him a weak smile. "Thank you, that is very sweet. But, unless you have some influence with my son's school, I'm afraid I'm on my own."

Mac shook his head slowly. "I don't have any pull at the school, but you are never on your own."

His smile was warm and genuine, and Sherry wanted to cry just from the sheer joy it gave her knowing someone else cared.

"Thank you." She wanted to say more, but their lunch arrived, and the moment passed.

They made small talk, and he told her about his experiences in school as a young boy. And about joining the Marines. She told him about marrying her high school sweetheart and that he was killed in a car accident. When lunch was over, she felt like she had known Mac all her life. He walked her back to the main entrance of the Port City's Industry building.

"I hope the rest of your day gets better." He said as he was preparing to leave her.

"It already has." She didn't care if she sounded flirty and she half hoped he took it that way. "I hope I get to see you before you go."

"I hope so, too."

"Thank you for lunch." She didn't want the afternoon to end.

"You're welcome." He smiled and turned away.

She watched him walk down the block, then she stepped into the building, her heart racing with excitement. What was she thinking? She had no time for a man. But another voice in her head said she should make time for this one. She smiled the entire elevator ride to the office. When the doors opened, Kay was standing there waiting for her.

Kay squealed, taking Sherry's hand, and dragging her into the office. "Tell me everything!"

"There isn't anything to tell."

"Really? Because I'm thinking when the very hot director of NCIS calls me to tell me he is taking you to lunch and you will be late returning to work, there is a story to be told."

Sherry laughed as she blushed, "Really, there isn't. I was sitting on the park bench reading my book like always and he saw me and asked if I would join him for lunch. I explained that my break was nearly over, so he called you."

"Where did you go?"

"Just over to Ling Nam's."

"I see, and what did you talk about?"

Sherry was finding it hard to remain nonchalant about the whole thing, and Kay was the one person who would probably understand more than anyone else. She beamed. "He told me about what he was like in high school and joining the Marines. I told him about losing Chris and that Wyatt was having some trouble in school."

"Wow." Kay sat back, that is a lot to cover in one lunch date.

"I don't think it was really a date."

"Trust me, Mac doesn't just randomly go to lunch with just anyone, he is more of a loner."

"Do you think he'll call?" Sherry was on the edge of her seat.

"I'd bet on it."

Chapter Four

"How was school today?" Sherry asked over dinner

"It was okay." Wyatt took a bite of macaroni and cheese. "Did you talk to Ms. Johnson today?"

Sherry took a deep breath. "I did..."

"Great! When can I move to different classes?"

"She said they wouldn't be able to make the change until January."

"January?" Wyatt whined.

"I called and left a message for the principal to see if there is anything that can be done. But we might be stuck with it until after the holidays."

"That's too far away." Wyatt pouted.

"It really isn't. Halloween is in a few weeks, then you're off for Thanksgiving and then Christmas. And in November school is closed for a couple of other holidays and a teacher workday so you really aren't going to be in there very much, anyway."

Wyatt poked at his food. She could hear the thud, thud, thud of him kicking the table leg.

"Wyatt, listen, we will deal with it as it comes. But I'm glad you told me what was going on so I could start doing something about it."

"I guess."

Her temper flared a little. She wasn't raising him to be a spoiled, entitled brat. "I'm sorry, what did you say?"

"Yes, ma'am."

"Please eat your dinner, unless you want it for leftovers tomorrow."

Wyatt ate the rest of dinner in relative silence. It was killing her to see him so unhappy, but she had few options at the moment.

Finally, after homework, dinner and one hour of TV, Wyatt was asleep. She allowed her thoughts to drift back to lunch with Mac. Sherry wondered if he would, in fact, call her. Tomorrow was Saturday, and the office was closed. He was supposed to be fishing and had no way to reach her. He hadn't asked for her number, and she hadn't offered it. Mac must have just been being polite when he said he would be in touch. She felt a little sad but lifted her chin. She really didn't have time for a relationship, but it had been nice to feel wanted even for a short while by an attractive man.

She had more important things to think about now, like all the errands she had to run tomorrow, including a soccer game for Wyatt. He had asked to go hang out at a friend's house afterward which would afford her the time to get the weekly shopping done.

Mac drove back to his hotel feeling conflicted about the day's turn of events. He was happy to see Kay and spend some time alone with her, but it was different this time. She was clearly in love with Ethan and there was none of the spark between them that had been there before. Then there was Sherry. Ah, yes, Sherry, vulnerable, determined with a definite stubborn streak. He felt drawn to her the moment he saw her and not because she was so obviously upset, but in the way she lifted her chin at the sight of him, determined not to allow weakness to show through. Although, the ruined make-up gave her away. He smiled to himself at the memory. Yes, Sherry had been a surprise. He had wanted to ask for her number but was afraid she would say no. He was sure he could get it from Kay. Kay had surprised him too with the job offer and at first, he was ready to dismiss it out of hand, but now that he had time to reconsider the offer, he wasn't so sure he should rush to refuse it. He had come here seeking answers about him and Kay, and he had gotten them. There was nothing there any longer. Even if Kay hadn't proven that point for him, Sherry did. He couldn't be so in love with Kay and feel the way he did right now about Sherry.

He took out his phone and sent a text to Kay.

"Need a favor."

"You name it." Came the immediate reply.

"I need Sherry's cell number."

A moment later, the number appeared on his screen, followed by a smiley emoji. He shook his head and saved the number on his contact list. Was it too early to call? He had just seen her earlier in the day. Was it too late in the evening? Would she be helping her son with homework?

In the end, he went downstairs to the restaurant and ordered dinner.

Wyatt was up early Saturday morning playing video games with his friends online. Sherry made a cup of coffee and took a couple of sips, leaning against the kitchen counter. She had tossed and turned the night before, her mind filled with thoughts of Mac and the problems Wyatt was having at school. She looked around the kitchen. If she had to sell this house to put Wyatt in a private school, then it might not be the worst thing in the world. She still saw shadows of her late husband everywhere. It was the only home that Wyatt had known, but a change from that might do him good as well. His therapist said that he had made wonderful progress with his grief and could reduce the frequency of office visits unless Wyatt felt differently. Wyatt had been eager to move on and reduced the office visits to once a month.

She took one more sip of coffee, then started breakfast. This morning she was making pancakes and bacon. Wyatt was going to need plenty of energy today.

"Breakfast is ready," she called out a few minutes later.

"Okay."

Wyatt came in and sat down at the kitchen table and helped himself to butter and syrup for his pancakes. Sherry joined him with a smaller stack and no bacon.

"Mom, can I be home schooled?"

Sherry looked at him curiously, "home schooled? What brought that on?"

"One guy on my soccer team is home schooled, and it sounds fun."

"I'm sure it does, but honey, I work all day. How can I do both?"

"I could come to work with you."

"I wish you could, I really do." Her heart was breaking for her son. "I will figure something out. Maybe a different school?"

"What school?" He perked up.

"I don't know, we will have to find you one, maybe a private school."

"Will I still be able to play soccer?"

"We'll make sure they have soccer, and you can always play with the rec teams."

"Okay, that might work."

Satisfied for the moment, he ate his breakfast and got ready for soccer. Sherry packed a cooler with drinks and snacks to share with the rest of the team.

An hour later she was ready. "Wyatt, time to go."

"Coming!"

She heard him bumping around upstairs. "Mom, I can't find my shoes!"

"Did you look under your bed?"

"Yeah."

"Closet?"

"Yes!"

"Wyatt, if I have to come up there and find them...." She started up the stairs.

"Got'em!"

She sighed as Wyatt raced down the stairs.

"Sorry, mom."

"We don't want to be late, put them on in the car."

Adding to her frustration, traffic was especially heavy getting to the sports complex. Once they arrived, Wyatt was out of the van and running to meet up with the team, leaving her to lug the cooler and folding camp chairs.

"Need a hand?"

Amy Barton, Sherry's best friend, walked over to offer her a hand.

"Oh hi, thank you." Sherry smiled, grateful for the help.

"They get so excited, don't they? Remember when we had that kind of energy?" Amy laughed.

"Barely."

Sherry set up her chair and put the cooler where the boys could easily grab a snack, then sat down to watch the warmup and chat with Amy. Wyatt had just scored a goal when her cell phone beeped with a text message. Fishing it from her jeans pocket, she looked at the screen and blinked.

"Is everything okay?" Amy asked, concerned.

Sherry looked over at her. "Yeah, I think so." The text from Mac read 'Can I call you?'

Sherry quickly responded, "I'm at a soccer game. When did you want to call?"

"Text me when you're free."

"OK."

She slid the phone back in her pocket and wondered why Mac was texting on a Saturday and how did he get her cell phone number.

Amy reached over and touched Sherry's arm. "You okay?"

"Yeah, a man I met yesterday just sent me a text."

"You are just mentioning this now? I need details." The game forgotten; Amy's attention was on Sherry.

"I met him at work. He is a friend of my boss, and he took me to lunch."

"Is he nice? Is he cute?" Amy was practically bouncing up and down in her chair.

"Yes, and hell yes."

A cheer went up from the other parents, drawing Sherry's attention away from the conversation for a moment. Wyatt and the rest of the team were coming off the field. Sherry looked over to Amy. "Wyatt knows nothing about this." She hoped Amy would understand.

"It's strictly between us." Amy reassured her and then greeted her son Robbie as he and Wyatt ran over.

"Looking good out there!" Sherry said, handing Wyatt a drink and a banana.

"Did you see me score, mom?"

Sherry beamed, "I did. You're doing an awesome job out there today!"

After a few minutes, the boys were headed back onto the field, and Amy looked over at Sherry. "Spill!"

Sherry giggled, "He came in to give my boss a security analysis for our building. While I was sitting on a bench reading a book he asked if I would have lunch with him."

"Did you?"

"Yes, we went to Ling Nam's and talked for an hour!" Sherry smiled widely at the memory.

"What did you talk about?" Amy was enthralled.

"He told me about where he grew up, I told him about Chris and Wyatt."

Amy looked surprised. Sherry didn't talk about her dead husband very often. "You did?"

"Yeah, I'm not sure why, it just sort of came out."

Amy grinned, "He must be easy to talk to."

"He is, which is kind of weird, but I felt like I had known him all my life when by the time we returned to the office."

"And he just sent you a text?"

Sherry instinctively touched her pocket where her phone was. "Yeah, and that is funny too, because I didn't give him my number."

"Then how did he get it?"

"My guess is he got it from Kay. I told you they were friends, and I wouldn't put it past Kay to encourage him to call."

Amy sat back in her chair, turning her eyes back to the game for a moment. "Wow."

"Yeah, tell me about it." Sherry mirrored Amy and turned her attention back to the game. But her mind kept drifting to Mac. What would it be like to have that deep, gravelly voice whisper in her ear? To have those ice-blue eyes staring at her in candlelight? Another cheer drug her back to the present. The game was over, and it was time to get back to reality.

Robbie and Wyatt ran over after they congratulated the other team for a game well played.

"Congratulations, boys! That was an awesome game!" Sherry cheered them.

"Thanks, mom. Can I go home with Robbie now?"

"If Ms. Barton is ready for you, if not I'll drop you over later."

Amy smiled, "He can come with me now, that is fine."

Sherry looked down at Wyatt. "Did you bring a change of clothes? I know you aren't planning on wearing those dirty clothes in Ms. Barton's house all afternoon."

Wyatt looked forlorn. "No ma'am, I didn't think to bring a change of clothes."

Sherry smoothed his hair down. "Well, then it is a good thing I did."

Wyatt looked up, eyes bright, "Did you?"

"Yes, and if you help me carry this chair and cooler back to the car, I will give them to you."

"Yes, ma'am!" Wyatt and Robbie grabbed up the cooler and chairs and ran off to the parking lot.

With the boys running ahead, Amy leaned over and whispered, "Are you going to call him later?"

"Who?"

"The man you had lunch with, as if you didn't know." Amy grinned.

"Yeah, I think I will." Sherry said, making the decision then that she wanted to talk to Mac again.

Amy put an arm around her and gave her a little squeeze. "Good for you, girl."

"I've got to run some errands while Wyatt is at your house. Do you need anything from the store?"

"That is sweet of you to ask, but I think I'm okay."

Wyatt was bouncing from one foot to the other, waiting for her to get to the minivan.

"Sit down and take those dirty shoes off. Here are your clothes." Sherry handed him a duffle bag.

Wyatt kicked off his soccer shoes and pulled on his sneakers.

"Ready?" Amy asked him.

"Yes, ma'am."

"You be good for Ms. Barton."

"I will, mom." Wyatt called as he and Robbie raced to Amy's SUV.

Sherry sighed, "If he gives you any trouble call me."

"Relax, Wyatt is a good kid. He is always respectful. Besides, they will go straight to Robbie's room and play video games until dinner time. I won't even see them."

"Okay, thanks. I'm looking forward to an afternoon to myself even if it involves grocery shopping."

"No problem."

Sherry watched as Wyatt and Robbie climbed into Amy's car, then she sat behind the wheel of her ancient minivan admiring Amy's sleek SUV and sighed. No point in dwelling on it. If she was going to find Wyatt a new school, a new car was out of the question. She pulled out her phone and checked her shopping list. She would go to the store and call Mac after she put away the groceries. Maybe she would treat herself to a pint of ice cream.

She pulled out of the parking lot of the sports complex and headed for the store. The parking lot was packed and there were balloons near the entrance, a clear sign that today was not the day she should be shopping. Her get in and get out quickly plan was about to come to a screeching halt. She loathed sale days with food samples and people more interested in browsing than shopping. She took a deep breath, grabbed a cart from the corral in the parking lot, and plunged into the crowded store.

The lines were long at check out, but they at least had several lanes open, and things seemed to be moving quickly. She hurried as much as she could to get everything on her list and avoid the free samples of everything from brownies to wine. Once she got through the checkout line, despite the rude cashier who had a passion for popping her gum, she breathed a sigh of relief. She loaded up the van and returned the cart to the corral. An older couple was walking past her van on the way to their car, so she sat and waited before turning over the motor. When she turned the key, nothing happened, just a clicking sound. She tried again, click, click, click. Nothing.

"Great!" She got out and lifted the hood to see if the battery cables were loose. Everything seemed fine. She got back in and checked to see if she had left her headlights on, but the switch was in the off position. "Dammit."

As she sat there scrolling through her contact list for the roadside assistance number, her phone rang. She didn't recognize the number.

"Hello?"

"Hi, it's Mac. Did I catch you at a bad time?"

Her temper flared for a moment. She had planned to call him later. "Yeah, it's kinda a bad time. My van seems to have died and I'm stranded in the grocery store parking lot."

"Where are you? I'll come to get you."

"That's sweet, but I have a carload of groceries."

"I can handle that. Where are you?"

She sighed, well getting a ride home with Mac would be better than riding in a tow truck. She looked around. People were waiting for her parking spot. Her cheeks flamed red. "I'm at the store on Apollo Drive. You can't miss it. There are streamers and balloons out front, and the parking lot is packed."

"I'm on my way. Which aisle are you parked in?"

"Aisle C about halfway down near the cart return."

"Sit tight."

She sighed. This is not how she had imagined this afternoon when she scheduled herself some alone time. She thought she might soak in a hot tub of water with a pint of ice cream talking to Mac on the phone. She dialed the number for the roadside assistance and explained the situation to them. Then she got out and put her ice cream in the cooler from the game, hoping to save it.

"Hey lady, are you leaving or what?" a man called from his pickup truck.

"No, my van won't start, sorry."

"Need a hand?" He offered.

"No thanks, help is on the way."

He waved and pulled away in search of another spot. Ten minutes passed and Mac pulled up and rolled down his window.

"You, okay?"

"I guess so, tow truck is on the way."

"Okay, let's get your groceries in the trunk." He maneuvered his car as close to hers as he could and popped the trunk on the shiny Chrysler 300.

"Is this yours?" She couldn't help asking.

"No, rental."

"You rented this to go fishing with?"

"Well, it isn't like I can take it out on the water." He chuckled.

"Good point."

She reached in and grabbed a couple of bags to help but Mac was already making quick work of it.

When they were done, Mac closed the trunk. "I'll go park somewhere and come back. Will you be okay until then?" He said, looking around the parking lot.

She smiled, "Yes, I'll be fine."

He nodded, got in the car, and pulled off. Sherry checked her phone. She had a text telling her the tow truck driver was just minutes away. She leaned against the back of the van and closed her eyes.

"Want me to have a look?" Mac's voice startled her. She hadn't expected him back so soon.

"Yes, just not how I planned to spend my day."

"I bet."

The tow truck came into view, lumbering down the drive aisle, then pulled to a stopped when Sherry waved. Cars were backing up behind him already and Sherry groaned.

"What's the trouble?"

"Won't start."

"Does it click or make a noise?" The driver asked, walking to the front of the van.

"Yes."

"Can you turn it over for me?"

She got in and turned the key. The same click, click, click she had heard before was all she got in return for her efforts.

"Probably your alternator, do you have a place in mind you want me to take it?"

"Keith's over off Pine."

"I know the place. If you leave me the key, I'll take care of it."

She was hesitant, but what choice did she have? She removed the key from her key ring and handed it over.

Mac reached his hand out to her, "Come on, I'll drive you home."

"Okay, thanks. Let me just call Keith and tell him my traitorous van is on its way in."

Mac gave her a small smile and nodded. He stepped a few feet away to give her some privacy.

When she was done, she walked over to him.

"All set?" He asked.

"Yes, finally."

He showed her to the car and safely navigated his way through the parking lot. "Which way?"

"Left." she said, feeling anxiety building in the pit of her stomach. She just realized Mac was taking her to her house, a house that needed a good dusting and vacuum. She gave him the turn-by-turn directions and he pulled into the driveway of her Cape Cod styled home. The yard was neat and tidy. She and Wyatt had recently spent a weekend painting the trim work and the rails along the steps and porch.

"We can go in the back door; it is closer to the kitchen."

"You lead the way." Mac popped the trunk and grabbed the cooler first.

They got all the groceries into the house and started unpacking them to get the cold items into the fridge or freezer. Sherry's phone rang again.

"Excuse me. " She stepped into the living room. "Hello?"

"Sherry, it's Keith. I've got your car. It is likely the alternator. I'll put it on the machine to make sure, but I probably can't get it to you until Monday afternoon at the earliest."

"Okay, how much is an alternator?"

"If that is all it is you're looking at about…,"

Sherry could hear him punching the numbers into the old adding machine she knew sat on the desk in the office.

"Around $300 parts and labor."

"Okay, well please fix it, but call me if there is anything else wrong that has to be fixed right away."

"Sure thing."

She clicked off and sighed.

"Everything alright?" Mac asked from the kitchen.

She had forgotten about him for a moment. She plastered a smile on her face.

"It was just the repair shop telling me they got the car in, and they will probably have it ready Monday afternoon."

Mac watched her as she pretended it was no big deal. The house was nice and neat as a pin, but it couldn't be easy on just her salary.

"How will you get your son to school on Monday and yourself to work?"

She tried to be nonchalant about it. She hated asking other people for help, but she would have to arrange for Wyatt to get a ride with Robbie and she would have to get a ride with someone at the office.

"I'll work something out."

"I can help you if you will let me."

"How?"

"Well, I can drive you and Wyatt on Monday and then pick you up and take you to get your car when it is ready."

"Don't you have to go back to work?"

"I'm the boss. I can take an extra day if I need to."

Sherry was dumbfounded. She had only just met him and while it was true, she really liked him and felt more comfortable around him than she had with a man in a long time. she didn't understand why he would do such a thing.

"Why would you want to do that?" she blurted out.

"Because I believe we are becoming fast friends and I can't leave town knowing a friend is stranded."

"That is really nice of you."

"Then it is a deal. Now, a more important question."

She looked at him, puzzled. "What's that?"

"Where do the canned foods go?"

It felt good to laugh.

They sat sipping a soda at the kitchen table.

"My son should be home soon."

"And I should go before he gets here."

The sadness in her eyes was palatable. "I'm sorry. I just don't know how he would take seeing me with a man other than his father. We've never talked about it."

Mac reached over and patted her hand. "No point in rushing things." He stood up to go. "Can I call you again?"

Sherry couldn't hide the big stupid smile that spread across her face. She nodded, "Yes, I'd like that." She walked him to the front door. He was standing at the bottom of the steps just as Amy pulled into the driveway, blocking Mac's car. Sherry could see Amy grinning from behind the wheel.

Wyatt jumped out of the SUV with his backpack and ran up on the porch. "Mom, can Robbie stay over tonight?"

"Well, I don't know. Did you ask Robbie's mom?"

"Yeah, she said it was up to you."

Sherry looked up as Amy was getting out of the SUV and heading for the house. This was not how she wanted this to go.

Wyatt turned to face Mac. "Who are you?"

"Wyatt, manners!"

"My name's James McIntyre, but my friends call me Mac." He held out his hand.

Wyatt shook it and sized him up. "I'm Wyatt."

"It is nice to meet you, Wyatt."

"What are you doing here, Mac? Are you a friend of my mom's?"

Sherry watched with pride as Wyatt took on a protective role.

"I am a friend of your mom's and Ms. Dandridge. Do you know Ms. Dandridge?"

"Sure, Kay is mom's boss."

"That's right, I was in town visiting and was in the area when your mom's van broke down."

Wyatt turned to Sherry. "What happened to the van, mom?"

By this time, Robbie and Amy were standing behind Mac.

"Mac, this is Amy Barton and her son Robbie."

Amy smiled sweetly and shook Mac's hand. "Nice to meet you. Then she turned to Sherry. What happened to the van?"

"Alternator died in the grocery store parking lot. Luckily, Mac was able to give me and the groceries a ride home."

"That was lucky." Amy gave them both a knowing smile.

Sherry changed the subject quickly. "So, if Robbie wants to stay tonight, it's fine. I'm not going anywhere."

"No, you have enough on your plate."

"Amy, it's fine. The car is at Keith's. I am stocked up on food. Take the night off. I've got this."

"Alright!" Robbie cheered and joined Wyatt on the porch. But Wyatt wasn't celebrating just yet. He was keeping an eye on Mac.

"What do you do for a living?" He asked.

"Wyatt Samuel, we do not interrogate our guests!" Sherry admonished.

Mac laughed, "It's okay." He turned to Mac and Robbie. "Have you ever heard of NCIS?"

The two boys looked at each other for a minute. I think so, isn't it like Navy Cops." Wyatt answered.

"That is exactly what it is." Mac nodded.

"You are a Navy cop?" Robbie asked.

"I'm the Director of NCIS. I'm in charge of all the Navy cops."

"Cool!" Both Wyatt and Robbie exclaimed.

Mac chuckled.

"Are you staying for dinner?" Wyatt asked.

"No, I need to get going."

"Oh." Wyatt was clearly disappointed.

"But, since your van is going to be in the shop, how about I give you a ride to school on Monday and your mom a ride to work?"

Wyatt nodded.

"Okay, see you then." He turned to Sherry. "You have my number. Call me if you need anything."

"I will." Sherry rubbed her neck and gave Amy a pointed stare.

"Oh well, I should go too, it was nice to meet you." Amy waved and headed back to her SUV.

Sherry stood on the front porch and waved as Mac backed out of the driveway. She turned to see Wyatt and Robbie watching her.

"You boys hungry?"

"No, not really." Wyatt answered.

"Okay." She opened the door and herded the two boys into the house.

CHAPTER FIVE

The weekend rushed by too quickly and before Sherry realized it, it was Sunday evening and she still had laundry to do. At dinner, the house finally quiet. Wyatt sat picking at his food.

"Is something wrong with your dinner?"

"No." He started kicking the table leg. After a long moment, he looked up, "Can I ask you something?"

"Yes, of course."

"Is Mac your boyfriend?"

She wanted to tell him it was none of his business, but they were always open and honest with each other and now was not the time to shut him out.

"No."

"But you want him to be?"

"I'm not sure. I like him. He is a delightful man."

"Why aren't you sure?"

"There are a lot of reasons."

"Am I one of those reasons?"

Damn, her kid was too smart.

"You are certainly one very important reason."

"Why?" Wyatt laid his fork down and concentrated on her.

"Well, because this is not something we have ever talked about, and your feelings are important too."

"What do you mean?"

"Well, suppose Mac was my boyfriend, and we spent a lot of time together. Maybe he started spending a lot of time over here and wanted to spend time with you. How would that make you feel?"

Wyatt's brow furrowed in deep thought. "Do you mean, would I get mad if you had a boyfriend that wasn't dad?"

She fought back a tear. "Yes."

"I think it would be okay to have a new dad. I mean, I know my real dad can't come back. He's gone and I think a new dad would be better than not having a dad at all."

Sherry cried, and she got up and went to hug her son, her loving, understanding son.

"I don't know that Mac is new dad material. I only just met him, but I'm glad I know how you feel. Because you know I would do nothing to hurt you."

"I know, mom. I love you." He hugged her again.

She smiled. Maybe she was doing something right. She had a wonderful, good-hearted son.

Sunday evening after dinner, her cell phone rang while she and Wyatt were watching a moving. She looked down at her phone.

"Who is it, mom?"

"Mac."

"Your gonna answer it, right?"

"You want me to?"

He nodded.

"Okay, you keep watching the movie."

She tapped the screen on her phone. "Hello."

"Hello, is this a bad time?"

"No, just watching a movie with Wyatt."

"I can call back."

She got up and walked into the kitchen. "No, now is fine."

"Everything okay with Wyatt?"

"Yes, he was asking about you."

"Is that a good thing?" Mac wasn't sure how her son would have reacted by coming home and finding a strange man in his house. He knew Wyatt had a tough time without his dad.

"Yes, I think so." Sherry didn't want to tell him the rest of it. She didn't want to presume this was a relationship if you could even call it that at this point.

"We still on for tomorrow?" Mac asked, not sure what else to say on the subject.

"Yes and thank you again. I feel bad that you are missing work because of me."

"Nothing to feel sorry about. They can get along without me. It isn't like I do much these days other than review reports."

"Doesn't sound like you enjoy it very much."

"I don't, not anymore. I think I need a change."

"Is that why you came to Gates Point?"

"Partially."

The tone of his voice made her think there was more to it than what he was telling her, and she was pretty sure it had something to do with Kay.

"Does Kay know you're still in town?" She wasn't sure why she asked.

"No, I haven't talked to her since Friday."

"I thought you guys were having dinner together."

"Yeah, I guess that didn't work out. Ethan is probably tied up with a case."

"Do you know Ethan well?"

"Pretty well."

Then Sherry remembered Mac had been a part of the team that rescued Kay from kidnappers a couple of years ago, when their own corporate attorney was helping a competitor take over the company. Kay wouldn't stand for it, and they tried to kill her to get her out of the way. Mac had come down from D.C. to help find Kay and bring her home safely.

"You still there?" Mac's voice broke into her thoughts.

"Yes, sorry. I'm still here."

"I asked if you had talked to Kay this weekend?"

"Oh no, I haven't." She could almost see him nodding over the phone. "What time are you coming by in the morning? I can make you breakfast."

"That isn't necessary. I'm not much of a breakfast person, anyway. More of a coffee on the go kinda guy."

She laughed. "Okay, no breakfast."

"Dinner would be nice though." He said.

"I could do that." She smiled.

"I meant we could all go out, me, you and Wyatt."

"On a school night?"

"I promise to have you both home early."

"Okay, yes. Dinner would be lovely."

"Okay, I'll see you in the morning around seven?"

"Yes, seven is perfect."

"Good night."

"Good night." She smiled and ended the call.

Wyatt put the movie on pause and turned to her.

"What did he say?"

He said he would be here at seven in the morning to give us a ride.

"Cool."

"And that he wants to take the two of us to dinner tomorrow night."

"On a school night?" Wyatt looked at her hopefully.

"That is what I said too, but he promised to have us home early, so I agreed."

Wyatt whooped with delight. He jumped off the sofa and hugged her. "You're the best. I'm going to go upstairs and get ready for bed."

She looked at him in surprise. It normally took all manner of cajoling and bargaining to get him to go to bed on a Sunday night. He liked to squeeze every ounce of enjoyment out of the weekend.

"Okay, I'll be up in a bit."

"Okay." he said as he bounced upstairs to his room.

She smiled to herself. Maybe she needed to rethink her position on dating. The thought of having a man around seemed to excite Wyatt.

The next morning Wyatt was up bright and early. He brushed his teeth and was dressed before Sherry came upstairs to wake him.

"Good morning, you're up early."

"Yeah well, I knew our schedule was going to be different this morning, and I didn't want to be late for school."

She doubted seriously that was the reason, but she would accept it for now.

"Okay, make sure you get all your books and everything you need. Breakfast is almost ready."

"Yes ma'am."

She went back downstairs to put the food on the table. A few minutes later, Wyatt skidded to a halt in the kitchen doorway. He looked around for a minute and then sunk into a chair at the table.

"What's wrong?"

"Nothing."

She put bacon and eggs in front of him.

He took a couple of bites and looked at the clock. "Is Mac going to have breakfast with us?"

"First, it is Mr. McIntyre to you and second, no, he will be here at seven."

"I did some research last night."

She turned to face him. Who was this kid and what had they done with her son?

"Research on what?"

"NCIS."

"And what did you find out?"

"That they have been around since 1882, that's really old."

"Yes, it is."

"And it used to be called," he paused, trying to remember, "Office of Naval Intelligence."

"That is very impressive."

Wyatt giggled, "Naval Intelligence sounds like they investigate oranges."

Sherry laughed, "Eat your breakfast, funny guy."

Wyatt laughed too and finished his eggs and bacon.

"Okay, upstairs shoes, brush your teeth again and grab your stuff. Mr. McIntyre will be here any minute."

"Yes, mom."

Wyatt ran upstairs, feet pounding on the steps. He was getting so big and lanky.

A moment later while she was gathering her own things for work, the doorbell rang.

"I'll get it!" Wyatt called. He came racing down the stairs as Sherry walked into the living room. Wyatt opened the door.

"Hello."

Mac stood there smiling, "Good morning."

"Come in." Wyatt, acting the perfect gentleman, stepped aside. Sherry watching him thinking he had grown up overnight.

"Good morning." Mac looked in her direction.

She crossed the floor over to him. "Good morning, thank you again for giving us a ride."

"My pleasure. He looked over at Wyatt, that's what friends do, they help each other out when they need it."

Wyatt smiled.

"You about ready?" Mac looked at Wyatt.

"Yes, sir." He moved to grab his knapsack.

"Wyatt, do you have your wallet and lunch money?"

"Oh right. It's upstairs." He quickly retrieved his wallet and came back down.

"We all set?" Mac asked.

"Yes, I believe we are."

Once outside, Wyatt studied the car. "This isn't an NCIS car, is it?"

"What makes you say that?" Mac asked.

"I thought NCIS only drove Dodge Chargers, Chrysler Interceptors and Cadillacs."

"That is pretty impressive and you're right, this is a rental car."

Wyatt looked over at Sherry and beamed.

Mac opened the passenger door for Sherry. "Wyatt, can you take the back seat and be the rear lookout?"

"Look out for what?"

"You never know. But it is always good to have a man on your six."

"Yeah, I can do that."

Sherry shot Mac a warning look. She knew it would be easy for Wyatt to get obsessed with this, and she wasn't sure that was a good thing.

Mac slid behind the wheel. "Everyone strapped in?"

"Yes, sir." Wyatt answered.

Sherry smiled and nodded.

"I can tell you how to get there." Wyatt offered.

"Okay, buddy, you be the navigator."

Wyatt gave turn by turn instructions until Mac pulled up to the curb in the drop off lane.

"Thank you, Mr. McIntyre."

"You're welcome, Wyatt."

"See you, mom."

"Have a good day." She watched, as he spotted Robbie and the two of them walked into the school together.

Mac navigated the traffic away from the school and headed downtown.

"How do you do it?" He asked.

"Do what?"

"All of it."

She shrugged, "I don't know. I just do it. I don't really think about it."

He glanced over at her briefly but returned his attention back to the road.

"So, you've never had kids?" She asked.

"No, never married."

"Really?"

He looked over at her again and smiled. "Didn't seem fair in my line of work to get married and then be gone at all hours of the day and night. Moving from one field office to another."

She nodded, "I can imagine that might be difficult for some."

"Some agents make it work, but I just couldn't see myself doing that. I always thought I'd have time later for that, you know."

She nodded.

"What about you? Have you ever thought about getting remarried?"

"I hadn't given it much thought honestly. I work to pay the bills and try to keep things consistent for Wyatt. I didn't think he'd be so happy about a new father. Especially when he was younger."

There was a long pause and then Mac spoke, his voice a gravelly whisper, "What about now?"

Sherry felt her cheeks blush. "Now I think if the right man came along, he would be comfortable with me dating, possibly getting remarried."

"How do you know?"

"He told me."

Mac chuckled, "He did?"

"Yeah, last night at dinner after you left." Sherry thought about stopping there and not telling him the rest of it, but what the heck, "He said a stepdad is better than no dad, and he was doing a fair bit of research on NCIS last night."

"He was?"

"Yeah, gave me a complete history lesson this morning over breakfast."

Mac laughed out loud.

They arrived in front of the office building too soon. Mac pulled into the parking garage. Sherry directed him to her reserved space.

"Are you coming up?"

"Yeah, if you don't mind, I need to talk to Kay about something."

"I don't mind." She smiled at him.

"Wait here." He said, getting out of the car. Then he came around and opened the door for her.

"Thank you." She had forgotten what it was like to be treated with respect by a man. They were standing so close in between his car and the car in the next space. The energy between them was electric, the air practically crackled with it. She wanted to kiss him. But that was crazy. They hadn't really been on a date. She barely knew him. But he was kind, he had come to her rescue and Wyatt liked him, what was holding her back? The sound of a car coming up the ramp made her jump. Mac closed the car door.

"Well, we should go upstairs. I hear your boss is a tyrant." He laughed.

They were fortunate to be the only ones in the elevator as they rode to the top floor. Kay wasn't in yet, and for a moment, Mac looked conflicted.

"Why don't you talk to me while I get settled until Kay gets here."

Mac looked around, and she thought he might decide to leave instead.

"Sure, okay."

"Good, I'll make coffee in Kay's office."

He stood at the doorway and watched her, not entering the office completely. She suspected he was monitoring the elevator.

"So, you are going to meet with Kay this morning?"

"Yeah, I thought I'd talk to her for a minute."

She pressed the button on the coffeemaker and turned to face him.

"Do you still have feelings for her?"

"No." He answered quickly and confidently.

She fought back a smile. She believed him.

He cleared his throat and added, "I thought I did at one time, but my feelings for her are as a friend, the same as they are for Ethan. No more."

"And you're one hundred percent sure about that?"

He turned his head to face her. The boldness of her question surprised him.

"Yes, I'm sure."

"Is that what this trip was about to make sure you didn't have feelings for Kay?"

He shifted his weight, uncomfortable with the question.

"Yes, partially."

They walked back out to her desk.

"What about you?" He challenged.

"What do you mean?"

"Is there room in your life for a man?"

Before she could answer, the elevator door opened, and Kay stepped out. She looked up to see the two of them facing her.

"Is there something wrong?"

"No." Sherry said, getting back to her computer, "You have an impromptu meeting this morning."

Kay stepped forward. "I see," as she looked from Sherry to Mac. Staring up at Mac, "Am I to assume the meeting is with you?"

"Yep."

"Well, smells like the coffee is done, come on in and sit down."

Mac let her go through the door first. He glanced back over at Sherry and cocked an eyebrow. She knew he was going to expect an answer to his question later, and she needed to decide if she was ready to answer it. When the door clicked into place, she let out a sigh of relief.

She opened her email and got to work.

After an hour, Mac emerged from Kay's office. "I need to run. I'll see you at five."

"Okay." she nodded.

"Call me if you need me before then."

She smiled and nodded. "I will." She watched until the elevator door closed. When she turned her attention back to her desk, Kay was standing in the doorway to her office, watching her.

"We need to talk." Kay said, crossing her arms.

"About what?" Sherry tried to look innocent, and she wondered what Mac had told Kay. She would guess not much. Mac seemed to be a private person and didn't strike her as the type to tell anyone about their business. Kay, on the other hand, wasn't above any means necessary to get Sherry to tell her what was going on.

"You can start by telling me why Mac is still in town and why he was here when I got here this morning."

"Well, you'll have to ask him why he is still here, and he told me he wanted to talk to you this morning."

"He tell you what he wanted to talk about?" Kay asked.

Sherry realized Mac hadn't told her, and she hadn't asked. "No."

"Well, I'll tell you." Kay unfolded her arms and walked over to Sherry's desk. "He asked if I'd be willing to hire him as head of security."

"Well, you were going to ask him, weren't you?" Sherry had a feeling that was part of Kay's reason for asking Mac for a security assessment.

"That is beside the point."

"Why?"

Kay looked at her puzzled, "Why what?"

"Why is it beside the point? It was your plan, after all. He just beat you to it."

"Sherry, is something going on between the two of you?"

"Did Mac say there was?"

"No, and even if there was, you know damn well he wouldn't say anything. He is too much of a gentleman for that. But I thought we were friends and so I am asking you."

Sherry closed her eyes and took a deep breath.

"I'm not sure."

"Not sure about what?"

"I'm not sure what is going on between us, and until today I wasn't sure how he still felt about you."

Kay's eyes widened, "Me?"

"Yes, you. I thought he came down here to see you because he still had feelings for you."

Kay shook her head, "I can assure you he doesn't."

"Yeah, I know."

"How do you know?"

"Because I asked him."

Kay smiled, "Really? You asked him point blank?"

Sherry giggled, "Yeah I did."

"Come in here and tell me about it."

CHAPTER SIX

It was mid-afternoon when Sherry got the call from Keith's auto repair that her car was ready. She gave him her credit card over the phone in case she couldn't get there before they closed. Keith promised to hide the key under the rear floor mat. He gave her a break on the price. She was grateful even though it was still $250 she hadn't planned on spending this month.

At five o'clock, the elevator door chimed, and Mac stepped off wearing dress slacks and a button-down shirt with the collar open. Sherry sucked in a breath. No man in history had ever been as good looking, she thought to herself. Then she noticed Ethan walking next to Mac.

"Uh, Kay?"

"Yes?"

"Are you expecting anyone this evening?"

"No, why?"

"Oh no reason, I guess I just have two handsome men here taking me to dinner." She giggled, and Ethan tossed her a smile and a wink.

"Hey Sherry."

"Hey."

Kay poked her head out of her office door, "What are you talking about.... oh!"

Sherry looked from Kay to Ethan and to Mac.

Kay smiled, "Well, this is a surprise."

"Why didn't you tell me Mac was in town?" Ethan walked over and kissed Kay on the cheek.

"Well, he was here on Friday, and I didn't know until this morning he was still here."

"Well, we decided that two single guys here in Gates Point were going to go find the two prettiest women and have some fun."

Sherry and Kay both laughed.

"Okay, I'll bite. What's the deal here?" Kay asked.

"No deal, Ethan and I want to have dinner with a couple of beautiful women." Mac grinned at Sherry.

"What about Wyatt?" Sherry asked.

"We are picking him up on the way." Mac reassured her. "Ready?"

"Oh, I'm ready, I wouldn't miss this for the world." She grabbed her purse from the desk drawer.

Ethan gave Kay a sultry look, "what about you Ms. Dandridge, are you ready?"

"Absolutely." Kay walked casually back to her desk, grabbed her bag, and the foursome took the elevator to the parking garage.

"We'll meet you there." Mac called out to Ethan.

Ethan nodded and slid behind the wheel of his Dodge Hellcat.

Once in the car Sherry looked over at Mac, "What have you been up to today?"`

"Oh, not much, just catching up with friends, something I should have done sooner, but I got distracted." He glanced over at her.

"You told Ethan you were coming to work for Kay before Kay could tell him, didn't you?"

His face took on a serious look. "Yes."

"Why? Didn't you think Kay would tell him?"

"I'm sure she would have, but I couldn't be sure of the timing, and I didn't want something to blow up in both our faces. Ethan knows Kay and I dated, and I wanted to make sure I told him about the job before I go back to D.C. and quit."

"Are you really going to quit and move down here?" She found herself more excited at the prospect than she should have been.

"Is that a problem?"

"No."

"I didn't ask how you feel about my coming to work at Port Cities."

"I don't think it is any of my business."

Mac's face was a mask. She couldn't tell what he was thinking, but it made her regret her words.

"I don't want to influence you on a decision that important." She tried to reassure him.

He nodded once and drove in silence the rest of the way to pick up Wyatt.

The look of sheer delight on Wyatt's face when they pulled up made Sherry smile.

Wyatt grabbed his gear and ran to the car. "Hi Mr. McIntyre!"

"Hello Wyatt, how was school today?"

"It was okay." Wyatt looked over at Sherry, "Hi mom, is the car still in the shop?"

"It's fixed. We just haven't had a chance to go over and pick it up yet. But Mr. McIntyre and Mr. Craddock have arranged for us to go out to dinner tonight. Do you have clothes you can change into in your bag?"

"Yes ma'am!"

"Okay, run inside and change quickly; we don't want to be late."

Wyatt grabbed his duffel bag and ran inside to the bathroom to change.

"He seems like a great kid." Mac said, leaning against the car and watching the other kids as they climbed into a variety of minivans and SUVs driven mostly by moms.

"He is. He had a hard time with the loss of his father, but any kid would."

"Does he mind me picking him up?"

She laughed lightly, "No, he doesn't."

"Did you two talk about it?"

"We did." she nodded.

Mac came to stand in front of her. He had a serious but apprehensive look. "What did he say?"

"Well, he thinks I should date."

"Really? He said that?"

"Not in those exact words, but that was the sentiment."

"And what about you?" Mac asked.

"Me?" She knew he was looking for the answer to his question from this morning. She struggled for the answer.

"Do you think you should date?"

She sucked in a breath, staring into those ice-blue eyes made her forget where she was. She had the urge to reach out and touch his face.

Her hand moved towards his. He reached out and touched her hand lightly.

"Okay, I'm ready!" Wyatt called, jogging from the building.

Sherry gave Mac a sympathetic smile, "Guess we better go."

Wyatt climbed into the backseat without waiting for Mac and Sherry.

"All buckled up?" Mac looked in the rearview mirror.

"Yes, sir."

"What about you?" Mac looked over at Sherry.

"Yes."

Wyatt giggled in the back seat.

Mac pulled out of the parking lot and headed back downtown.

When they arrived, Sherry texted Kay to let them know they were there.

"Come on in, we got a table."

Ethan stood up so they could easily spot them. "There they are." Wyatt pointed out.

"Hi, Mr. Craddock." Wyatt said, approaching the table.

Ethan held out his hand to shake Wyatt's, "Hello there young man, how've you been?"

"I'm good. Are you still catching bad guys?"

"Absolutely."

"Hello Wyatt." Kay smiled.

"Hello Ms. Dandridge."

Once they were all seated, a server brought water and menus for everyone.

Wyatt looked at the menu for a moment and then gave Sherry a nervous look. She knew he was concerned about the prices listed.

She leaned over and whispered, "It's okay."

He gave her a doubtful look and refocused on the menu.

Mac noticed Wyatt's anxiety. "Wyatt, have you had the steak here?"

"Uh, no."

"I hear it is superb. Want to try it with me?"

"Um, I think I'll just have the burger and fries."

"Are you sure? My treat for going out on a limb with me."

Wyatt frowned. Sherry looked over at him and nodded slightly.

"Thank you, Mr. McIntyre, but I think I would rather have the burger."

"Fair enough."

The server arrived to take their order, "For the ladies?" The server looked at Kay.

"I'll have the fish."

The server nodded, "excellent choice." He turned his attention to Sherry. "And for you, ma'am?"

Sherry glanced at the menu one last time. "I'll have the shrimp alfredo."

The server nodded and looked at Wyatt. "For you, sir?"

Wyatt looked up surprised, "Oh, I'll have the All-American burger, with fries."

"Would you care for bacon on your burger?"

"Yes, please."

The server nodded, "wonderful choice, I had that for lunch, it was delicious." He turned to Mac and Ethan.

Mac went first, "Make it two." He winked at Wyatt. The server looked to Ethan, "Make it three."

"Fish for the lady, shrimp alfredo for you, ma'am."

Sherry nodded.

"And for the gentlemen, All-American burgers with bacon and fries."

Mac nodded in the affirmative to the server.

Wyatt smiled. Sherry knew he was relieved, but it made her sad her son had to know about having to order cheaply off a menu and try to not be embarrassed in front of friends.

Ethan and Mac peppered Wyatt with questions about school and soccer, while Kay and Sherry talked about work and the most recent romance movie until their meal arrived.

After dinner, Mac drove Sherry to pick up her car at the repair shop. Wyatt got out of the back seat and put his duffel on the back seat of the minivan.

"Are you going to come over to our house?" Wyatt asked.

Mac gave him a small smile. "No, I have to go back to work in the morning, so I have to drive to D.C. tonight."

"Aw, really?" Wyatt was clearly disappointed.

"Tonight?" Sherry was surprised, "that is a long drive."

"It won't be too bad this time of night. Traffic should be light."

"Still, I feel bad, we shouldn't have kept you so long."

"I wanted to take you both to dinner. I wouldn't have missed it for anything."

Wyatt was listening to their conversation and was bouncing from one foot to the other, "will you come back to visit?"

Mac looked down at him, "Yes."

"When?" Wyatt pressed.

"Wyatt, don't be rude."

"I didn't mean to be rude."

Mac put his hand on Wyatt's head. "I didn't take it as rude; I took it as a compliment."

Wyatt gave Mac a weak smile.

"Maybe if it is okay with your mom, when I come back, we can go to a hockey game. Would that be cool?"

"Way cool! Thank you for dinner."

"My pleasure." Mac reached out to shake Wyatt's hand.

Wyatt climbed into the van.

"I'll follow you home."

Sherry shook her head, "You don't have to do that."

Mac let out a breath slowly and controlled. She could tell he wasn't used to people disagreeing with him. She suppressed a smile, wondering what he would say next.

"It would make me feel better, if I know you got home safely."

She nodded, "Okay."

She made sure she didn't lose Mac in traffic, although she was sure he could stay with her no matter what. Wyatt was quiet in the backseat.

"Everything alright, back there?" She asked.

"I guess."

"Did you enjoy dinner?"

"Yeah."

"Are you tired?"

"Yeah."

She nodded, even though he couldn't see her.

"Are you upset that Mac is leaving?"

"Aren't you?" He demanded.

"Of course, but he has a house and a job he has to attend to."

"Do you think he will come back?"

"Yes, I do."

"How do you know?"

"Because I am your mother and I know things." She smiled.

"I hope you're right." He mumbled.

The week dragged by and Sherry hadn't heard from Mac since Wednesday. As far as she knew he was still planning on visiting this weekend, but she hadn't discussed it further with Wyatt despite his asking her every day if Mac was coming to take him to a hockey game. She couldn't bear to get his hopes up and have them crushed. Mac was the first real male influence in his life since his father died. She was terrified things might not work out between her and Mac, and it would devastate Wyatt. But she also didn't want to get into a relationship just so her son would have a stepdad. It was too complicated, and she was halfway hoping Mac didn't show up this weekend. Better to let Wyatt suffer the loss now when it would hurt less than to let this relationship go too far and crush his little heart.

Kay stepped out of her office as Sherry was packing up her things.

"Do you have anything planned this weekend?"

"No." Sherry snapped.

"Oh, I'm sorry. I assumed you would spend it with Mac."

"I'm not sure that is a good idea." Sherry fumbled with her keys.

"Hey, hold on, is everything alright?"

"No, yes. No."

"Want to talk about it?"

"Not really."

"Sherry I will not pry but if you want to talk, I'm here."

"Thanks. Sorry, I'm just a little...," Sherry sighed, "I'm fine."

"Okay."

"See you Monday."

Sherry drove home cursing at herself for letting a man make her this upset. She felt bad that she had snapped at Kay. Now she was going to have to apologize. How did life get so complicated?

She picked up Wyatt and Robbie from soccer practice.

"Mom, you should have seen us. I made three goals in practice!" Wyatt called out as he and his friend raced to the van.

"That's great! Robbie, how did you do?"

"I scored too, but mostly I blocked the other team from scoring on us."

"Good job!" Sherry praised them both.

"Mom, can Robbie come home for dinner?"

She was thankful that Wyatt had something to focus on other than Mac. "I'll call his mom and ask."

"Awesome!"

Wyatt and Robbie high-fived each other in the back seat.

She clicked off the phone, "Okay, Robbie, your mom says you can stay for dinner, and she'll pick you up at eight o'clock."

"Thank you, Ms. Davis."

She smiled, happy that Wyatt was content to talk about video games with Robbie and not pepper her with questions about Mac.

Sherry was in the middle of cooking dinner when the doorbell rang. She checked the time, and it was too early for Amy to be picking up Robbie. She opened the door to find Mac standing there in a suit and holding a bouquet of flowers. Her breath caught in her throat.

He gave her a lopsided grin, "Hi."

"Please come in. I was just cooking dinner. Will you stay?"

"I don't want to impose."

The thoughts and reasons she shouldn't be in a relationship left her head. All she could think about was how happy she was to see Mac.

Mac glanced at the table set for three. "Are you expecting someone else?"

"No." She grabbed another place setting, "Wyatt has a friend over. They are upstairs."

"Can I help?" Mac offered.

"I've got it." She added silverware to the table. "How was work?" That simple question made her feel like she had stepped into an alternate universe, asking Mac how his day was, like it was natural, and it felt right.

Mac leaned against the doorframe admiring her form, "It was interesting."

A sound that could have been a herd of cattle stampeding through the house interrupted their conversation as Wyatt skidded to a halt with Robbie right behind him.

"Mr. McIntyre!"

Mac turned to greet Wyatt with a broad smile. "Hey buddy, how are you doing?"

"You remember my friend Robbie."

"Hi Robbie." Mac shook Robbie's hand.

"Wyatt says you are in charge of NCIS, is that true?" Robbie said

"Yes."

"Cool!" Robbie looked at Mac in admiration.

"Are you staying for dinner?" Wyatt asked.

"Yes, he is. You two go wash your hands and no peppering Mr. McIntyre with questions during dinner, please."

"Yes, ma'am." Wyatt mumbled and turned away, "Come on, Robbie."

Sherry waited for them to go before turning back to Mac.

"Sorry, he is just super excited to see you."

"I don't mind, I wish you were that excited to see me."

Her cheeks reddened. "Why do you think I'm not?"

He gave her a smile but didn't trust himself to say anymore.

Over dinner Wyatt continued to ask Mac questions, but he tried not to overdo it. Mac happily answered them all.

After dinner, Robbie and Wyatt went to the living room to watch TV.

"Can I help with the dishes?"

"You don't have to, if you'd rather watch TV with the boys."

"I'd rather help you." His voice was soft and low, and it sent chills up her spine.

Just as they were putting the last plate away, the doorbell rang.

"Robbie, that is probably your mom." Sherry called from the kitchen.

"I'll get it." Wyatt shouted.

"Hi mom," Robbie waved from the sofa.

"Hi Ms. Barton, my mom is in the kitchen."

"Hi Sherry, oh...." Amy stopped at the door.

Sherry tried to act nonchalant," Amy, you remember Mac?"

"Of course, nice to see you again."

Mac smiled and gave her a nod. "Nice to see you."

"Did I come at a bad time?"

"Not at all, we just finished dinner."

"Oh, thank you for feeding Robbie, I appreciate it. "

"Excuse me. I'll let you ladies talk." Mac folded the dish towel and then went to the living room with the boys.

Amy leaned in close. "Girl, if you don't want him, I'll leave my husband."

"Paws off!" Sherry laughed, "I think I'll see where this goes."

Amy gave her a knowing smile, "well if you need Wyatt to spend the night at our house, I'll understand."

Sherry swatted at her friend, "Stop, you're going to make me blush."

Sherry and Amy joined Mac and the boys.

"Robbie, grab your stuff, it's time to go."

Robbie got up slowly, "Okay."

Mac looked down at Wyatt and quietly asked, "Do you think Robbie would like to go to the hockey game with us this weekend?"

Wyatt's eyes got big, "Yeah!"

Mac turned to Amy; I'm going to take Wyatt to a hockey game on Sunday afternoon. Is it alright if Robbie goes with us?"

"What time on Sunday?"

"Game starts at four."

"If he can be home by seven, I think that will be okay?"

"Thanks, mom!" Robbie gave Wyatt a high five.

"What do you say to Mr. McIntyre?"

"Thank you, sir."

"You're welcome, see you Sunday."

After Robbie and Amy left Wyatt turned his attention to Mac. "Want to watch a movie?"

"Okay, but can you stay up later?"

Wyatt laughed, "Yeah, it's the weekend, so I can stay up late."

Mac looked to Sherry.

"You can stay up for a little while longer but not too late."

"But mom..."

She gave him a stern look.

Wyatt turned to Mac, "we better just watch the movie, that look is not good."

Sherry bit her lip to keep from laughing.

"Are you going to watch the movie with us?" Mac turned to Sherry.

"Yes, after I make the popcorn."

Mac and Wyatt settled on the sofa, and she watched how easily her son responded to Mac's presence in their lives. It was as if the relationship between the two of them was far more advanced than her relationship with Mac.

CHAPTER SEVEN

The movie ended and Wyatt was sound asleep on the sofa next to Mac. Sherry smiled.

"I knew that would happen." She got up to wake him.

"Don't wake him, I'll carry him upstairs."

"He's a little big to be carried to bed, I think."

"Nonsense." Mac stood up and lifted Wyatt with ease. "Where's his room?"

"Top of the stairs to the right." Sherry followed Mac up to Wyatt's room. To her surprise, Wyatt never woke. Mac laid him on the bed and put a blanket over him.

Sherry smiled. It was a perfect picture. Mac standing over him protectively. It was an image she never thought she'd have again.

"You, okay?" Mac interrupted her thoughts.

"Couldn't be better." She smiled and led the way back downstairs.

When they were in the kitchen washing the popcorn bowl, Mac came over to stand next to her.

"I didn't mean to insert myself into your family time tonight."

"Don't be silly, you didn't, you are always welcome here."

"I'd really like to spend some time with just you."

His voice was husky in her ear, and it made her skin tingle in ways it hadn't in a long time. She felt like she was losing herself to him and she wasn't sure she was ready to fall in love with him, although she couldn't explain why, even to herself.

She hesitated, but when he didn't move, she turned. He was standing so close she had to look up. She only needed to take a half step more and she would be close enough for him to wrap those muscular arms around her and bring her into him. Sherry knew if she did, she would be lost to him forever, and she couldn't do that again. She wasn't sure she could live through another heart break.

Mac seemed to sense her hesitation. "Sherry, I won't hurt you."

"I know."

"I mean it."

She swallowed, "I know."

"Is this moving too fast for you?"

"No, not really."

His brows knitted together. "Maybe we should sit down and just talk."

She breathed a sigh of relief. "That would be nice."

Mac went to the sofa and pulled her down next to him. He turned so she could lean against him just a little.

"What do you want to know?"

She wondered how he could read her mind.

"Other than Kay, do you date much?"

"No, not at all. You?"

"No, not at all."

"So, we are both pretty new at this." He affirmed.

"Yes, I guess so." Her heart was racing.

"That doesn't mean that we can't have very strong feelings, even though we haven't had feelings for a lot of other people."

Sherry smiled to herself. "That's true."

"But it is kinda scary. Trusting your feelings with someone else."

She closed her eyes. He was good; he was really good.

"You feel nervous about a relationship, too?"

"Scared to death, but also not because I know you are the one." He said, while stroking her hair.

Sherry bolted upright. "What?"

Mac stayed in his relaxed position and smiled up at her.

"Don't you feel it?"

Sherry had to admit she did, but that was what scared her. She stared into his eyes.

"Yes," her voice was barely a whisper.

"But you're still afraid?"

"Yes," she was feeling less afraid, just knowing he understood.

He nodded, "That is okay." He pulled her close to him again with her back leaning into the curve of his body.

They sat quietly for a while, with Mac slowly and gently stroking her hair. It was very relaxing, and she nearly fell asleep.

"I should probably go. It wouldn't look good if I was still here when Wyatt got up."

"I doubt he would mind very much." Sherry smiled. "Where are you staying?"

"The Holiday Inn near to here."

She nodded as he walked to the door.

"Can I see you tomorrow?"

"Yes, Wyatt has a game and...."

"Why don't you call me if you have time to get together."

"Mac, it's not that I don't want to see you."

"No, I get it. You have a busy life."

"I do, but that doesn't mean I don't want to spend time with you, this is just," Sherry sighed, "It's new and I haven't figured it out yet."

"You don't have to have it all figured out. Come with us to the hockey game."

"Are you sure? Sounds like it might be a guy's thing."

"It could be an 'us' thing. Sherry, it's you I want to spend time with, and I get you are a package deal and that is okay, but I am spending more time with Wyatt than I am with you."

"I know, I know."

"So come to the game with us."

"Okay." She nodded, "I'll call you tomorrow."

He kissed her forehead lightly and left.

Sherry stood on the front porch for a long time after he left.

She was torn. She wanted to spend more time with Mac, but she was reluctant to give her heart over so quickly. Mac seemed ready to be all in on a relationship. Wyatt clearly liked him. So, what was her problem?

"Mom, is Mr. McIntyre coming to the game today?"

"I didn't ask him."

"Why not?"

"Because I'm sure he is busy. He is taking you to a hockey game tomorrow, isn't that enough?"

She sounded irritated, and she didn't mean it, not to Wyatt. She glanced in the rearview mirror to see him looking out the window.

"You like Mr. McIntyre, don't you?"

"Yeah, he is cool. Don't you like him?"

"Sure, I like him, I just have a lot of things to do and don't have as much time to spend with him as you do."

"You're coming with us to the hockey game, aren't you?"

"Yes, I am."

Wyatt nodded.

"Do you mind if I go with you and Robbie, or do you want it to be a boys only thing?"

"I want you to come too." He insisted.

She nodded and pulled into the parking lot closest to the soccer fields. "Ready?"

"Yeah, let's get 'em!" Wyatt shouted, opening the van door, and jumping out.

Amy walked over from her van and together they carried chairs and a cooler with snacks.

After the boys were on the field, Amy turned to Sherry. "So where is that gorgeous man today?"

"No idea. Haven't talked to him." Sherry tried to keep her eyes on the game.

"And why is that?"

"Because I haven't decided how I feel about him just yet, and I have a lot to do today. I will see him tomorrow when we go to the hockey game."

"Okay, I have so many questions. First, what do you mean you haven't decided how you feel about him? Second, and I get you have a lot to do, but why can't he be part of it?"

"The only time I have spent with him since that first lunch has been with other people. We haven't spent any time alone, well except after Wyatt went to bed the other night. So, it is hard to figure out how you feel about someone when you don't spend any time with them."

"That is an easy fix but go on." Amy nodded to her.

Sherry frowned. She was hoping for more empathy.

"Second, I still need to figure out what to do about Wyatt and his school situation. If the school isn't willing to work with me as his mother, then I am going to have to put him in a private school, and that cost money. Money, I don't have. Which means I'll probably have to sell the house and move."

Amy reached over and squeezed Sherry's arm. "Honey, I'm so sorry. Is there anything I can do?"

"I don't know if there is anything anyone can do."

Amy looked out at the boys on the field, "I will do whatever I can to help. I'd hate for Robbie and Wyatt to not go to school together."

"I know me too."

"Okay, back to Mac. I know you haven't had a lot of quality time with him, but still, you have to know if you even like him.

Why else would you let him spend so much time with Wyatt?"

Sherry sighed, "Of course I like him. And yes, I know he's freaking gorgeous!"

"Now you're talking!" Amy laughed.

"I guess if I am honest, it isn't that I don't know how I feel about him. It is I don't want to let myself feel that way, because my life feels like it is in shambles and when do I have time to date?"

"Now, you're talking sense. If you want some quality time with Mac, then Wyatt can stay at my house for a night or a weekend. You guys go have some fun."

"Thanks, you're the best."

The boys ran over. "Can we have something to drink?" Robbie asked.

"Sure." Amy opened the cooler and handed them drinks.

After they ran back to the field, Sherry took out her cell phone and sent Mac a text.

"Hey, at a soccer game, wanna meet me here?"

"Sure, where?"

She gave him the name and location of the park.

"Do you mind if Wyatt came home with you after the game?" Sherry asked.

Amy grinned wickedly, "Not at all."

"Thanks."

Then she opened the grocery app on her phone and set up a delivery.

The game was nearly over when Mac pulled into the parking lot. Sherry watched as he walked towards her wearing a hoodie sweatshirt and a pair of faded jeans. He had never looked so handsome as he did at that moment.

"Holy hell." Amy whispered, "If you don't have time for him, I sure do."

"You're married."

Amy sighed. "I could change that."

Sherry laughed. "You're terrible!" She stood up to greet Mac. "Hey, glad you could make it."

"Hey." He bent down and lightly kissed her cheek.

Sherry could feel Amy's eyes on them. Mac turned to her, "Nice to see you again."

"You too. Can I get you a chair from the car?"

"Oh no, I'm fine." He gave Amy a dazzling smile.

Mac stood behind Sherry and placed his hands on her shoulders. The warmth spread through her body, and she hoped Mac couldn't tell how her body responded to his touch. She could feel Amy watching her too, and she did her best to avoid eye contact.

Wyatt stole the ball from the other team and Mac cheered him on. A time out was called, and Wyatt came running over.

"Hi Mr. McIntyre, did you see that?"

"I did, that was awesome!"

The whistle blew, and Wyatt raced back into the field.

"He's an outstanding soccer player." Mac commented.

"Yeah, he really enjoys it."

Soon the game was over, and the boys returned to the sidelines, feeling dejected because their team lost.

"You played a good game." Mac offered.

Wyatt protested. "But we lost."

"Yes, but did you have fun?" Mac asked.

"Yes."

"And did you play your best?"

"Yes." Wyatt repeated.

"Then it was a good game."

Wyatt nodded.

"Wyatt," Amy cut in, "Do you want to come hang out with Robbie this afternoon for a while. Your mom and Mac need to run errands."

Wyatt looked torn.

"It will be fun," Robbie encouraged. "Plus, my mom promised to bake cookies later."

That got Wyatt's attention. "The chocolate chip ones?"

Amy nodded.

"See ya later, Mr. McIntyre."

Mac laughed, "See ya later."

Wyatt and Robbie raced to Amy's SUV.

"I never thought I could be replaced with a cookie." Mac feigned disappointment.

"You've never had one of Amy's cookies." Sherry laughed.

"Good thing she didn't promise you one, or I'd be all alone this evening."

They all laughed, and Amy waved goodbye as she left to catch up with the boys.

Mac turned to Sherry, blocking her view of the parking lot. "So, what do you want to do this afternoon?"

She peered up into his eyes, "I have nothing planned."

"I see." He gave her a devious grin. "Well, we can't leave your car here, so why don't I follow you back to your house and we can drop off your car and decide what we want to do."

She smiled back. "Okay, see you there."

She was relieved to have a few moments to collect herself.

Mac pulled into the driveway behind her and got out of his car.

They walked into the house together. "Have a seat, I'm going to freshen up a bit."

"Okay." He sat down on the sofa and waited patiently. The house smelled like a combination of something floral and citrus. He had noticed it previously. He stood up when he heard Sherry coming up the hallway. Her bedroom seemed to be on the first floor and Wyatt's was upstairs of the little Cape Cod.

She walked into the living room wearing jeans and a floral print shirt under a deep blue sweater. Her hair was pulled back in a clip, with a stray piece drifting across her face as she walked.

"Wow."

She paused, "What?"

"You are so beautiful."

She blushed and fought the urge to say, 'this old thing?' and it would have been true. She couldn't remember the last time she had bought new clothes for herself.

"Thank you."

Mac strode over to her. "I'm glad we have some alone time."

"Me, too. What would you like to do?"

Mac cradled her face in his hands. Sherry sucked in a breath. His hands were so warm and gentle, despite the calluses she felt.

"I just want to..." He stopped and leaned down close to her. His lips so close, she couldn't resist. She leaned into him, letting their bodies touch ever so slightly. Then it happened. Her mind exploded, white lights dancing on the edge of her vision as Mac's lips gently touched her own. As she reached up to wrap her arms around his neck, he pressed them more firmly against hers. She responded with a soft moan. It had been so long since she had been kissed and, if she was honest, she had never been kissed like this before.

When Mac stepped back, he stared down into her eyes. "I didn't mean to be so forward; I just couldn't help myself. You are so beautiful and I'm afraid I lost my self-control there for a moment."

"I think I did too." She gasped. She appreciated the fact that he was a gentleman, but right now, a gentleman was the last thing she wanted.

"Please don't think I go around forcing myself on unsuspecting women."

She tried to reassure him. "The thought never entered my mind."

"Let me prove I'm not a cad." He took a step further back.

Sherry's body screamed in disappointment. "What did you have in mind?"

"How about lunch along the water and a walk on the beach?"

"Okay." She nodded, knowing that this was the best course of action, or she was going to get herself in a situation she wasn't really prepared for no matter how much she wanted it.

Mac drove to the old fort and parked next to the marina. There was a casual seafood restaurant next door.

Mac looked over at her. "You like seafood?"

"Absolutely," she smiled.

"Great." He came around to open her car door.

The hostess seated them at a window with a view of the marina. The server brought beer and an order of oysters on the half-shell at Mac's request.

With only a granola bar for breakfast, Sherry realized she was starving. "These look delicious."

They each took an oyster and Mac offered her the hot sauce. She splashed a little on to her oyster and then swallowed.

Mac did the same.

Sherry closed her eyes, "Hmm, these are good." She took a sip of beer and relaxed a little. It was good to be in the company of an adult. The empty oyster plate was removed, and their entrées were being served as her phone buzzed.

She looked at Mac, "I'm sorry I need to check this."

"Of course."

She pulled her phone from her purse. A text message from Wyatt popped up.

"Mom, can I spend the night here?"

"Is it okay with Ms. Barton?"

"Yes, she said to text you."

"Yes, you may."

A second text message popped up, this one from Amy. "I told him to text. Where are you?"

"Thank you, I'm at lunch overlooking the water."

"ooolala," was the last message from Amy and her phone went silent.

"Everything alright?" Mac asked.

Sherry tried not to blush. "Yes, Wyatt is spending the night at Robbie's house."

Mac leaned forward "So, you're free to have an adults only evening?" he asked in a low voice.

"It would appear so." She tried to stifle the smile that was slowly spreading across her face.

They ate their lunch while talking of those things normally spoken over a meal, nothing too detailed, light-hearted stories of days past or how they had each met Kay.

By the time dessert was offered the conversation turned to Wyatt and her concerns about how he was being treated at school.

"I want him to be the best he can be and while he was having some difficulty last year, this year he seems to have been able to overcome that, but I feel like the school isn't allowing him to progress and I don't want them to hold him back." She confessed.

"I agree. If he has overcome his challenges, he should be rewarded by allowing him to attend the classes where he can learn the most." Mac studied her. "What will you do if the school refuses to move him into different classes?"

"I've started looking around at private schools, but that will probably mean I will have to sell the house to put the money towards tuition."

"Is there no other way? Have you asked Kay for a raise?"

"No, because if I do, Kay will give me the raise and pay for Wyatt's school. I want to handle this on my own. I want to raise my own son." Her words sounded more defiant than she meant them.

"Hang on, no one is suggesting that you aren't doing a fantastic job raising your son, but it is okay to have help in one form or another once in a while."

"I'm sorry, I didn't mean to snap at you like that, you're right of course, but you don't know how Kay can get. She loves to help people, but it is an addiction with her, and she doesn't always know when to stop."

Mac frowned, "What do you mean?"

"I mean, she loves helping people, and that is a wonderful thing. I can't tell you how many of her employees have benefited from her generosity and most of them don't even know the help came from Kay. And she means well. But I must do this. I have to prove to myself I can raise my son on my own."

Mac wanted to say more, to tell her she had already done all of that, but now was not the time and this discussion was not the reason he wanted some alone time with her today.

The check arrived and Mac paid before the server left. Sherry offered to pay for her own meal.

"Ready to have a walk along the beach?"

"Absolutely, I love the water."

"Let's go." Mac stood and put his hand on the small of her back as they left the restaurant. The seawall led from the marina to the beach so they could leave Mac's car in the parking lot.

Chapter Eight

S herry and Mac strolled down the seawall, allowing the speed walkers, cyclists, and joggers to pass them by. As they got close to the fishing piers, Mac paused and pointed.

"Look off the end of the pier."

Sherry followed his gaze. "Oh!" she exclaimed as she spotted the pod of dolphins as several of them broke the water. "It never gets old seeing them." She leaned against the concrete wall.

They watched them in silence for a long while, sharing in the magic of watching creatures who belonged to a different world, a realm beneath the waves. Finally, she looked up at Mac and found he was watching her rather than the dolphins. She smiled.

"You are so incredibly beautiful," he ran his thumb along her forehead, smoothing the creases she made when he said things like that to her. "You don't believe me, do you? But you have a light, this wonderful energy that shines out into the world."

"No one has ever said things like that to me before."

"Maybe they couldn't see it."

She thought about it. Chris had been a loving husband. He had never been short-tempered or unkind, but even he had never spoken to her this way.

"Oh Mac, you are so kind and such a gentle soul." She reached up to touch his cheek, but he captured her hand and kissed it lightly.

"I have a confession," he said, walking again.

"Oh?"

"I have another reason for bringing you here other than just enjoying a wonderful afternoon with you."

"I can't wait to hear it."

"As you know, I accepted the offer from Kay to come work for the company."

"Yes, we all talked about that at dinner last week."

"Yes, and I went back to DC to turn in my papers and plan to sell my house."

A thought struck her, and a cold lick of fear slid down her spine. "You haven't changed your mind, have you?"

He looked at her in surprise; he was glad that she seemed eager for him to move here.

"No, I haven't changed my mind. In fact, I start work on Monday. But my question was I am looking for places to rent and I wondered if you would be upset if I rented a place not too far from you?"

"No, why would I mind where you live?"

"We haven't spent a lot of time together, and I would like to change that, but I also don't want to make you feel smothered or trapped."

"That is very thoughtful, but I've lived next door to people that I only speak to once a month, so I think you're safe."

Mac blinked at her for a moment. "Also, I know we are going to keep this professional at work, but I am really going to enjoy seeing you every day and I don't want that to hinder our relationship outside of work."

She laughed lightly.

"What?"

"Mac, I think you are over thinking this."

"Maybe, but Sherry I have some strong feelings for you, and I don't want to do anything to mess things up. I don't know if you have feelings for me and I understand you might be cautious. That is okay. You set the pace for this relationship, and I am patient."

"You are a very sweet man, and I have feelings for you. But I am also not sure how this is going to work. I think right now you and my son have a better relationship than we do and that is good. Any man I decide to date must understand that Wyatt and I are a package deal, and you understood that from the beginning. But I don't want Wyatt to get hurt because of our relationship. So please keep that in mind that while I think it is doubtful you and I wouldn't get along; if we stopped seeing each other, Wyatt is going to get hurt too."

"I understand, and I promise you I would never hurt either of you. Not even if you hated my guts and never spoke to me again. I'd make sure that Wyatt understood he would always have a place in my heart no matter what happens between us."

"And that makes me look like the bad guy!"

"What? Wait, why are we even talking like this? Unless this relationship is not something you want at all? If that is the case I will walk away now before we are more invested than we need to be."

Tears stung her eyes, and she reached out for his hand. "No, that isn't what I want. I don't want you to leave. I just...." The tears spilled down her cheeks, and she turned away, embarrassed.

Mac let her have a moment, then stepped up behind her and gently wrapped both arms around her. "In one breath I promised never to hurt you and in the next I've made you cry."

Sherry sniffled. "It isn't you. You are so sweet and kind. And it is all just me. I'm so confused and there is just so much going on at once, I don't know what to do."

He gently turned her to face him. "The first thing you have to do is to never feel you have to apologize to me for your tears. The second is to stop trying to do it all on your own. Everyone needs help sometimes and there is no shame in that at all. It is a brave person who can ask and allow their friends to help them when they need it."

"It just seems like too much is happening at once and I feel like I can't have fun, when my son is struggling at school."

"Have you talked to him lately about how things are going?"

"Not this week."

Maybe check in with him and make sure things are not still going at bad as there were."

She sniffed, then she nodded.

"God, you must think I am the worst. This is the second time you've seen me cry."

"Not at all, it just means I know you care and are passionate about the people you love." He wrapped her in a comforting embrace. "Come on, let's go down on the sand and walk close to the water."

She smiled up at him, grateful for his understanding and falling for him that much more. He was so perfect.

"It seems like all we've done since I met you is talk about my problems. What about you? Beyond high school I don't know that much about you." Sherry asked casually as they walked along the water's edge, avoiding the water as it rolled up the beach.

"There isn't much to tell that you don't already know. I joined the Marine's, when I left there, I went to work at NCIS, and here I am."

"You didn't date anyone after high school? Never kissed a girl?" She teased.

He frowned thoughtfully. "I have dated a few women here and there, but nothing serious. I've just never had a job that I felt like I was willing to give up until now."

"Why does it have to be all or nothing?"

"Because long hours or months on deployment are hard on relationships for both parties, and I didn't think it was fair to bring someone else into that. I chose that life for me, not for someone else, and it takes a very rare person who can handle the stress of months alone. Just didn't seem right."

"And after the Marines?"

"Well, at first, NCIS wasn't a lot different. I worked long hours, weekends, worked in different countries and different cities. It was like being in the military and getting transferred, just not as intense."

"And again, you didn't feel that was the type of environment for a long-term relationship?"

"Not really."

"And you thought that decision was yours alone to make?"

"Well, yes, and no. The few women I dated seemed to be okay with the short-term relationships, so yes it was my decision. But, let's say, for example, I had met you ten years ago. Things might have been different."

Sherry gulped. She wasn't expecting him to bring her into it.

He laughed at her expression. "I might have been willing to ask you to wait for me while I was deployed or to move to Spain with me or something."

"I might have said, yes."

He was his turn to be surprised.

"I mean we'll never know, of course, but I think I would have been willing to follow you to Spain." She grinned.

He nodded, "good to know."

They walked the three miles to the end of the beach. The afternoon had slipped quietly into evening and the sun was setting as they walked back, the lighthouse on the old fort and the one off the coast were both flashing their warnings to the ships coming in and out of the port. The temperature was dropping quickly, but neither seemed to notice.

When they arrived back at Mac's car, he turned on the heated seats.

"Oh, that feels wonderful!" Sherry sighed, sinking further into the soft leather.

"They do come in handy." He sat for a moment looking at the water. "I'm not ready for this day to end."

"Me either."

"You said Wyatt was spending the night with Robbie?"

"Yes." Sherry wondered where he was going with this question.

"Without sounding too forward, do you want to come back to my hotel with me?"

She glanced at him from the corner of her eye. Her heart skipped a beat. She had no intention of sleeping with him, but a thrill flashed from her stomach to her thighs.

"I'll be a perfect gentleman, I promise."

She bit her lip. She wasn't sure she wanted him to be a gentleman because that would mean she could blame the way she felt on his wickedly sexy ways, and not her wonton desires.

"Sure, and I promise to be a lady."

The look in his eye told her he was having the same thoughts as she. He grinned as he backed out of the parking space and drove to his hotel.

When he had told her he was staying in a hotel near to her, she had imagined the little motel that had been in place since the 1950s. No, Mac was staying at the Harbor Inn Resort, which was on the west side of the city, but not exactly in her neighborhood. It was new and very expensive. She wondered how much NCIS Directors made a year.

The valet came out to park the car and the carpet in the lobby was so thick she felt like she was sinking up to her ankles.

"I feel underdressed." She whispered.

They took the elevator to his room and any thoughts of being awkward and having to sit on his bed to have a conversation went out the window when she opened the door to a small suite. There was a living room with a small bar and coffee machine, a table and chairs, a sofa and a wall mounted flatscreen. A balcony and a short hallway she assumed led to the bedroom and bath.

"This is quite impressive."

"They seem to cater to executives or people staying more than a couple of nights. It's pretty comfortable."

"I'll say." She walked over to the sliding glass doors and peered out at the skyline. His room faced the river and so there wasn't the haze of lights from the city, just the bridge and a few scattered lights on the opposite shore.

"I could get used to a view like that."

He joined her. "It is nice." He opened the sliding glass door and the cool evening air rushed into the room, bringing the smell of the salt water with it.

Sherry closed her eyes and breathed deeply, "I can't ever imagine living somewhere that doesn't smell like that."

Mac watched her with fascination. Her features were so delicate, her lips were sculpted perfectly and were the color of a pink rose in full bloom.

"It is comforting." He said, wishing he could take her in his arms and make love to her amidst the smell of the sea and the sound of the waves. Then he cleared his throat, "can I get you something to drink, wine perhaps?"

"Oh, I'd better not."

"I'm driving, if you want to have a glass." He smiled.

Sherry thought about it for a minute. Why not have a glass of wine? Wyatt was safe at Amy's. She had all night, and it would be nice to do something for herself for a change.

"Okay, yes, wine would be lovely." She followed him over to the small bar while he opened a bottle of red wine and poured two glasses.

Handing her a glass, he raised his own, "to new friends."

"Yes, to new friends."

She tasted the wine letting it slide down her throat and warm her from the inside.

"Shall we?" He motioned to the sofa.

She nodded and followed him.

They sat in silence for a few minutes. The wine and the salt air were helping her to relax more so than she had been in a long time. She felt like she was doing something naughty, because since her husband had died every moment of her life was devoted to Wyatt. Not that it hadn't been that way before, but there had been a shared commitment to raising their son and now she was on her own. She never once thought about doing something for herself. But, in this moment, sitting in a hotel room with a man who was kind, not to mention so handsome, she was trying very hard not to throw herself at him like some kind of wanton hussy. She was raised not to be too forward with men, but because she married her high school sweetheart, she never learned the subtle art of flirting. It had never crossed her mind, but tonight she regretted not having learned more about what to do or say when alone with a sinfully handsome man.

Mac shifted, so that he was facing her and put his glass down on the table in front of the sofa and took her free hand in his. Sherry stared up at him a little confused and not sure how to respond.

"I need to confess," he started.

She gave him a sweet smile, "Okay."

"I'm no good at dating. As you probably guessed, I know nothing about what you might call flirting. I'm a direct kind of guy. I say what I mean and mean what I say."

"I got that impression, yes."

"I'm lousy at trying to figure out what to do on dates, what a woman would enjoy doing. But what I know with no doubt is how I feel about you."

Her breath caught in her chest.

"But I'd like to try, I realize you don't have a lot of time and our dates might have to include a certain eleven-year-old soccer player, but I'm okay with that as long as I can steal a kiss once in a while."

She felt her body heating up despite the chilly fall air blowing in off the river. She reached for the table to put her glass down Mac took it for her, putting the glass on the table without even looking.

"There's no eleven-year-olds here now." She heard herself saying.

"No, there's not. There is only the most incredibly beautiful woman I have ever met."

Mac leaned forward, and she found herself drawn to him like a magnet. This kiss was less tentative than the first. It was gentle, but more urgent. She ran her hands over his close, clipped hair while he supported her head with one large, steady hand. The kiss was heated and slow, urgent, yet gentle.

Mac reached behind her with his free hand and turned off the table lamp. Then pulled away and stood up.

"I want to kiss you in the moonlight." He took her hand, leading her to the balcony, turning off more lights as they went. Mac led her outside and then pulled the curtain closed behind them to soften the remaining. The balcony was private from the other hotel rooms and their kiss passionate and desperate.

Her hands caressed his face and shoulders. His five o'clock shadow was rough on her face, but she didn't care. It had been so long since a man had touched her this way that her body was responding faster than her brain could process what they were doing.

He left her lips to caress her neck with his mouth. A moan involuntarily escaped her lips as his hands traveled down her back to grip her hips and pull her closer. She stared up into his eyes. They were intense with passion and desire.

Sherry ran her hands down the front of his sweater, breathing in his cologne mixed with his own scent. She closed her eyes. She felt lightheaded with lust and was on the brink of doing something she could very well regret in the morning. Suddenly, Mac's hands slid to cup her bottom, and he lifted her up, placing her back against the wall of the balcony.

His kiss was passionate, his tongue desperately seeking hers. Her body responded without any prompting from her. When their lips broke apart, they were both panting.

"Sherry, you make me want to do things I shouldn't." His voice growled in her ear, sending chills down her spine at the suggestion.

"Who says you shouldn't?"

"Don't tempt me, please." His voice softer, "I promised to be a gentleman, and I'm afraid I am about to break that promise. "

She closed her eyes and prayed that he would break his promise and quickly before she had time to rationalize what they were doing.

Mac slowly stepped back so that she could get her feet back under her.

"Sherry." He closed his eyes, "You have no idea how much I want to take this farther, but I don't want to rush you. I want you to take your time and let you decide how you feel about me."

She bit her lip. She knew he was right. He was so right, but she also wished he wasn't, that he wasn't so completely reasonable.

"You are so sweet." She reached up to touch his face.

"I care about you, and I don't want to mess this up before it even gets started."

She kissed him lightly. "How are you this perfect?"

He laughed, "I'm far from perfect." He took a step back. "How's your Skee ball game?"

"My what?"

"I saw there was one of those traveling carnivals in town. Wanna go check it out?"

She laughed. "Sure!"

CHAPTER NINE

M onday morning came too soon, after a weekend filled with traveling carnivals, romantic walks on the beach and a hockey game, both Wyatt and Sherry were exhausted.

"Mom, I'm too tired."

"I'm not at all surprised, but so am I and I'm going to work, so you sir, are going to school."

There was more grumbling, but he got up and headed down the hall to the bathroom while she headed to the kitchen to make coffee, lunches, and breakfast. She had been exhausted after the hockey game and then dinner with Wyatt and Mac. The entire weekend had been a whirlwind of emotions. But she got Wyatt to school on time and herself to work before Kay, which she took as a personal win under the circumstances.

Sherry was reading the emails that had come in over the weekend when the elevator door opened, and Kay and Mac stepped off into the foyer. She suppressed a smile. She was sure Kay wasn't happy to find Mac sitting at the curb in front of her house this morning. Mac told her over dinner it was his intent that Kay have proper security and if that meant he had to handle that himself until he got enough people on board then that was something he was prepared to do. He had not shared that detail with Kay when outlining his security plan, and she was sure it was to avoid the argument he would get from Kay. From the smug look Mac was wearing and the look on Kay's face, she was certain that argument had taken place on the way to the office and Kay had lost.

The speculation about that conversation helped her keep the hint of jealousy that threatened to rear its ugly head at the sight of Kay and Mac together.

"Good morning," she greeted them.

Mac turned down the hall to his new office. "Good morning," he said as he passed her desk.

Kay frowned at her, "Morning."

Sherry ducked her head to keep from laughing. She gave Kay a minute before she made coffee and give her a rundown on her day.

She kept her back to Kay while she fiddled with the coffeemaker.

"How was your weekend, Sherry?" Kay asked.

Sherry turned to face her and walked over to sit down in front of Kay's desk.

"It was good." She smiled.

"What did you do?"

"Hmm, let's see. We went to a hockey game."

"Hockey? I didn't know you liked hockey."

"Don't know a thing about it, but Wyatt likes it and now I am learning a little."

"Is Wyatt going to play hockey in the soccer off season?"

"Please don't even say it!" Sherry held up a hand. "I can't only imagine what that gear costs."

Kay smiled. "Well, it is good for him to try different things."

"True but tell that to my bank account." She laughed.

"How are things going with his school?"

"No changes yet, I am going to call them back again today and give them one last chance to do what is right for my son and if we can't come to an agreement, then I will have to find a private school for him." She sighed, "then I will need to figure out how to afford that and take him away from his friends. I just don't know what to do, honestly."

"Is there anything I can do to help?"

Sherry thought about Mac's words and how help wasn't necessarily a bad thing. "I just don't know yet, but once I figure out what I need to do, I'll let you know."

Kay smiled, "Okay."

Sherry changed the subject, "so", she drew out the word, "How was your ride to work this morning?"

Kay leaned forward. "Did you know about that?"

"Know about what?" She played innocent. "I saw the look on your face when you and your new head of security got off the elevator. I only assumed he picked up where Eddie left off."

"It is ridiculous for a grown woman to be shuffled around like produce going to market."

Sherry laughed out loud.

"What is so funny?"

"Well, first, I believe the term is chauffeured, not shuffled."

Kay's eyes narrowed. "That's easy for you to say. You're not the one being escorted from my door to the car."

"I wouldn't mind, being shuffled like that." She laughed again.

"I think Ethan was in on it." Kay sighed.

"I'm sure he was," Sherry continued to laugh. "What I think is ridiculous is a woman who has been a target twice, wouldn't want a little security."

"But, by having a security guard around me all the time makes me feel trapped and also like the bastard is still winning because he caused me to change my lifestyle."

"I think being kidnapped and nearly being killed twice should make you change your life to a degree. You're not hiding, you still work in the office and you still go out to dinner with friends. You are just using some common sense. Besides, you're the one who lives with an FBI agent. It doesn't get more secure than that."

Kay glared at her and then laughed, too. "I guess you're right. I hadn't thought of it quite like that."

"However, you do need to stop being so bullheaded and talk to Mac. I'm sure there is something you can work out short of him putting a security guard on your porch at night."

Kay held up her hands in surrender. "Okay, I'll have a talk with him."

"Good, now I have work to do." Sherry got up and left.

When Sherry left work that evening to pick Wyatt up from school; she found Wyatt waiting for her.

"Hey buddy, what's up?"

"Practice ended early."

"Why didn't you call or text me? Are you okay?"

"Yeah, I just sat and did my homework while I waited."

"Is school going any better for you?"

"I guess, but the classes are still really easy. But I have had no more problems with the other kids recently."

"That's good. I'm still working on the class situation. If the school won't change you to different classes, would you be willing to change schools?" She looked at him in the rearview mirror.

"I don't know. Would I still get to play soccer and see Robbie?"

"You could still play on the recreation league team, but not the school team. And Robbie is on that team with you, and you live close enough to hang out with him outside of school now. The new school might have a soccer team, too."

"That might be okay."

"Well, it isn't a decision we have to make yet. I have an appointment tomorrow with the principal and we'll see how that goes."

"Can I come to the meeting?"

They pulled into the driveway, and she turned to look at him after putting the van in park. "Is that something you want to do?"

"Yes, you'll be talking about me."

"Okay, but you are to listen and let me do the talking. While you will have a say in what we do the decision is mine to make. It is my job to do what is best for you long term. Okay?"

"Yes ma'am."

"Okay," she nodded.

He smiled, "Since I already did my homework, can I play video games until dinner?"

"Yes, you may."

"Awesome!" He said, jumping out of the van.

She went inside to change clothes and start dinner.

The holiday season was about to start. Halloween was only two weeks away, and it was all downhill from there, Thanksgiving and Christmas. She had made no plans yet, and she needed to think about what they would do for the holidays. Her parents had retired and moved to Florida. They always invited her and Wyatt to come there, but she didn't like the idea of flying during the holidays and driving was out of the question. She could invite her parents here, but in all honesty, she really didn't want to have house guests and now that she was dating Mac, she wasn't ready to answer questions about him.

She took the chicken out of the fridge and put it in the oven to roast and prepped some broccoli and cauliflower to roast along with it.

Her phone buzzed with a text from Mac.

"Hey, how was your day?"

"Good. How was your first day?"

"Interesting."

She sent a laughing emoji, "I bet."

"Can I call you later after Wyatt goes to bed?"

"Yes."

She smiled at the phone and laid in on the counter. It rang this time with a call from Amy.

"Hello?"

"Why haven't I heard from you until now?" Amy's words came out in a rush.

"What do you mean, I saw you yesterday when we picked up Robbie and again when we dropped him off?"

"Exactly, and nothing after. What happened Saturday night? What happened after the hockey game?"

Sherry smiled. She found she wanted to tell Amy everything. "I have so much to tell you!" Sherry walked into the living room looked up the stairs to see if Wyatt was still involved with his game and then settled onto the sofa. "Okay, I have to talk fast because dinner is in the oven."

Amy sucked in a breath, "Oh well, get to talking girl, I want details."

"On Saturday after the soccer game we went to his hotel, because he hasn't found a place here yet, and we had a glass of wine, and things started getting romantic."

"What do you mean by romantic?"

"Well, we were sitting on the sofa, and he started telling me things like how beautiful I was, and we kissed."

"Oh my god, then what? Did you do it on the sofa?"

"What? No, we're not in high school. He turned off all the lights and took me out on the balcony and he told me he wanted to kiss me in the moonlight."

"I think I am going to die right here. What did you do?" Amy whispered with excitement.

"I let him." Sherry remembered the heat of the moment and wondering again what would have happened if Mac had taken things further. Would she have let him take it to the next logical step?

"Things got pretty passionate after that. He had me up against the wall and I really thought that things might, well, you know, right there on the balcony."

Amy was practically breathless. "Did you?"

"No."

"Why not?"

"Because Mac stopped; he said he didn't want to rush me or the relationship. He wanted me to be comfortable and not regret anything we did."

"Wow, that was really sweet."

"I know, right? He had promised to be a gentleman if I came up to his hotel room and he honored that. Although, I kinda wish he hadn't."

"You're scandalous!"

"I'm also thirty-three and not getting any younger. Do you have any idea how long it has been since I have been touched by a man?"

"No."

"Since Chris died."

"Are you serious? You haven't been with anyone else in that long?" Amy sounded shocked.

"No, and you know I haven't because I would have told you if I had."

"Seriously, that is honorable, having a proper mourning period and all, but this is the twenty-first century you have to take care of you."

"I haven't been with someone because of any old fashion notions, but when the hell have, I had time to meet anyone, much less date?" Sherry whispered so Wyatt wouldn't hear her. "I've got a son to raise, my boss was kidnapped and nearly killed so there has been a lot going on the past few years."

"Well, you have had more than your share of tragedy and excitement, I'll give you that."

"And I want to make sure Mac is the one."

"How do you not know he is the one? Wasn't there like a lightning bolt or something, isn't that how it works?"

Sherry thought about it for a minute. "On the physical attraction side, yes, it was like a lightning bolt. I thought I was alone in a room and suddenly there he was, looking more gorgeous than any man should look. But there has to be more to it than that."

"Well, of course, he has to be kind, sensitive, and not bossy. He must like kids and preferably your kid; your kid must like him. He needs to respect you and the life you've already built for yourself. Have I missed anything?" Amy said sarcastically knowing that Mac had already met each of those qualities.

"You've made your point, yes he is all of those things and more."

"Then, girl, what are you waiting for?"

"I honestly don't know, to make sure it is all real and not just something I want to see that isn't there."

"Trust me, it's there." Amy reassured her.

"I know, at least I think I do."

"Are you seeing him tonight?"

"No, he is going to call after dinner. Oh, did I tell you he started work in my office today? So, we are keeping the relationship a secret, but he walks past my desk throughout the day."

"What? No, you didn't tell me that. How could you not tell me that?"

"Oh, the timer just went off in the kitchen, gotta go." Sherry clicked off the phone laughing, knowing her friend was going to want more details. Her phone buzzed with a text from Amy.

"You suck!"

Sherry laughed and pocketed the phone.

"Wyatt! Time for dinner!" She called from the bottom of the stairs.

A few minutes later, she heard him thundering down the stairs. He slid into the kitchen in his stocking feet.

"Whoa there, be careful."

"I am." He said, grabbing the silverware and helping to set the table without being asked.

"What as you in such a good mood?"

"I just beat Robbie in our game."

"Oh okay, I trust that is a good thing."

"It is." Wyatt began explaining the object of the game and how he and Robbie could play online against one another. It sounded interesting and slightly over her head.

Over dinner Wyatt brought up the subject of Mac.

"Did Mr. McIntyre start his new job with you today?"

"He started his job at the company. But he is in a different office than me."

"You get to see him, right?"

"Not really. He is very busy."

"Do people at work know you are dating him?"

She looked up at him in surprise. She was fascinated by the things he knew and cared about.

"No, they do not, and we would both like to keep it that way if you don't mind."

"So, it is like a secret."

"Yes, exactly."

"Why?"

"Because, sometimes in the workplace there are rules against co-workers dating each other."

"Do you have that rule?"

"I don't know if our company has that rule, because I have never dated anyone I worked with before."

"Oh." Wyatt ate more chicken and thought about her answer.

"I don't think teachers are allowed to date each other."

"Why do you say that?"

"Because there was a math teacher and a gym teacher that people said were dating and then the gym teacher left."

"Were they your teachers?"

"No, it was just a rumor in school."

"And what do we know about rumors?"

Wyatt rolled his eyes. "They are hurtful and often not true."

"That is correct. I'm glad you remember that."

"And you don't want people spreading rumors about you and Mr. McIntyre."

"No, I do not."

"I won't tell anyone."

Sherry smiled sweetly. "Thank you, since you're my best friend, I knew you wouldn't tell."

Wyatt smiled and took a bite of broccoli.

After dinner, she was eager to get the dishes done and Wyatt off to bed.

"Can we watch TV tonight?"

"I'm not really in the mood. How about as a special treat you watch TV in your room tonight and I will read a book down here."

"Alright!"

"But I'll be up at nine o'clock to make sure the TV is off, and you are getting ready for bed. It is still a school night."

"Okay, mom." He bounced up the stairs.

She waited until she was sure he was engrossed in his TV show, and she sent Mac a text.

"Wyatt is watching TV upstairs if you want to talk."

She waited almost half an hour before getting a reply. Finally, when she didn't think she could take the waiting anymore, the phone rang.

"Hello?"

"Hey, it's Mac."

"Hi."

"Sorry I didn't get back to you right away. I was on the phone trying to recruit some security staff."

"Former Marines?"

"No such thing."

"I thought you stopped being a Marine to work at NCIS."

"I basically changed jobs, once a Marine always a Marine."

"Oh, okay." She was getting the impression she had a lot to learn about Mac and his life, that she would not get sitting around sipping wine.

"Was your father in the military?" Mac asked.

"Uh no, he wasn't, which I know many people find strange because this area has such a large military presence. My family is from here and my dad owned a hardware store, until the big box stores moved in and pushed him out."

"I love those small local hardware stores. You can find some really cool stuff in them you can't get anywhere else."

"Yeah, that is true. It is amazing what those big stores don't carry. But he couldn't compete with the prices even though their products are cheaply made. He bought and sold local, and he was proud of it."

"I'm sorry he had to go out of business."

"It's okay. It all worked out. My parents live in Florida now and are having the time of their lives."

"Do you see them often?"

"Not really. Sometimes we see them around the holidays. We used to fly down but, I don't think I'm up for that this year and I doubt they will come here. So, not sure when I will see them again."

"Do you want me to drive you down there?"

"No," she said a little too quickly. "But thank you."

Mac paused, and she was grateful he didn't pursue that part of the conversation. Instead, he switched to a more personal topic, "When can I see you again?"

She smiled to herself, savoring the thought of their passionate kissing, "Tomorrow at work."

"That's no good. I want to spend time with just you."

"I don't know, I want to spend time with you too, but it is tricky to schedule time like that."

"I know, and I'm sorry if I seem like I'm pressuring you. I just really want to sit and put my arms around you."

She smiled at the thought, "Maybe you can hang out with us this weekend and we'll get some alone time after Wyatt goes to bed." She whispered carefully.

"Sounds like a plan."

"I need to go check on Wyatt. See you tomorrow?"

"See you tomorrow."

Chapter Ten

T he next morning, Sherry parked her car instead of pulling into the drop off lane at Brookstone Middle School. She sat for a quiet moment and then turned to Wyatt. "You ready for this?"

"Yes."

"Remember the rules?"

"Yes, you have the final say and all decisions are final."

"Alright then, let's go."

They walked through the doors of the school past groups of kids mingling in the hallways, greeting friends, and gossiping. They passed a group of older boys,

"Hey Wyatt, is your mommy going to walk you to class?"

"Just ignore them, mom. I do."

"Good for you, son. Good for you."

They entered the principal's office and were met by the receptionist. "Can I help you?"

"Yes, I have an appointment with Principal Monroe, and I would also like a copy of the school's policy on bullying and harassment."

The receptionist blanched, "We have a zero-tolerance policy on bullying and..."

"Really? Who enforces that policy because my son and I were both just harassed in the hallway by a group of boys who seem to have nothing else to do with their time."

"Let me get Mr. Monroe for you."

"That would be nice."

Sherry stood in front of the desk and waited, ignoring the worn fabric and wood guest chairs and the scarred end tables with the two-year-old magazines strewn across them.

"Mr. Monroe will be out in just a minute if you'd like to have a seat."

"No, thank you. I'm sure we won't be waiting that long."

The receptionist was giving her a tight smile and tried to go back to work. Sherry was more than aware of how uncomfortable it was when someone stood at her desk while waiting to speak with Kay and under difference circumstances, she would give this lady some professional courtesy and go sit down. But not today. Today she was ready for a fight and Mr. Monroe and Brookstone Middle school were about to find out she gave as good as she got.

She looked down at her son standing straight and tall next to her.

"Do those boys bully you like that every day?" She said loud enough for the receptionist to hear her.

"Not every day, but twice a week. I mostly just ignore them because they do that to everyone, not just me."

"I see, and did you tell a teacher or someone in this office?"

The reception looked up at Wyatt and then to Sherry, who was making it a point to ignore her.

"I used to tell my teacher, but she did nothing but tell me to ignore them, so I quit telling her about it."

"I see." Sherry pegged the receptionist with a stare before asking, "Do you have that policy available?"

"Oh yes, ma'am. I'm printing it right now."

The printer on the corner of her desk whirled to life. A moment later she was handed a sheaf of papers.

"Ms. Davis?"

"Mr. Monroe, I presume?" Sherry looked up.

"Yes, please come in." He glanced down at Wyatt. "Why don't you run along to class while I speak with your mother."

Wyatt puffed out his chest. "No, sir."

Sherry spoke up. "This conversation involves my son, and he will sit and listen quietly while we discuss if he is going to continue to attend this school or not."

She heard a door close behind her and turned to see another parent had entered the office and was looking from the principal to Sherry and Wyatt.

It was obvious Mr. Monroe was not pleased, and he quickly ushered the two of them into his office.

"Please have a seat." He said, closing the door behind them.

This time, Sherry sat down. Wyatt did the same.

"Please tell me what this is all about."

"My son is in developmental classes. I feel he no longer needs them and I would like to have him transferred into the regular classes starting next semester."

"I see," Mr. Monroe said, typing on his computer. "I see your son tested into those classes; are you telling me that his development issues have been resolved?" He peered over the top of his glasses.

"Yes, that is what I am telling you. My son's issues resulted from a car accident, and he has been working here and outside of school to overcome those issues and I believe he has done so."

"I see." He peered over at Wyatt. "We can't just transfer him because you feel he is cured."

"No, I would hope not, but you can retest him and place him in more appropriate classes."

"Have you spoken to his guidance counselor?"

"Yes, I have several times and she keeps putting me off. I came here today to get an answer. Are you going to do what is best for my son's education and retest him?"

Mr. Monroe removed his glasses and folded his hands before speaking to her again.

"Ms. Davis, I'm sure you can understand that we cannot simply set up a test every time a parent thinks their child is gifted or a prodigy or something."

Sherry sucked in a breath before straightening her spine, a sure sign that things were about to take a turn in the conversation.

Mr. Monroe sensing were about to get more tense in the room spoke quickly. "Tests cost money. We can test Wyatt again at the end of the school year and see how he does."

Sherry weighed her options. There were so many things that she wanted to say to the weasel faced man sitting behind the desk giving her a condescending look.

"Well, I'm afraid that is going to be quite impossible Mr. Monroe," she tried to match his tone and arrogance.

"Why is that?"

"Because my son will no longer be a student at this school. He will attend a private school next semester where the faculty and staff care about his education and well-being." She stood up. "The members of the school board will know exactly why I am removing my child from this school."

"What do you mean?"

"I mean, that I have a copy of your so-called zero tolerance bullying policy right here and I can tell you I wasn't in the building five minutes before both my son and I were harassed by a group of your students, but what can one expect with no school resource officer in sight, no teachers or staff in the hallway to enforce any rules or regulations. I'm sure that some of the other parents of the students in my son's class could tell a similar story about how their child is treated here and would enjoy the opportunity to address the school board with me at their next meeting." She stood up. "Enjoy your day, sir." Then she looked down at Wyatt. "Let's go." She strode out of the office with her head held high. The exit from the building was without further incident. She unlocked the van.

"Mom, I have to go to class."

"Not today, you don't. If you don't want to."

Wyatt stood there and blinked at her in disbelief.

"I think we need a mother and son day. What do you think?"

A smile slowly spread across Wyatt's face just the way his dad used to smile. "Yeah!"

"Hop in kid, we're both playing hooky today."

She slid behind the wheel and took out her cell phone.

"Hello Kay, it's Sherry. No, everything is fine, but I need to take the day." She glanced over at Wyatt and made a face. "I'm sorry for the short notice but things didn't go well with my meeting this morning and I think Wyatt and I need a day to weigh our options." She paused while Kay talked some more. "I'll be in tomorrow. Thanks Kay."

"You will not get in trouble, will you, Mom?"

"No, not at all. Kay is just worried about you."

"Is she going to have Mr. Monroe fired?"

Sherry laughed. "I don't think Kay's influence stretches that far into the schools. But I'm sure she would if she could." Sherry started the van, wondering if Kay really could have Mr. Monroe fired. Kay had a way of surprising her in the most interesting ways. She backed out of the parking space and thought she should have text Mac, but that would have to wait until later.

"What should we do today, kiddo?"

"I don't know, maybe the zoo?"

"The zoo it is, let's go home and change clothes first."

"Okay." Wyatt smiled at her but there was still a worried look in his eyes.

She was feeling more relaxed already. They changed into jeans and comfy shoes and drive the nearly forty-five minutes across town.

They arrived just as the zoo was opening. "Hey look, we might be in time for some of the animal feedings," she pointed to a schedule posted as they entered the visitor center.

"Cool!" Wyatt ran over to the schedule and read down the list. "Mom, looks like we can see the otters and then the tigers!"

"Let's go."

They strode off along the trail to the otter enclosure.

They were leaving the otters and headed for the tigers when Sherry's phone buzzed with a text from Mac.

"Everything alright?"

"Yeah, just taking care of some stuff with Wyatt and his school."

"Okay, call me later?"

"Yes." She smiled.

They arrived just in time at the tiger habitat.

"Oh wow, did you see that?" Wyatt asked as the zookeepers tossed some meat into the enclosure.

"That looks pretty scary to me." She said, watching the tiger shred the meat off a large bone. She shuddered to think what poor animal had given his life for this meal.

"No mom, it's cool."

"If you say so."

They stood and watched the tigers a while longer before Wyatt got bored. "Let's go check out the giraffes."

"Lead the way."

They spent two more hours at the zoo until Wyatt showed signs that he was getting tired.

She knew he might be doing better in school but sometimes he still suffered from sensory overload. "Wanna leave and go get lunch?"

"Yes, I think so. I'm kinda hungry."

"You got it."

"Can we get burgers and fries?"

"Hmm, okay because it is a special mother/son day, but not at some drive thru. I know a really cool place with the best milkshakes."

"Really?"

"Yeah, I used to go there when I was your age."

"Wow, really?"

She laughed, "Yeah."

They pulled into the parking lot of the Blue Diner, a classic silver rail car diner that had opened in the 1950s.

"This place is cool, mom."

A server in a retro uniform came over to take their order. They both ordered burgers, fries, and a chocolate shake.

"You know, this is going to completely ruin our dinner." She said after the server left.

"It's okay mom, that way you won't have to cook tonight." He smiled sweetly, and she wondered how she got so lucky to have such a wonderful son.

"I enjoy cooking for you."

"I know, but you do it all the time. I know I get tired of doing the same things all the time. Don't you?"

She marveled at him, "Yeah, like what kind of things?"

Wyatt gave her a devious smile, "Like cleaning my room and going to school."

"Well sorry kid, you need to have a clean room and to learn things and you need to eat, so I guess you're stuck cleaning your room and going to school and I'm stuck cooking dinner."

"You get off easy."

"Hey, you only have to clean your room, I have to clean my room, the kitchen, the living room....,"

"Okay, mom. I get it."

"We could trade if you wanted to. I'll clean your room one day and you make dinner."

He thought about it for a minute. "Okay!"

"Really, you want to cook dinner?"

"Yeah, but not tonight."

"No, not tonight." Sherry changed the subject, "What do you want to do for Halloween?"

"I think I am too old for trick or treating."

"Okay, are any of your friends having a party?"

"I don't think so."

The server brought their food, and they ate in silence for a few minutes.

Wyatt took a break from his burger for a moment. "Is Mr. McIntyre coming over again soon?"

Sherry swallowed a French fry. "Do you want him to?"

"Yeah. I like him. He's cool."

"Yes, he is." Sherry agreed.

"Do you like him?"

"Yes, I do, he is a delightful man."

"No, I mean, is he like your boyfriend?"

"What makes you think that is your business, young man?" She tried to sound serious, but Wyatt saw through her and just laughed.

"It's okay, I have a friend at school whose mom has a boyfriend because his parents are divorced."

"That is unfortunate."

Wyatt shrugged "Not for him. He gets double the presents at Christmas and for his birthday."

"I'm sure he'd rather have his mom and dad."

Wyatt shrugged again and turned his attention to the milkshake.

"Mr. Monroe was kind of a jerk today, wasn't he, mom?"

"I know Mr. Monroe wasn't a nice man, but please, still speak of him respectfully, Wyatt."

"Yes, ma'am."

"But, yes, he was not very nice at all the way he treated us today and I'm sorry that I blurted out that I was going to pull you out of school, but I don't want you to be treated disrespectfully, either. You deserve the best education possible, and I will make sure you get it."

"Private schools cost a lot of money, don't they?"

"I'll worry about that part. You just worry about being the best you can be."

Wyatt laughed, "You sound like a commercial."

Sherry laughed too.

"I will look at some options on-line and then we will go visit them. How does that sound?"

Wyatt nodded and finished his milkshake.

"Ready to go home?"

He nodded.

Sherry paid the bill, and as they drove home, Wyatt was nodding off in the backseat. She felt like she could use a nap too. She hadn't had a nap in years. When they got home, Wyatt announced he was going to his room. Sherry sat down on the sofa with her laptop. It was nearly four thirty when the sound of her phone woke her up.

"Hello?"

"Sherry, it's Kay. Are you alright?"

"Yeah, sorry. I fell asleep."

"Oh, I'm sorry I woke you. I was just worried about you and Wyatt."

"We're fine. I had a meeting with his principal this morning that didn't go well and so we had a mother and son day. I'll put in a leave slip in the morning."

"Don't worry about it at all. I'm just glad you guys are okay. I'll let you go, and we'll talk tomorrow."

"Okay."

She laid back on the sofa and closed her eyes, knowing she probably wouldn't be able to go back to sleep. She was wrong.

"Mom? Mom?"

Wyatt was shaking her arm. She opened one eye. The room was dim.

"What? Oh, Wyatt honey, are you alright?"

"I'm fine, I was worried about you and Mr. McIntyre is here, he is worried about you too."

"What?" She bolted upright. Mac was sitting across from her in a chair, his brow knitted together.

She turned back to Wyatt. "Are you sure you are, okay?"

"Yes, mom. I took a nap and then played video games until Mr. McIntyre got here."

"Thank you, sweetie."

Wyatt turned to Mac. "Would you like another water?"

"No thank you, Wyatt."

"I'm going to go back to my room."

Mac nodded, "good job" and gave Wyatt a fist bump.

Sherry smoothed her hair and tried to collect herself. When Wyatt was in his room, she looked over at Mac.

"I tried to text you and then call. When you didn't answer, I became worried. Sorry for just dropping in but I needed to know you were alright."

"I can't believe I slept that long. What time is it?"

"It's nearly eight o'clock."

"Oh, my gosh!" She stood up, "Excuse me just a minute." She ran upstairs. "Wyatt, are you hungry?"

"A little."

"Okay, come down and entertain Mr. McIntyre, while I make us dinner. Then it is going to be off to bed."

"But mom...."

"You have school tomorrow."

"I thought I didn't have to go back."

"I'm sorry sweetie, but you have to finish out the school year."

"But..."

"No arguments."

She came back to the living room, shaking her head. "One minute he is still my sweet baby boy, the next he is on the brink of turning into a surly teenager. It is like he is caught in the middle."

"Well, I'm afraid you can't avoid the teenage years, and probably not even the surly part."

"You're a lot of help." She looked at him with her hands on her hips. "Want some dinner?"

"Yes, please." He smiled.

She went to the kitchen, turning on lights as she went.

"So, talk to me. What happened today?"

She sighed, "I had an appointment with the principal this morning and I took Wyatt with me. I lost my temper and announced that I would pull Wyatt out of school at the end of the semester."

Mac leaned against the door frame and crossed his arms. "That was a bold statement. How did Wyatt take it?"

"Not as bad as I thought. But I think as long as he gets to play soccer, he will be okay."

"What are you going to do?"

"I don't know, I do not know how I am going to afford a private school." She sank down at the table and put her head in her hands. "What am I going to do?" She heard the chair next to her scrape across the floor. Mac placed his hand on her back.

"Don't worry, we'll work something out."

"Why is it you are always seeing me at my worst?"

"If this is your worst, then I think you're doing okay. I have seen people at their worst, and this is nothing."

She looked at him.

"Not that what you are going through isn't serious, but it is fixable." He added quickly.

"I suppose you have a point."

"No, I'm just saying, badly, that I do not think of this as your worst. I see a mom who cares about her son." He took her hands in his and looked her in the eye, "There is absolutely nothing wrong about that."

CHAPTER ELEVEN

Tuesday morning, Sherry dropped Wyatt off at school and headed to work. She needed to interview schools in the area. She wondered how much work would be waiting for her when she arrived.

She stepped off the elevator to find Kay waiting for her.

Kay greeted her with a smile, "Good morning."

"Morning. What are you doing here so early? Did something happen yesterday when I was out?" Panic lacing her voice.

"No, no. I just thought I'd come in and help you out a little."

Sherry was immediately suspicious. "Help me out how?"

"Well, first, this coffee is for you." Kay handed her a cup.

"Thank you." Sherry sat her purse down on the desk.

Kay continued on, ignoring the look Sherry was giving her. "I've made my own, so you don't need to worry about that. I also opened my mail yesterday and sorted it." Seeing the horrified look on Sherry's face, Kay held up her hands. "I filed nothing or threw anything away, I just put it all in neat piles on my table for you."

Sherry managed a smile. "Thank you, that was very thoughtful."

"Tell me what happened. I know you had an appointment with the school yesterday."

"Well, the short version is that I lost my temper and told the school principal that I would take Wyatt out of the school at the end of the school year. So now I have to find him a school."

Kay looked concerned. "What does Wyatt think about that?"

"He just wants to see his friend Robbie and play soccer, other than that I think he will be happy to leave."

"Well, that's good I suppose, do you have any schools in mind?"

"One I can afford." Sherry said in between sips of coffee.

"Let me see which ones we have scholarships at. That will at least give you some information about the school before you have to decide to go visit them."

"Thank you, Kay."

Kay smiled, "Okay, next topic of discussion." Kay crossed her arms.

Sherry looked up, concerned Kay, had learned about her relationship with Mac.

"Ethan and I would like you and Wyatt to join us for Thanksgiving dinner."

Sherry let out a sigh of relief.

"We wouldn't want to impose."

"I wouldn't invite you if it was an imposition." Kay cocked an eyebrow at her. "Unless you have other plans."

"No, we do not have plans. I still don't know what we are doing for Halloween, much less Thanksgiving."

"What's the problem with Halloween?"

"Well, Wyatt says he is too old for trick or treating, and I asked if he was going to any parties, you know, like at a friend's house or something. But he said he didn't know of any parties. I was trying to decide if I should take Wyatt and a few friends to a haunted maze or something."

"Sherry, you are taking on too much."

"I can't let an eleven-year-old sit at home and do nothing on Halloween."

"You can if that is what he wants to do." Kay laughed.

"You are no help." Sherry turned her attention to her desk.

"Now, I need to get to work before you do my job too and you decide you don't need me."

"Sherry, I will always need you."

"Thanks, Kay. I mean that."

Kay smiled and returned to her office.

Sherry sunk down in her chair and logged onto her computer to see how many emails she had to read from the day before.

An hour later, Mac walked past her desk to the elevator. She looked up as it was closing in time for him to give her a quick wink. She smiled and ducked her head.

When she finished with the emails, she got up to retrieve the mail from Kay's office.

"Have you seen Mac?" Kay asked, hanging up the phone.

"What?"

"Have you seen Mac today?"

"Uh, yeah, he just got on the elevator."

Kay frowned. "Did he say where he was going?"

"No, is everything alright?"

"Yeah, I just need to talk to him about something. If you see him, can you tell him I need to see him if he has time?"

"Sure." Sherry chided herself for reacting too quickly. If she wasn't careful, she was going to give them away.

It was nearly noon when Mac re-appeared. Sherry was just gathering her things to go find a quiet place for lunch.

"Oh hi. When you get a minute Kay asked if you could come talk to her."

"Sure, is she in now?"

"Yes."

"Thanks." He strode to Kay's office.

Sherry looked back over her shoulder as she got on the elevator in time to see the office door close. What was that about? She wondered. If they wanted to talk in private, they both knew she was leaving for lunch. She didn't like the thoughts that were playing at the edge of her mind. She walked down the street to the coffee shop with free Wi-Fi, ordered a coffee, and a cup of soup before digging her laptop out of her bag and began her research into local private schools.

There were five, two of them included middle school and high school grades. The other three stopped at the eighth grade, which mean Wyatt would have to change schools again. She started with the two schools that included high school. She nearly fainted when she looked at the tuition. Both schools were accredited and had sports programs and good academic programs. One had a very strong reputation and plenty of kids of high-profile members of the community attending that one. They boasted about their graduation rate and college acceptance rate. That school looked ideal, but she wondered how much pressure was put on the students there and if that would help Wyatt at all. She moved on to the other three and started ranking them in her mind based on cost and academic programs.

She walked back to the office, trying to figure out how she would pay for any of these schools. She wanted the best for Wyatt, but she couldn't afford the two that she thought would be the best. Maybe she could get a part-time job. Working away from home in the evenings wasn't possible. She couldn't leave Wyatt with Amy or someone every night. But maybe she could get a job working doing transcription or something. Anything that might help. Who was she kidding? Those schools were so expensive even a part-time minimum wage job wouldn't cover it. She needed to think of something. Maybe she could mortgage the house or get a loan. She would check with the bank to see if she had any options there.

When she returned to the office, Kay's office door was open, and Mac was nowhere to be seen. She felt a pang of disappointment but focused on her work the rest of the afternoon. At 4:30, her computer pinged with a new email from

Kay. It was a list of the schools that had Port City Industries scholarships for children of the company's employees. Her hand trembled a little as she clicked to open the list and see the amounts. She didn't want to get her hopes up, and she knew if there was a way for Kay to help, she would, but she couldn't allow someone else to provide for her son. He was her responsibility.

She scrolled through the list the scholarships were very generous and if awarded one, she might send Wyatt to her first choice, but the scholarships were awarded at the beginning of the school year she didn't see anything for a mid-term entry; she wasn't even sure they would accept Wyatt mid-term. What a mess she had gotten them into.

"Everything alright?" Kay asked.

"Yeah, just everything seems overwhelming at the moment. I shot my mouth off and now I have to find Wyatt a school by January."

"Did you get the list I sent?"

"Yes, but it looks like the scholarships are awarded at the beginning of the year, so they will help next year, but I will need to figure out what to do to for the rest of this school year."

"I'm not sure that is a hard and fast rule. Call the head of Tidewater Academy, I find him to be a reasonable man. I'm sure if there is a way, he will work with you."

"Okay, I'll call him tomorrow."

"I'm headed out. I'll see you tomorrow." Kay smiled.

"Is everything alright with you?" Sherry asked.

"Yes, of course. Why?"

"Because you never leave early."

Kay laughed, "Then I am overdue."

"Yes, you are." She refrained from asking where Mac was. He normally drove her home. Or maybe she was ditching Mac. Sherry watched as Kay got on the elevator alone. She got the sense Kay was up to something. She pulled out her phone and texted Mac.

"Is everything okay?"

"Sure, why?"

"Because Kay just left without you."

"Yeah, I know. Someone else is taking her home tonight."

"Oh?"

"Can I call you later to explain?"

"Sure."

She put her phone back in her purse. There was just too much going on right now. She didn't have time for whatever was going on between Mac and Kay, and she really didn't care. She had to focus on Wyatt right now.

She packed up the rest of her things and headed home.

After dinner, Sherry's phone rang.

"Hello?"

"Hi, it's Mac."

"Hi, how was your day?"

Despite was she told herself earlier about not caring what was going on with Mac, she was happy to hear his voice.

"Listen, I hate to spring this on you last minute. But I need to go to the Connecticut yard for an issue they are having there. I wanted to see you first, but I'm afraid I need to leave right away."

"Oh, you don't have to apologize. You have a job to do." She hoped the relief in her voice wasn't obvious. "How long will you be gone?"

"Probably two or three days. I'm not really sure until I get there."

"Okay, be careful."

"You, too. I'll text when I can."

"Okay, look forward to it."

They clicked off. She stared down at her phone. It was just as well. She didn't need the added distraction.

She pulled out her laptop and sent emails to Wyatt's doctors, asking for an appointment with them to discuss his progress and any potential issue with changing schools. It was a little late for that question, but she could still change her mind if necessary.

When she was sure she had done everything she could for the day, she checked on Wyatt and went to bed.

Wednesday went by in a blur. She talked to both of Wyatt's doctors. They both agreed under the circumstances that a change of schools might be best for Wyatt. Both agreed with her choice of Tidewater Academy and agreed to make whatever recommendations were required. They assured her that Wyatt had made significant progress and if he was up to the challenge, then she should let him try. Only time would tell if he would fully recover from his injuries. Emotionally, he was more than capable of handling the change. Sherry relaxed, a little more confident that she was doing what was best for her son.

At dinner that night Wyatt was kicking the table leg again, something he did when he had something on his mind.

"Is everything alright at school?"

"Yeah, same old stuff." He picked at his salad.

"You'd let me know if I need to go down there, right?"

"Yes ma'am. I'd like to see you give Mr. Monroe what for, again."

"Well, while I stand by what I said, I should not have lost my temper and I hope you are more reserved with your temper and not take after your mom."

He smiled. "I'll try. Why hasn't Mr. McIntyre been over lately?"

"He is out of town for work in Groton, Connecticut."

"I miss hanging out with him."

That was the crux of the problem, Sherry thought. Wyatt was missing Mac. She was too, even though she was stubborn to admit it. "Maybe later we can text him and see if he has time to chat online."

"Really?"

Sherry smiled, "Yeah."

"Awesome!"

The promise of talking to Mac was enough to get him to eat his salad and the rest of his dinner. He went upstairs to finish his homework while she did the dishes. She sent Mac a quick text.

"Do you have time to talk tonight?"

It was nearly an hour later before the reply came. She was just about to force Wyatt to go to bed.

"Hey sorry, yes, I'd love to chat."

"Do you mind if Wyatt says hi?"

"Of course not."

She went upstairs, "Wyatt? Are you still awake?"

"Yes."

"Got a call coming in for you."

She handed him her phone just as it rang. Wyatt clicked it.

"Hey buddy!" Mac's face appeared on the screen.

Wyatt smiled so widely, Sherry thought it would reach his ears.

"Can you see me alright?"

"Yes, sir. Can you see me?"

"I sure can. Is your mom there?"

"Yeah, she is sitting on the other side of the room."

"Okay."

She heard Mac's voice drop to a whisper, "No talking about secret guy stuff then."

Wyatt laughed and shook his head.

"How's school going?"

"It's okay. I'll be glad when it is over. Mom says I don't have to go back."

"She said you don't have to go back to school ever?"

Wyatt frowned, "No, just never back to that school."

"I see, and what do you want?"

"I don't want to go there anymore. They have me in classes that are boring, and no one does anything about the bullies."

"And what do you do about the bullies?"

"I ignore them, because giving them my attention gives them power."

"Good man."

Sherry beamed. She didn't realize that Wyatt had talked to Mac about the kids in his school, but hearing this, she was glad he did. She wondered why Mac hadn't mentioned it.

"Have you played any soccer since last weekend?"

"We've had some practices. I have a game this weekend. Do you think you will come and watch?"

"If I can get my work finished up here, I will be there."

"What are you working on? Is it secret ship building stuff?"

"Not exactly. It is more like keeping the secret ship building stuff safe, so that people don't get to the secrets."

"Cool! Are you hunting bad guys?"

Mac laughed, "No, I look for ways the bad guys might try to get in and I think of ways to prevent that from happening."

"So, what would you do if someone broke in and tried to steal the plans or something?"

"Well then, I would try to find out how they got in and then hopefully find out their identity."

"And would you go after them?"

"No, I'd let Mr. Craddock and the FBI do that part."

"Oh," Wyatt looked thoughtful.

"Do you use security cameras and retinal scanners?"

"In some cases, yes."

"That is really cool. I saw this movie once about a spy and he had to break in to get the stolen secrets back and he poked this guy's eye out so he could use it to get into the vault."

"Oh gross, where did you see that?" Sherry asked.

Wyatt laughed, "I'm not telling besides, there are worse things in my video game."

"Maybe I need to look at your video games more closely."

"Mom!"

"Hey Wyatt, why don't you let me talk to your mom and explain things."

"Okay, thanks Mr. McIntyre."

"You're welcome. Hold the phone close."

Wyatt grinned. "When it is just me and you talking, you can call me Mac. Okay?"

Wyatt pulled the phone back and nodded.

"Okay, let me talk to your mom."

Wyatt grinned and nodded. "Good night, M... Mr. McIntyre."

"Night, buddy."

Wyatt handed Sherry the phone.

"Okay, you get some sleep, school tomorrow."

"Night, mom."

"Night." She closed his door partway and looked down at the screen. "And you are going to tell me what all the secret guy stuff is all about."

Mac laughed. "Then it wouldn't be a secret."

"Uh, huh?" She walked downstairs to her bedroom and partially closed her door.

"We alone?" he asked.

"Yes."

"God, I miss you, I'm sorry I didn't have time to say much before I left."

"What's going on up there?"

"They had to fire one of the engineers and they think he might have taken some files with him when he left."

"So, you are tracking him down."

"Yeah, I did."

"Is he still in one piece?"

"Of course, he is."

"What did you do to him?" Sherry thought Mac was probably not someone you'd want to piss off.

"I got the files back and had him arrested."

"Wow, you've been busy." Sherry leaned back against the pillows on her bed.

"It's been interesting. I'm going to set up some more security measures while I'm here. I probably won't be back until Friday."

"Okay, just be careful."

"You too, no more telling off school principals until I get back."

"I think I'm done with that for now."

"How is it going with the school search?"

"I think I have decided on the school. The money is still an issue. I was thinking about a second job."

"No, Sherry, you can't do that. You need time to spend with Wyatt. Let me help before it gets to that point."

"I'm not at that point yet."

"You let me know if it comes to that, okay?"

"I will, I promise."

"I wish I was there to hug you and tell you it will all be okay."

"Me, too."

"I'll make up for it this weekend."

"And how are you going to do that?" she giggled like a schoolgirl.

"Can't tell you, it's a surprise."

"Okay, well call or text when you can."

"I will. Miss you."

"Miss you too." With that, he clicked off.

She sank deeper into the pillows. This was all too good to be true. Was it real? Was Mac really that perfect? She wanted to believe it was true.

She closed her eyes for a few minutes before changing her clothes and before she knew it, the alarm was ringing.

Chapter Twelve

"**M**om! Mr. McIntyre is here!" Wyatt called out as he raced out the front door. Wyatt looked around to make sure Sherry wasn't outside yet.

"Hi, Mac."

"Hey Wyatt," they fist bumped, "Good to see you."

"You too. How was your trip?"

"It was good. I think things will be safe up there for a while."

"That's good. Hey, after dinner you want to play video games? I beat Robbie this week and made it to level forth-five on Sky Reacher."

"You might get too good for me, but I'm up for it."

"Sweet!" Wyatt bounded up the steps and opened the door just as Sherry was about to step outside. Wyatt stepped back and watched.

As much as she tried to fight it, Sherry's heart leapt into her throat at the sight of Mac standing there, looking up at her.

"Hi," Mac's voice was raspy at the sight of Sherry.

"Welcome back."

Mac slowly ascended the steps onto the porch. He stopped just inches from Sherry.

"I missed you."

Wyatt stood grinning, watching the two of them.

"I missed you, too." Sherry breathed.

"Are you sure?" Mac searched her eyes. He hoped she had missed him as much as he had missed her.

She smiled and nodded, "Yes."

Mac drew her close and kissed her. He heard Wyatt whisper, 'yes!' He smiled and stepped back from Sherry. "I'm glad."

"Want to stay for dinner?"

"I was hoping you would say that." He looked over and winked at Wyatt.

"Have you been home yet?" Sherry asked, leading Mac inside.

"No, I came straight here from the airport."

"Well, sit down. You must be exhausted."

"Not really. Want some help in the kitchen?"

She eyed him suspiciously. "You cook?"

"Not really, but I'm great at following orders and chopping vegetables."

"Wyatt, go do your homework."

He protested, but then looked over at Mac. "Yes, ma'am."

"We'll, play games after dinner." Mac reassured him.

"Okay." Wyatt ran upstairs.

"That was impressive."

"Not really, you're the parent, I'm just the cool boyfriend."

"Meaning, I'm the bad guy."

"Not at all. It means you have all the power and authority. I'm just here for a free meal and hanging out."

Sherry laughed, "Well, it is good to know where I stand."

Mac looked over his shoulder to make sure Wyatt was out of sight before putting his arm around her waist and pulling her close. He bent over and growled in her ear.

"I'll tell you exactly where you stand, even better I'll show you." He kissed her ear and then turned her loose.

Sherry was breathless, "I just might let you, too." She gave him a wicked smile and turned to the refrigerator. Opening the door, she let the cool air wash over her skin. When she turned back around, he was watching her closely, taking in every movement.

"Do you know how to cut an onion into a flower?"

"No." He grinned and shook his head.

"Do you know how to cook a steak?"

"That I can do."

"Okay, here are the steaks." She handed him a container, "I am going to make this onion into a bloom and then air fry it."

"I don't know what you just said, but I'll stay out of your way while you do it."

She laughed, "Okay, you handle the steaks, I'll take care of the veggies."

Mac was anxious to get caught up on what she had been doing while he was gone. "Have you decided about the schools, yet?"

"We have some appointments next week. I know where I want him to go, but as always, it is a matter of financing. But if he can get accepted, I'll just have to find a way."

Mac concentrated on the steaks and remained quiet.

Sherry changed the subject, "How are things going with hiring additional security?"

"Pretty well actually, Kay is pretty much letting me run that and gave me a generous budget, so I have a couple of people starting next week in our office and some interviews lined up for some additional IT staff who specialize in security."

"That sounds exciting."

"Yeah, it is. I'm proud to say I stole one or two from NCIS and recruited a few more from the private sector, so we'll see how it goes."

"Do you know all of them or had you worked with them in the past?"

"Yes, I either served with them or we worked together while I was at NCIS, so they are all people I know personally."

"Well, that should make things easier."

"You have to start with people you can trust. And I trust these people with my life."

"That's pretty serious."

"You need to know the people you work with have your back; to be there to support you when you need it. If not, you are going to be in a lot of trouble."

Sherry paused holding the knife mid-air above the onion. "That sounds very military."

"It is, but it applies to everything I think."

She was curious, "don't you trust your friends to be there for you if you need them, no matter what?"

"Yes, a few close friends yes." This time Mac set the steaks aside and turned to face her "And how many of them would you trust in Wyatt's life?"

Sherry looked up at him. "I would trust Wyatt's life to Amy, Kay and you."

He looked at her and blinked. "That's good." He nodded.

Finally, they were close to having dinner ready. "I'm going to go get Wyatt for dinner." She announced.

She went upstairs and knocked on Wyatt's door. "Wyatt?"

"Yes?"

She opened the door. He had his head bent over a book and he looked frustrated.

"Everything alright?"

"I'm not sure I understand this." He said, sitting back in his chair.

"Okay, why don't you take a break and come eat dinner and then we can look at it together."

"I want to get it done so I have time to pay video games with Mac, I mean Mr. McIntyre."

"School comes first and I'm sure once you've had something to eat, we can tackle this no problem."

"Okay, thanks mom."

She left him to wash his hands before coming downstairs.

"Everything okay?"

"He is just having a little trouble with his homework, and he is worried it will cut into his gaming time with you."

"Oh, hmm. What subject is it?"

"Geography."

"That's not so hard. I'm sure I can help him if you don't mind."

"I don't mind if you don't." Sherry smiled.

Over dinner, Wyatt filled Mac in on his soccer practices and the latest news with his video games. To his credit, Mac gave Sherry fleeting glances while staying focused on Wyatt.

After homework and video games with Wyatt, Mac leaned back on the sofa next to Sherry.

She looked over at him and took his hand. "You must be exhausted."

"I'm good."

He pulled her across this lap. "This is the most relaxed I have been all week."

"I'm sorry Wyatt bombarded you with questions tonight, but he missed you."

"You never have to apologize for Wyatt asking me anything and I'm more interested in whether or not, you missed me."

She looked into his ice-blue eyes, "I missed you." She leaned in and kissed him.

She pulled back, "More than I thought I would."

"So, my charm is wearing you down." He smiled.

She giggled lightly, "Yep, I'm not sure how much longer I am going to be able to hold out."

"Don't bother, you won't be able to resist me much longer and it will just be easier for you to fall head over heels in love with me now and save time."

"Do women often just fall head over heels for you?"

"I don't think so."

"But wouldn't you know?"

"Not necessarily."

Sherry leaned back and looked at him, seriously. "Why wouldn't you know."

"Because, unless I was madly in love with them, why would I know or care how they felt about me?"

"I guess you have a point." She thought about it a minute. "And you've never been in love before?"

"No, not really. There have been people I cared about, but again the…"

"Lifestyle," she answered for him.

"Exactly."

"And you care about me, but your lifestyle is more conducive to a relationship?"

"Well, my lifestyle is currently more conducive to a relationship, but even if it wasn't, I think I would make it work or change my life so that it did work."

She looked at him in surprise, "You'd do something that drastic."

"To be with you? Yes. And I already have." He smiled.

"Why?"

He looked at her curiously. "Sherry, don't you get it? I'm in love with you."

She looked at him, "You've never said that before."

"No, I haven't. I didn't want to pressure or rush you. You didn't seem like you felt the same way, and I wanted to give you space. But you should know."

Sherry sat stunned for a moment, her thoughts swirling around in her mind. All her feelings rising to the surface and demanding to be recognized.

"But you hardly know me."

"I know what my heart feels, and I am looking forward to learning about the rest."

She knew he meant every word, and she wanted to give herself over to him right then, but something was holding her back and she couldn't let go of her heart just yet.

"Mac, I care for you deeply."

"That is good enough for me right now. If you don't mind me hanging around."

She laughed, "I don't mind at all." She kissed him again.

He settled her back against the arm of the sofa with her legs across his lap. "Do you want someone to go with you when you visit the schools?"

"I appreciate that, but I can't ask you to take off from work, not when you are trying to get the security department up and running the way it should. I think we have been lucky in ways other than the direct attacks on Kay, but there are so many other ways our company could come under attack, and your work is too important."

"Nothing is more important to me than you and Wyatt."

She smiled at him.

"I know," she stroked his cheek. "But I think I can handle a school visit."

"I'm sure you can handle it. That was never in question. The question was, do you 'want' someone to be with you?"

"I'll never say no to wanting you." She ran her hand through his hair. It was growing out a little from the military style cut. She hoped he didn't let it to grow out too much. She like it short, it suited him.

"Well, it is getting late, I should be going."

She was disappointed but didn't argue. She nodded and slid off his lap.

"I'm glad you're home."

Mac stood up, wishing he could break through that brick wall Sherry had put up around herself.

"Thank you again for dinner and letting me spend time with Wyatt," as he headed for the door. "I'll see you tomorrow."

She hated to see him go, but she couldn't bring herself to ask him to stay. She leaned against the door.

Mac leaned down to kiss her good night.

She smiled up at him, "Drive safely."

"Always." He bounded down the steps to his car.

She watched until he pulled out of the driveway. She should've been exhausted, but she knew she would not be able to sleep.

She took a shower and spent extra time with nighttime personal grooming. It was nearly one in the morning before she fell asleep.

Sherry stood at the bottom of the stairs holding her keys, purse, and a duffle bag with a change of clothes for Wyatt. "Wyatt, we are going to be late, let's go!"

"Coming, Mom!"

Mac stepped up on the porch. "The van is all loaded,"

"Thank you, I don't know what I would do without you."

"Let's hope you never have to find out." He gave her a charming grin. "Do you need me to go get him?"

"I can't imagine what he is doing up there."

Mac stepped just inside the door, "Wyatt buddy, do you need a hand?"

Wyatt magically appeared at the top of the stairs. "I'm ready!"

"Do I even want to know what was taking you so long?"

"No." Wyatt said matter-of-factly and headed for the van.

"How long did you say this stage lasts?"

Mac looked thoughtful, made a show of counting and then declared, "Into his twenties if you're lucky and some guys never outgrow it."

"Terrific!" she said, locking the door behind them.

Mac climbed behind the wheel of the van, and Sherry slid into the passenger seat. It felt strange sitting on this side of her own van.

"Why can't we take Mr. McIntyre's car? It is cooler than this van."

"For two reasons. The first, we have way too much stuff to take with us and so the van is roomier. And second, Mr. McIntyre doesn't want his car to smell like sweaty soccer players when this is all over."

Wyatt leaned back and looked out the window, giving his best surly pout.

"Are you kidding me?" Mac said to no one in particular. "These vans are hard to find these days. I'd have one if I could get one at a reasonable price, but any of them on the market that run cost an arm and a leg."

Wyatt's interest was piqued, "Why would anyone want one of these old vans?"

"Oh." Mac pretended he didn't realize Wyatt was listening, "Well, you see they are one of the last few vans on the road before they changed everything over to those crossover vehicles and SUV's. Now don't get me wrong those SUV's look sleek and everything but you've got no room. It is very hard to throw a decent party out the back of one of those new models. No headroom for us tall guys either."

Mac checked the rearview mirror. Wyatt was considering Mac's words. "And it's amazing what some people can do with these things. There is an entire website about people converting these into mini-RV's and they live in them full-time or use them for serious road trips. I mean, can you imagine going fishing or hiking and having a place to come back and lay down and rest or an actual bathroom, instead of some tree with poison ivy?"

Wyatt laughed, "I suppose." He twisted in his seat, sizing up the van. Sherry could only imagine what he was envisioning for her humble minivan with its sliding side door and paint peeling off the roof and hood.

"I'd paint the inside black with green rope lights and have personalized tags that said 'gamer'."

Sherry's mouth dropped open. She had never known Wyatt to be overly interested in cars and to have a plan for the van so quickly; she shook her head.

"Yeah?" Mac encouraged him.

"Yeah, and one of those projectors so I could use the side of the van outside as a screen and play my games outside. It would be my own big screen. Can you show me that website later, Mr. McIntyre?"

"Sure."

They pulled into the sports complex. Today the city-wide tournament and teams from different schools and clubs would be playing and the place was packed with cars.

"Wow, look at this parking lot." Sherry exclaimed. "Look for Amy, she said she would try to save us a spot next to her."

"There's Robbie!" Wyatt pointed out.

Mac followed Wyatt's directions until he saw Robbie running down the drive aisle.

"There!" Sherry pointed.

Mac swung into the space next to Amy's sleek SUV. He barely had the van in park before Wyatt was sliding open the door and hopping out. Several parents were already tailgating.

"Why don't you and Amy do your thing and we'll make sure the boys get checked in with the team." Mac offered.

Brad Barton, Amy's husband, and Robbie's father smiled as he shook Mac's hand, "Sounds good man, let's go."

Amy watched the four of them head off across the parking lot. "How is it that no matter how much help we bring with us, we get stuck doing everything?"

Sherry laughed, "It sure seems that way, doesn't it?"

"Let's get things set up. I want to hear all about the school you picked for Wyatt."

"Oh Amy, you should see it and they honestly have Wyatt's best interest in mind. They can be flexible in his classes if they need to be, and he goes next week for a placement test."

"Are you nervous?"

"Yes, more so than Wyatt. He is excited as long as he can still hang out with Robbie."

Amy looked thoughtful, "Robbie is worried Wyatt will make new friends and won't want to hang out with him anymore."

"Oh, I don't believe that, and we can make sure that they stay in touch. Robbie can come spend the night or a weekend with us and Wyatt is still going to play on the same soccer team."

"I think you're right. I think they have been friends for too long for anything like that to happen."

"Well, we just won't let it." Sherry squeezed Amy's arm to comfort her.

CHAPTER THIRTEEN
NOVEMBER

"**G**ood morning, Sherry." Kay greeted as she came off the elevator.

Sherry looked up and smiled as Kay's new security officer watched until Kay was safely in her office before heading down the hall to the security office suites that Mac had established on the floor.

Sherry got up and followed Kay into her office. "You sound like you had a good weekend."

"Ethan had the weekend off, so we were able to spend some quality time together."

"Oh, that is wonderful. What did you do?"

"We went out for drinks and listened to some music and...." Kay sat down at her desk and started digging through her bag. Kay's style wasn't one of a typical CEO. She carried a messenger bag that she had carried back when she was a photojournalist. She produced a cream-colored envelope made of heavy bond paper.

Sherry stopped making the coffee and walked over.

"What's this?"

"Your invitation to Thanksgiving dinner with Ethan and I." Kay smiled.

"You made formal invitations?" Sherry opened it slowly, "are you sure we will not be an imposition?" she asked studying the creamy paper with the words written in gold ink.

Kay stood up and walked over to Sherry. "How can it be an imposition when you are holding a handwritten invitation?"

Sherry smiled, "Thank you. We'll be delighted."

"Wonderful!"

To be honest, with so much going on with Wyatt's school issues and trying to pay for the new school, she had given little thought to Thanksgiving. Kay's invitation was perfect. She wouldn't have to cook an enormous meal and it would be less depressing than just sitting at home with her and Wyatt remembering past Thanksgivings. No, this would help them make new happy memories. She wondered if she should tell Kay about her relationship with Mac and ask if she could bring him as a date?

She sent him a quick text to get his thoughts on going more public with their relationship.

"Let's talk tonight." Was the reply.

She put her phone away; she wondered why she was concerned about an office romance, when she hardly ever saw him at work. He had established some offices up on the top floor for the security staff that worked in plain clothes, as he called it. The uniformed staff had an office on the first floor. It had taken more convincing to get Kay to hire security staff and not contract it out for the uniformed positions. But Mac convinced her the only way to ensure a genuine sense of security was to invest in people that would be loyal to the company. There would be a significant risk for stealing or selling secrets or other bad acts if the security officers didn't have a vested interest in the company. Mac was also putting security at the other two out-of-state facilities as well. He handpicked the plainclothes security agents and only the best of those were allowed to drive Kay, to which she still protested heavily. But she was outvoted. Ethan supported the idea of her having a bodyguard/driver as well.

A few minutes later, Mac and Kay's driver, Mateo "Matt" Garcia, came down the hall headed for the elevator. Neither man looked in her direction and it gave her a chance to admire Mac without his knowing it. She admired the way he could wear a suit and be just as sexy as he was in a pair of jeans and a skintight t-shirt. The elevator door opened, and she dragged her eyes away from Mac and back to her work. She heard the elevator door close.

"I saw that." Kay said from her office door.

Sherry looked up in surprise.

"I see the way you look at Mac."

Sherry's face felt hot, but she tried to be nonchalant.

"Like when?"

"Like just now." Kay smiled.

Sherry began to protest, but Kay stopped her.

"It's okay. He is hot as hell."

"Kay, I wouldn't want to infringe on your relationship with Mac."

"My relationship with Mac is both as a friend and professional, but it is certainly not romantic, so you are not infringing on anything." She got a devious look on her face. "Maybe I need to invite Mac to Thanksgiving dinner, too. Get you guys talking and see what happens, you never know."

Sherry almost giggled out loud. She managed to keep her innocent composure until Kay went back into her office. Sherry had her own devious thoughts; this Thanksgiving was going to be more fun than she imagined.

She found she was feeling more of the holiday spirit and less weighed down by life now that Wyatt was all set to enter Tidewater Academy after the first of the year. She was feeling more comfortable with a long-term relationship with Mac. The ironic thing was they seemed to spend less time together lately.

He was busy with work until he felt like things could run on their own. She hoped that would be soon, but they just seem to have their timing all wrong lately. And now that soccer season was over, she had more time in the evenings. It was just her luck.

Her phone buzzed. "Hello?"

"Hey there." Mac's voice was smooth and sultry over the phone.

"How was your day?"

"Not over yet unfortunately."

"You've been working a lot lately. Are you sure you not just avoiding me?" The words escaped her lips before she could stop herself. "I'm sorry I shouldn't have said that."

"You should always say what you feel."

"No, I shouldn't. At least not until I thought about it first." Sherry sat down at the kitchen table; the vegetables she was chopping forgotten for the moment.

"I'm here to listen."

"I know you are you are always there for me. And it is my turn to be here for you. You've got a lot on your plate right now and I truly understand that; it just feels like, our timing is off right now."

"It will get better I promise." Mac reassured her.

"Oh, did you get an invitation to Thanksgiving dinner at Kay and Ethan's?"

"Yeah, I did. I found it on my desk."

"Heads up. Kay is trying to play matchmaker between you and me for Thanksgiving. Wanna have a little fun with her?"

Mac chuckled into the phone. "You bet I do!"

"Okay good. I'll let you get back to work."

"Okay, talk to you later, and Sherry?"

"Yes?"

"I miss the hell out of you."

"I miss you too."

She clicked off and was still sitting at the table, smiling, when Wyatt came into the kitchen.

"Are we having dinner soon?"

"Oh, yeah, sorry, got sidetracked. Wanna help?"

"Sure."

"I'm thinking spaghetti this weekend. I'll simmer the sauce all day on Sunday. What do you think?" She asked.

"I love spaghetti. Will Mac be able to come to dinner?"

"Well, I hope so, we will certainly ask him."

"Cool."

"Mac and I are going to need your help with a little joke on Ms. Dandridge. Are you up for it?"

"Yeah! It's not a mean joke, is it?"

"No, not at all."

"Okay, then what do I have to do?"

"Kay has invited you and I to Thanksgiving dinner. She also invited Mr. McIntyre, and she is going to set us up on a date."

"Because you guys are a secret and Ms. Dandridge doesn't know you are dating?"

"That's correct, so when we go to dinner, act like you don't know Mr. McIntyre."

Wyatt shrugged, "Okay."

"You don't want to do it?"

"No, I'll do it. I just don't understand why you just don't tell her."

Sherry looked deflated.

"We will; we were just going to have a little fun with it." Sherry let the subject drop.

Wyatt was quiet the rest of the night and went back to his room after dinner without watching TV. Sherry was grateful for the lack of television but was concerned about Wyatt. She was learning to let him have his space, but it was hard.

It was after midnight when her phone lit up with a text.

"I'm outside. Are you awake?"

"I'm still up. Come to the door. I'll let you in."

She got up and put a robed on over her shorts and t-shirt, then tiptoed to the front door.

Mac stood there in a sweater and jeans, smiling at her. "Hey."

"Hey." She smiled, her heart racing at the sight of him.

"Wyatt asleep?"

"I hope so. Wanna come in?"

"I don't want to wake him, but I had to see you."

She smiled. "We can go into my room. He won't be able to hear us talking from there."

"Is that what we are going to do?" He gave her a sultry grin.

"For now." She smiled back, heat flashing through her body.

He followed her to the back corner of the house. It was on the opposite side of Wyatt's room, so it offered a little privacy.

"I'm sorry we have spent little time together lately. I wanted you to know I miss you." He started in a low whisper, not wanting to take any chances and wake up Wyatt and have to explain why he was doing in his mom's bedroom.

"I've missed you, too."

"Sherry, I don't have all the answers about how our relationship is going to work. But I'm ready for more when you are."

"More? What does that mean?" She asked.

"I'm not sure what it means or how we do it, but I know I can't stand not going able to see you outside of work every day, I don't like going more than a few hours talking to you just to see how your day is going or if everything is alright with you."

She smiled and reached out to take his hand. "I feel the same way." She looked away for a moment.

"Why do I feel there is a 'but' in there?"

"But while I feel all of those things, I'm also scared."

"I'm scared, too." He brushed a stray piece of hair out of her face and tucked it behind her ear for her.

"You are?" She was shocked.

Mac smiled warmly. "Yes, I'm scared. Scared you don't feel the same way I feel. That I'll screw this up somehow. I'm scared at the thought of living the rest of my life without seeing you every single day."

She looked at him and blinked. It never occurred to her that Mac would be just as scared as she was and for the same reasons. He always seemed in control.

"But you're always so calm, like nothing fazes you."

This time Mac laughed a little. "Are you kidding? I'm calm, cool, and collected on the outside, but when I'm around you, I'm a nervous wreck on the inside."

"It doesn't show."

"Good, I wouldn't want you to see what a mess I am when I'm around you."

"But that doesn't make sense. You're a Marine, a federal agent. You aren't afraid of anything."

"A firefight with rebels. A murderer pointing a gun at me doesn't scare me. But you," He put both hands on her shoulders, "You Sherry Davis, terrify me. The worst those other things can do is kill me, but you have the power to steal my heart and rip it out, leaving me hallow and alone. That terrifies the hell out of me."

"I'd never do that to you." She whispered, knowing he was about to kiss her sitting here on her bed.

Mac gently kissed her, not trusting himself to stop with just a kiss. A thin robe and the t-shirt under it were all that was between him and what he imagined was her soft skin. He wasn't sure he possessed enough self-control in this situation. She was all he thought about, even dreamt about, when he could sleep. But this isn't how he wanted it to be the first time he made love to her. He wanted it to be special, to be romantic and not in secret.

Sherry inhaled deeply. She knew this was not the ideal situation, but she told herself she would not fight it anymore.

Without her even realizing it, she had fallen hopelessly in love with Mac, and she knew he could break her heart and there was nothing she could do about it.

Mac pulled back just a little and rested his forehead against hers. "I should go."

Her heart sank.

"If I don't go, this might lead to something we aren't quite ready for and if I don't go now, I cannot leave." He growled.

"I know." Was all that she could say. She didn't even care if he knew how disappointed she was, but he was right. The time wasn't right.

"Is the time ever going to be right?" She asked, her body feeling greedy with need.

"Yes, I promise." He kissed her again and then stood up.

"But are we ready to answer questions if Wyatt finds me here in the morning?"

"Honestly, I think Wyatt wouldn't have a problem with it. I think he wants us to get on with it." She laughed.

"What do you mean?" "I told him about our prank on Kay for Thanksgiving and he didn't seem overly impressed with the idea and asked why we are keeping it a secret. He went to bed without asking to watch TV tonight."

"You want me to talk to him?"

"No, I'm just going to give him some space."

"Okay."

"I'll see you tomorrow?"

"Of course." She smiled up at him, again wishing he didn't have to go. She stood up on her tiptoes to kiss him. He pulled her close, feeling the heat of her body through the thin silk robe.

Sherry was nearly breathless when they broke away again. "I'll walk you to the door."

Mac nodded silently and led the way out. Once in his car he put it in neutral and rolled out of the driveway and started it in the street as to not wake Wyatt.

Sherry stood on the porch, watching him. There was no way she was going to sleep now. It was going to be a long day ahead. She sighed and took a shower and made coffee.

She had already had her breakfast by the time Wyatt was up. He plodded downstairs dressed, but his hair uncombed.

"Have you brushed your teeth? You obviously haven't combed your hair."

"I didn't feel like combing it." He plopped down in a chair.

"I don't care what you feel like, young man. You go back upstairs and comb your hair and brush your teeth."

He reluctantly got up and mumbled on the way up the stairs.

"And put on a new attitude while you're up there!" She called after him.

When he returned, he had at least combed his hair.

She was tempted to ask him if something was wrong, but she didn't want to baby him or smother him. Still....

"Do you have something on your mind today?" She asked.

"I'm sick of going to this school." He groused.

"It will be over soon." She said as she packed his lunch.

"Can I just buy my lunch like normal kids today?" He sighed.

"Yes."

She put the sandwich back in the fridge and put away his lunch bag.

"Is there a problem?"

"I'm too old to take my lunch to school like a baby."

"I take my lunch to work every day." She said without looking at him.

"That's different."

She was tired and not in the mood to argue with him.

"Here's some money."

He took it and stuck it in his pocket.

"You ready?" She asked. He nodded. "Let's go then." She grabbed her lunch and purse and headed for the door. By the time she got to work, she had drained her travel mug of coffee and went to Kay's office to make a pot without waiting for Kay to arrive.

It surprised Sherry when Kay got off the elevator alone.

"Good morning," Sherry greeted, "No driver today?"

"Oh yes, he is dependable as a cocker spaniel, but I left him downstairs and reassured him there would be no ninja assassins waiting for me in the elevator." Kay laughed.

"I already made coffee; I hope you don't mind."

"You know I don't." Kay stopped and looked at Sherry more closely. "You, okay?"

"Oh yeah, I'm fine. Just a late night and Wyatt is testing out those teen angst issues a little early."

Kay laughed, "Well, maybe the sooner it starts, the sooner it will be over."

"If I had that kind of luck, I would have hit the lottery a long time ago." Sherry rolled her eyes.

"Hang in there."

Sherry hadn't seen Mac around the office all morning. But, she was too busy to worry too much about it until she saw him racing to the elevator and when it didn't come fast enough; he took the stairs. She sat watching the staircase door close behind him, wondering what could be so important. Was there a problem in the building? It couldn't be too serious. No one had shown up to stand guard at Kay's door.

She checked her email for any warnings or alerts. A new notification system Mac's department had set up, said nothing. Next, she checked her phone for a text alert. No messages or alerts of any kind.

Maybe one tenant in the building was having an issue. While Mac's department wasn't necessarily responsible for individual tenants, he handled the building as a company asset.

CHAPTER FOURTEEN

F orty-five minutes later, Sherry's cell phone rang, Amy's
number flashed up on the screen.

"Hello, Amy, is everything okay?"

"Sherry, I felt like I needed to call you."

"What's happened? Are you okay? Is it the boys?"

"Sherry please don't be mad."

"Why would I be mad? What's happened?"

"Robbie and Wyatt got in a fight at school, Robbie called me,
and I went to the school."

"A fight! Are they okay?"

"Yes, they are fine."

"I'm on my way."

"Okay, come to my house. I brought them both here."

"Why didn't Wyatt call me?"

"I don't know, but that is the part I don't want you to get mad
about."

"I'm not mad that he is with you. I'm grateful he is safe."

"There is more to it than that."

Sherry had her purse in her hand and the phone to her ear as
she walked into Kay's office.

"Amy, can you hang on a second?" Sherry held the phone
away from her ear for a moment.

Kay looked up, concern on her face.

"Kay, I'm so sorry I need to leave. Wyatt was in a fight at school."

"Go, go!" Kay shooed her out of the office.

Sherry turned and headed for the elevator. "Okay, tell me the part I'm not supposed to be mad about."

"Robbie called me, but Wyatt called Mac."

"What?" Sherry shrieked as the elevator door closed.

"He said he was too afraid to call you. Somehow, he convinced the school to let him call Mac. But the school wouldn't let Mac take him, so I brought them both home with me. Mac is talking to Wyatt right now and neither of them know I am calling you."

"I'm getting in my car right now. Thank you, Amy. I'm not mad. But Wyatt is about to be in more trouble that he has ever been in, in his life!" She clicked off and started the car.

She didn't remember the drive to Amy's house. She was barely out of the car when Mac met her in the driveway.

Mac held up his hands as he approached. "I'm sorry I didn't tell you before I left work, but at the time I wasn't sure how serious it was."

Sherry took a deep breath. She tried to remember that this wasn't Mac's fault Wyatt called him and he was there for him. She was grateful for that much, at least.

"What happened? Is he hurt?" She felt hysteria creeping in.

"He is okay. He might have a black eye tomorrow, but other than that physically, he is okay."

"Did he tell you what happened? Was it those bullies?"

"Yes, it was the same boys that have given him trouble before. Apparently, they tried to steal his and Robbie's lunch money or what was left of it after lunch."

Sherry sighed, grateful that he wasn't hurt worse.

"So, listen," Mac tried to steady her, "The important things to remember before you go in there and talk to him is that he isn't hurt, he was defending himself and a friend, and the reason he called me was he was afraid to call you."

"But why?"

"I think you should ask him that."

"Did he tell you why?" Sherry was fighting back tears.

Mac nodded. "He did, but I think he needs to tell you himself. You don't need to hear it from me."

"Okay, where is he?"

"Inside."

Mac opened the door and let Sherry step in ahead of him. Wyatt was sitting on the sofa alone; Robbie and Amy were conspicuously absent. Wyatt's left cheek was red, and he would indeed have a bruise by tomorrow. She fought every urge to run to him and scoop him up. But she knew that would only embarrass him in front of Mac. She went over and sat next to him on the sofa.

"You, okay?"

"Yes ma'am."

"You want to tell me what happened?"

Wyatt sat staring at the floor for a long time.

Mac could sense they needed to be alone. "I'll be outside if anyone needs me." He stepped out onto to the porch.

When the door clicked shut, Wyatt looked up at her, "Mom, I'm sorry." He started to cry, and she hugged him. She knew he hadn't wanted to cry in front of Mac.

"It's okay, sweetheart." She stroked his hair.

Wyatt sniffled and pulled back, "I'm really sorry."

"I know, but I don't understand why you were afraid to call me?"

"Are you mad I called, Mac?"

She noticed his use of Mac's nickname, but let it slide for the moment.

"No, I'm not mad. I'm glad you had someone you could call, and I hope you know that no matter whatever happens Mac will always be there for you."

Wyatt nodded. "It was just kind of a guy thing, mom."

"Okay, is it a guy thing to be afraid to call me?"

"No, I was afraid you would be mad at me for fighting and I guess I was afraid you would be disappointed in me."

"Well, I'm not thrilled that you got into a fight, but from what I understand so far, you didn't start it and you were defending your friend. And while violence is not the answer, I am proud of you for standing up for your friend."

"I'm really sorry, mom."

"I know, son. But you did the right thing. You helped someone in need, you called someone you could trust, and you told the truth. I can't ask for any more than that."

"I'm sorry. I was afraid to call you. I should have known better."

She smiled down at him. "You did the best you could at that moment. I can't fault you for that, but I hope in the future you know I will never be mad at you for defending someone."

"No ma'am. I won't."

"Okay, do you want to tell me what happened and did the other boys' parents come and get them, too?"

"Usually, Robbie and I have lunch at the same time, and we sit with a group of kids that are kinda considered nerds because we play video games. We get teased about it. All of us bring our lunch, but Robbie and I decided we would buy our lunch." Wyatt looked down again. "It was dumb to worry about what other people think."

Sherry smiled reassuringly at her son.

"The bullies noticed that we didn't bring our lunch today and when we were leaving the cafeteria, they followed us into the hallway and started pushing us around, demanding money. We both said no, and that is when they started punching us and pushed Robbie to the floor and after that it was kind of blur."

"I can imagine."

"The football coach saw us and came over with another teacher and broke it up and took us all to the principal's office." He paused for a moment. "The other boys tried to say we started it, but there are cameras in the hallways, and it showed that Robbie and I were telling the truth."

"Good."

"Then we had to call our parents and wait, and while we were waiting, the police came and took two of the boys, Brad and Ryan because they have been in trouble before and the other two had to wait for their parents, too."

"I'm just glad you are alright."

"Me too."

"Is Robbie, okay?"

"Yeah, he is fine. He is probably going to have a black eye, too, and he has a busted lip."

"Oh no."

"Yeah, he has to wait for his dad to get home later. I'm glad I'm not him."

"Do you think Robbie's dad will be mad?"

Wyatt looked thoughtful, "I don't think so, but I guess Robbie is just worried about it like I was."

"I'm sure he is." Sherry gave him a hug. "You ready to go home?"

"Yeah."

"Okay, why don't you and Mac go ahead, and I am going to talk to Ms. Barton for a minute."

"Yes, ma'am." Wyatt got up to head for the door and stopped. "Mom?"

"Yes?"

"I'm sorry about this morning."

"Don't worry about, we all have bad days."

"Thanks!" He smiled and stepped out onto the porch with Mac.

Sherry got up and walked towards the kitchen. "Amy?" She called out.

"Up here, coming." Amy's voice sounded from upstairs. Sherry guessed she was probably in Robbie's room.

"Hey, everything okay?" Amy asked as she came down the stairs.

"Yeah, it's all good. How's Robbie?"

"He's still angry at those other boys and he has a split lip and probably a black eye by tomorrow. But I think he will be okay."

"Thanks so much for bringing Wyatt home with you."

The two friends hugged. "No problem. Is everything okay you know with you and Mac?"

"Oh yeah, I'm not upset. I'm grateful he cares enough to help Wyatt."

Amy smiled, relief showing on her face. "I'm glad. He is great with him, you know."

"Yeah, I know." Sherry smiled. "Well, I'd better go. Let me know if you need anything."

Amy hugged her friend again. "You, too."

Sherry called Kay on the way home. "Kay, it's me."

"Sherry, is everything okay?"

"Yeah, he's fine and luckily he didn't start it."

"Well, that is good."

"Listen, do you mind if I take the rest of the afternoon off?"

"No, no, stay home with Wyatt. Make sure he is okay."

"Thank you, listen, I'm really sorry for having to run out like that. I'll work this weekend."

"No, you won't. Life happens, don't worry about it."

"Do you want me to call and get a temp in there this afternoon?"

"You worry too much. I can manage an afternoon of answering my phone and if I can't then I'll take the rest of the day off too."

Sherry laughed, "Okay see you tomorrow."

She was grateful for Kay's understanding, but she still felt bad about leaving.

A few minutes later, she pulled into the driveway next to Mac's car. She found the two of them in the kitchen having a snack and a soda.

"Hi mom,"

Mac looked up, "Hey, everything okay?"

"Yeah, I just needed to talk to Amy and thank her and then I needed to talk to Kay about taking off the rest of the afternoon."

Wyatt looked up. "You're staying home?"

"Yes," she smiled.

Wyatt turned to Mac. "Can you stay?"

"Well, I left in kind of a rush. I might need to go back and finish up some things, but I could come back by later if that is okay with your mom." He looked up at Sherry. So did Wyatt.

Sherry looked at the two of them and laughed. "Dinner is at six."

"Yes!" Wyatt pumped his fist.

"Why don't you go get your homework done so you will be free to enjoy Mac's company when she comes back."

"Okay." Wyatt cleared the table and put the glasses and plates in the sink. Then he turned back to Mac.

"I realize I probably should have called my mom but thank you for coming to school to get me."

"You should always tell your mom what is going on, but I'll always be there for you." Mac smiled.

"Thanks!" With that, Wyatt ran upstairs.

Mac watched him go. "He's such a great kid."

"Yeah, he is."

"You've done a wonderful job, raising him."

"Thank you, it's been pretty easy until recently." Sherry shook her head.

Mac laughed. "Well, I'd better go before Kay catches on."

"That is what I was thinking. You will come back for dinner?"

"Wouldn't miss it."

"Good."

He kissed her and was gone. She sank down in the kitchen chair he had vacated. She was so tired. But no time to sleep now. She had to figure out what they were going to have for dinner. She had thought about tacos earlier, but now that Mac was joining them, she was going to need something more. Taking stock of the freezer and pantry, she decided on salmon.

True to his word, Mac returned by six.

Wyatt raced to let him in. "Hi, dinner is almost ready."

"Hey, okay. You put any ice on that eye?"

"Yeah, I held it on there while I did my homework."

"Good man, what's your mom up to?"

Wyatt smiled, "She's in the kitchen."

Mac smiled, "Smells good."

"It's fish." Wyatt led the way to the kitchen.

Mac stopped at the kitchen door and watched Sherry for a moment. He loved the way she moved, even just doing everyday things. "Hey there."

Sherry turned at the sound of his deep sultry voice, "Hi, yourself." She smiled. "You're just in time."

"Can I do anything to help?"

"No, Wyatt already set the table, so we're ready. You can help with the dishes afterwards." She gave him a flirtatious smile.

"I have water, tea, soda, beer, wine, to drink. What would you like?"

"Water will be fine, thank you."

She put three glasses of water on the table.

"Now, before we begin, each of us will tell the rest of us something positive that happened to them today." Sherry looked at Wyatt.

Wyatt looked sheepish for a moment. "I learned that I have someone besides my mom to help me when I get in trouble."

Sherry smiled and looked at Mac. "Yes, you do."

"You go next." Wyatt said to Mac.

"A positive thing that happened to me today?" He glanced at Wyatt and then Sherry. "There are so many things. If I had to pick one, I guess it would be that I know you both trust me enough to let me know if you need help with something."

Wyatt grinned from ear to ear. "What about you, mom?"

"I learned it is okay to ask friends for help."

Mac smiled at her and winked.

Sherry took a bite of the salmon. She didn't realize how hungry she was until then.

"This is delicious. You made this today?" Mac asked in between bites.

"Yes, well, I just put a little seasoning on the fish and popped it in the oven, not that hard."

"Mom, grows her own vegetables and herbs in the garden out back."

Mac looked at her with new appreciation. "Really?"

"Well, it is late in the season for much of anything to be growing, I will have to move the smaller herbs into the house for the winter." She said nonchalantly.

"I'm afraid I didn't have time to do anything special for dessert, but I have ice cream if you are interested." Sherry offered.

"Can I have ice cream?" Wyatt asked.

"Yes, you can have ice cream."

"With chocolate sauce and whipped cream?"

Sherry laughed, "Yes, a small bowl, though."

Mac looked around the table, "Why don't I do the dishes while Wyatt handles the ice cream and you, take a break."

Sherry stood up. "That is a wonderful offer, but you don't know where anything goes, and if I let Wyatt be in charge of the ice cream, we'll all be sick from a sugar overdose. But you are both welcome to help."

"Mac, I mean Mr. McIntyre, you wash, I'll dry and then mom can put them away." Wyatt got up and started collecting the empty plates.

"That sounds like a plan."

Sherry nodded. Working together the kitchen was clean again in no time.

Wyatt pulled out his favorite ice cream toppings, while Sherry retrieved the ice cream and bowls.

"I'll scoop." Mac offered.

"Okay, but just one scoop for me." Sherry cautioned.

Wyatt and Mac went to work while she watched. She wasn't trying to pretend to be modest in front of Mac, but she knew if ate too much sugar as tired as she already was, she would crash and be asleep by eight o'clock.

Wyatt and Mac were left in charge of the ice cream, while she went into the living room and turned on the TV knowing Wyatt would want to watch something with Mac before going to bed.

Her phone rang. It was the number from the school.

"Hello?"

"Ms. Davis, this is Assistant Principal Dunlevy. I hope I am not catching you at a bad time."

"No, Mr. Dunlevy, what can I do for you?"

"I wanted to follow up and see how Wyatt was doing."

"He will be fine, thankfully."

"That is good to hear. I'm sorry to be calling so late, but I wanted to make sure you understood the totality of the situation."

"I'm not sure I do." She turned towards the kitchen to see Mac and Wyatt standing there watching.

"Well, as you know we have a zero-tolerance policy against fighting, so I'm afraid Wyatt will have to be suspended as well as the boys who started the fight."

"Are you serious?" She felt her temper flare as her voice raised.

Wyatt looked up and whispered to Mac, "This will not be good, she is really mad."

Mac looked back at Sherry, concerned, and feeling helpless.

"My son had to defend himself. He was not fighting; he didn't start it."

"I realize that Ms. Davis, but school policy is clear…."

"No, Mr. Dunlevy, let me tell you what is clear. My son has a black eye from four thugs you let into that school, and I understand two of them have a record and were arrested today, not just merely suspended. My son was injured because you failed to protect him when he was in your care. Where was your zero tolerance, then?" Her voice had just about reached its limit. Mac came over and put his hand on her shoulder.

"I'm sorry you feel that way Ms. Davis."

"That is not only how I feel, Mr. Dunlevy, but that is how my attorney sees it. And you and each individual school board member need to be prepared to explain yourselves in court." She clicked off the phone and turned to throw it. Mac caught her arm.

"You'll regret breaking your phone. Throw a pillow instead." He handed her one from the sofa, but she only threw it on the floor and stormed out the front door.

Wyatt stood there wide-eyed. "I've never seen her that mad before."

Mac felt bad for him. "She is mad because she loves you and she is trying to protect you. She feels like maybe she couldn't today and that makes her angry. Your mom felt like the school has rules that don't follow common sense and those rules allowed you to get hurt and that makes her mad, but she is not mad at you."

Sherry went out into the front yard and screamed with frustration, then without a second thought, she punched in Kay's number.

"Kay, it's Sherry." She said as soon as the phone stopped ringing.

"Sherry's what's wrong?"

"I need a lawyer."

"Are you in trouble?" Kay's voice conveying her concern as clearly as if she was standing in front of Sherry.

"No, but they want to suspend Wyatt from school."

"Slow down, start at the beginning." Sherry took a deep breath and leaned against the hood of her minivan. When she got done telling Kay what had transpired, leaving out the parts that involved Mac, she felt a little better.

"Okay, why don't you weigh your options, find out if Wyatt can finish out the school year doing his classes online. He can't have that many days left anyway, with the holidays coming up. Then call his new school and make sure this will not create a problem with him there."

"I hadn't even thought of that. Oh god, do you think this will cause a problem for him at Tidewater Academy?"

"I don't know. Call them up and talk to them. If it is going to be a problem, let me know. I can help with that."

"Thank you, Kay. I appreciate your advice."

"Bring Wyatt with you to work tomorrow. We can find an office for him to work in until we get this straighten out."

"What would I do without you?"

"It's my pleasure. Please don't stress, we'll get it all worked out."

"Thank you, good night."

Mac kept watch from the window to make sure Sherry was alright but giving her some space to cool down. When he saw her headed back inside, he opened the door for her.

She smiled at him and looked over at Wyatt, who was sitting on the sofa.

"Hey sweetie, eat your ice cream, you don't want it to melt."

"Okay." Look at her with concern in his eyes, "are you okay?"

"I'm fine sweetie, sometimes I just get a little upset when I see people treating you in a way, I don't think you should be treated."

"I don't care if they suspend me, I don't want to go back there, anyway."

"I know, but that is not something you want on your record if you want to go to Tidewater Academy next semester?"

"Why? What difference does it make?"

"I don't know for sure that it will, but I am working on that. In the meantime, you are going to work with me tomorrow and do your schoolwork there."

"Really?" Wyatt was practically jumping up and down on the sofa.

"Yes, Ms. Dandridge says we can set you up in your own office." She laughed. "Now you and Mac watch TV and eat your ice cream."

"What about you?" Mac asked.

"I have a couple of phone calls to make, and I'll join you in a minute." She smiled and patted his arm.

Mac didn't like seeing her like this, but what else could he do? She wanted him to stay with Wyatt. He was sure it was because she wanted Wyatt distracted from all the details and implications of what was happening. It wasn't going to be easy. Wyatt was a bright kid, and he loved his mom fiercely. He was going to be very aware of what was going on.

"So," Mac picked up his bowl of ice cream and sat down next to Wyatt, "What are we watching?"

"Wanna watch a navy seal movie?"

"Sure."

They sat watching the movie, with Wyatt asking questions about some scenes in the background, as if they were actual places where Mac had been. He didn't want to give Wyatt too many details, but he answered the questions as best he could.

About an hour into the movie, Sherry emerged and took their bowls to the kitchen.

"Need some help with those?" Mac asked.

She smiled sweetly, "no, I've got it." She didn't mind a quiet minute alone in the kitchen. A few minutes later, she returned to the living room. Wyatt was falling asleep.

"Hey sweetie, why don't you go to bed, big day tomorrow."

"Okay." Wyatt stumbled off to bed.

"Come here." Mac held out his hand and pulled her down on the sofa next to him. He put his arm around her to comfort her.

"You gonna be, okay?"

She sighed heavily, "Yeah, I'm sorry for leaving you like that; I'm a terrible hostess."

"You are not anything of the sort. I hate standing by and doing nothing. I feel helpless."

"You are my rock." She whispered, leaning her head against his shoulder.

Five minutes later, she was asleep. Mac was content to stay there and let her sleep. Soon, his head nodded.

CHAPTER FIFTEEN

S herry woke at the sound of her alarm on her cell phone. She tried to roll over and found she couldn't move, and her neck was painfully still. She opened one eye, searching for her phone. The alarm was still beeping incessantly. Then it stopped. She opened the other eye and Mac's hand was covering the cell phone on the coffee table. She bolted upright and instantly regretted it.

"Oh!" She rubbed her neck. "What time is it?"

"Should be six, I think." Mac shifted over and then stood up, stretching his back.

Sherry looked up at him sheepishly, "I guess we fell asleep."

"I think so." He looked up at the second floor. "Maybe I should go before Wyatt comes downstairs, unless you want to answer questions about adult sleepovers."

Sherry bit her lip, "Maybe not just yet."

"I don't blame you, me either." He gathered her up in his arms and kissed her, "I just wish there was something to explain."

"I'm sorry, falling asleep on your shoulder isn't very classy."

Mac smiled and headed for the door. "Woman, you can fall asleep on me anytime."

She giggled and watched the door close behind him. Once he was gone, she raced to the bedroom for a hot shower. Hopefully, it would help work out the kinks in her neck and back. Despite having a cramped neck from sleeping in an awkward position against Mac's shoulder, it was the best sleep she had in a very long time. She tried to tell herself it was because she was so emotionally exhausted, but deep down, she knew it was because of Mac. Because he made her felt safe and like she wasn't alone in the world. She wondered what it would be like to sleep in his arms every night or would this feeling she had wear off after they were together for a longer period. She didn't think so. As terrifying as it was to risk losing it all again, Mac was worth the risk.

She hopped out of the shower and dressed. To her surprise, when she walked into the kitchen, Wyatt was already there.

"You're up early."

"I still get to go to work with you today, right?"

"Yes." she said, smiling.

"I started the coffee for you." He pointed.

"Thank you," she eyed him suspiciously. "You're excited to go to the office with me. I thought you would think it was boring."

"Well," he shrugged, "I mean, there will be a lot of old people there, but you will be there, and Ms. Dandridge and Mac!"

"That is true and thank you for not counting me in with the 'old people'." She laughed.

"What do you want for breakfast? We have pancakes, eggs, waffles."

"Cereal will be fine; we don't want to be late."

She laughed out loud, "Okay."

She set a box of cereal, a bowl and milk on the table. "You want toast with that?"

"No, thank you."

She put the lid on her travel mug of coffee. "What should we take for lunch today?"

Wyatt looked up confused, "Aren't we going to have a business lunch?"

"Do you think I go out to lunch every day?"

"Yeah."

"No, don't I take my lunch every day?"

"You do?" He looked disappointed. "I thought you told me that just to make me feel better."

"No, I take my lunch every day."

"What about taking clients out to lunch and stuff like that?"

"Where did you get that idea?"

"I saw it on a documentary show at school and Jason at school told me that his dad is an accountant and takes clients to lunch."

"Well, you'll have to talk to Ms. Dandridge about her power lunches. I am the office manager, and I don't go to lunch with clients."

"Oh."

"Eat your breakfast." She pointed to his bowl and then started packing lunches for them.

When they entered downtown, Wyatt was glued to the window, looking at all the buildings and people. Sherry pulled into the underground parking garage and parked in her space.

"Wow, you have your own parking space?"

"Yeah, I do."

"Cool!" Where does Mac park his car?"

"First, it's Mr. McIntyre. Second, remember we don't tell people that Mac and I are dating, and finally, I do not know where he parks."

"But Mac said when we are alone, I can call him Mac."

She frowned at him but didn't argue the point further.

"And I promise not to tell anyone that Mac is your boyfriend." He grinned and opened the car door.

They got on the elevator, and she pressed the button for the twenty-fifth floor.

"We are going to the top floor?"

"Yes."

Wyatt smiled.

The elevator doors opened, and Wyatt followed Sherry while scrutinizing his surroundings. Kay greeted them from her office door.

"Good morning, Sherry and Wyatt."

Sherry looked at her in surprise. "Good morning, you're here early."

"I wanted to make sure I was here to greet our new intern." She reached out her hand to Wyatt.

"Good morning, Ms. Dandridge." Wyatt shook her hand.

"Why don't the two of you come in and sit down and we can talk about Wyatt's time here."

Sherry looked at Kay suspiciously. Wyatt looked up at Sherry with concern. She smiled and put her hand on his shoulder and nodded to reassure him that everything was okay.

Kay led them to the conference table, "Have a seat anywhere you like, Wyatt."

"Now, Sherry, after I got your call last night, I contacted a friend of my who is an attorney and told him everything I know about the situation. He has agreed to come down later today and meet with you."

Sherry knew this wasn't worthy of a conversation at the conference table.

"Thank you," Sherry said slowly.

"What he told me was that Wyatt is not required to go back to that school if he doesn't want to."

"Yes!" Wyatt smiled.

Sherry rolled her eyes and gave Kay an evil look. "And what about failing for missing too many days? What about getting into Tidewater Academy; what about his grades?"

Kay gave Sherry a patient smile. "Yes, I thought of those things too and I don't want to jeopardize Wyatt's entrance into a new school or have him fall behind in his schoolwork. But I, just like you, don't want to see him bullied anymore either."

Sherry waited for the other shoe to drop.

Kay continued on, "I have a friend that works at Tidewater Academy and spoke with her confidentially about Wyatt." She held up her hand, "Sherry I know what you are thinking, I should have discussed it with you before taking any action regarding your son and you are correct. That is why anything I say from this point on, is not set in stone and can be amended. But Tidewater Academy would look favorably upon Wyatt's initiative if he were to spend the remaining part of the semester taking part in a special internship for future leaders of tomorrow." Kay paused and beamed.

Sherry looked at her in surprise. "An internship for an eleven-year-old?"

"Yes, the program is open to all ages and there is an age group including eleven-year-olds." Kay smiled sweetly back at Sherry.

Sherry sighed, "Okay, so if Wyatt takes part in this internship before he is enrolled in Tidewater, how is that going to help him?"

"The program is an independent program and not tied to a specific school. He would receive a grade from his employer which would be forwarded to his new school."

"I see." Sherry looked over at Wyatt, who was watching her and Kay closely. "And what about his other subjects, science, math, social studies?"

"Yes, that is where my friend the attorney comes in," she smiled, "he will ensure that Wyatt's school provides a very safe and educational online environment for him to receive lessons, and the tests he needs to complete out the school year to receive a passing grade." Kay turned to gaze at Wyatt. "Provided he puts in the work."

Sherry looked from Kay to Wyatt. "Wyatt, can you go hang out at my desk for a few minutes and I talk with Ms.

Dandridge?"

"Okay." He stood up reluctantly and looked at Sherry with pleading eyes. As he walked past Kay, he whispered, "Nice try."

When Sherry was certain the door was closed, she looked at Kay.

"Are you serious about an internship for an eleven-year-old? I appreciate it Kay, I really do. How late did you stay up creating this?"

Kay feigned surprise and put her hand on her chest.

"Don't play that with me. I know you too well. I've helped you set up too many things like this for other people to not recognize it."

"First, the internship program is legit. You can google it and the fact that his school doesn't advertise it broadly is another reason I agree he shouldn't be in that school."

Sherry felt her cheeks flush. "Okay, I'll give you that one. But you still had to have called Tidewater Academy."

"I did, and I said as much just a moment ago. I needed to know they would accept the internship credit before offering it to you, if it was going to be worth anything."

Sherry swallowed Kay and thought of everything.

"And how is this attorney of yours going to make the school board or the school do anything they don't want to do?"

"Well, I leave that to him, but I believe he is drawing up papers for a lawsuit right now, which I'm sure he will discuss when he gets here this afternoon."

"A lawsuit?"

Kay looked determined, "Yes, to sue the principal, and the school board for their treatment of Wyatt and the situation and for putting him in danger."

"Do you think that will work?"

"I don't know, but I would bet money that it will at least convince them to let Wyatt finish out the year at home."

Sherry stood up and went to the window. "I don't know."

Kay let her have a moment. Then asked, "What do you mean you don't know?"

"I mean yes, I am mad at the school and yes, I want to talk to this attorney, but is pulling him out of school the right thing to do? Am I teaching him to run away from his problems?"

"I think you are trying to keep your child safe and remove him from what is clearly an unsafe environment."

Sherry turned to face Kay, "How do I teach him to stand up for what is right?"

"I think you already have. That is why he was in the fight. He was standing up for what was right and defending a friend and himself."

Sherry took a deep breath. "I suppose you're right."

Kay got up and met Sherry at the window. "I can't imagine what it must be like to raise a child alone. But I do know you're doing a fantastic job."

Sherry smiled, "Thank you and thank you for helping me with all of this."

"What are friends for?" Kay smiled.

"You're right, I just don't know what I could ever do to repay you."

Kay laughed. "Are you kidding? I'm a photojournalist. What do I know about running a company. You run this place Sherry, not me."

Sherry laughed, "Nice try but I don't think so."

They walked to the door arm and arm, "Well, guess I'll give Wyatt the good news, he is going to be super excited."

"I would be, if I were him." Kay put a hand on Sherry's shoulder. "I'm always here if you need me."

"Thanks, seriously."

When Sherry opened the door, Wyatt was sitting on the sofa with Mac. Sherry paused for a moment.

Mac stood up. "I found this young man out here alone. He said he was waiting for his mom, is that you?" He looked at

Sherry.

"Yes, thank you."

Wyatt looked from Mac to Sherry but said nothing.

"Well, you're in excellent hands now, young man. It was nice to meet you." Mac gave Wyatt a fist bump.

"Yes sir, nice to meet you too."

Mac smiled and left without another word.

Wyatt looked at Sherry. "Do I have to go back to school?"

Sherry studied him for a moment, wondering how he had grown up so fast.

"Yes, you have to go to school."

Wyatt slumped back down on the sofa.

"Just not that school. You will work here with me every day, you will to your schoolwork online for the rest of the semester and then you will go to Tidewater academy and be the best student you can be."

Wyatt jumped up and came over to hug her.

"Thank you, mom."

She hugged him back. "You're welcome. But you better thank Ms. Dandridge, too."

To her surprise, Wyatt walked over and hugged Kay. "Thank you."

Kay looked confused for a moment. "You're very welcome." She smiled at Sherry, "I emailed your mom a sample internship schedule you guys can discuss and let me know what you decide."

"Yes, ma'am."

Once Kay had returned to her office and things had quieted down a bit, Wyatt looked over at Sherry, "Thanks, mom."

Whatever doubts she had this morning, in that moment, she knew they had done the right thing for her son.

CHAPTER SIXTEEN
THANKSGIVING

K ay was up early, excited at the idea of having friends over for Thanksgiving. Besides Mac and Sherry, Ethan had invited Logan Watson and his fiancé, Blake Morgan. She hoped having couples would encourage Mac and Sherry towards each other. She thought they would make a wonderful couple, but she knew Sherry was shy and they might need a little nudge. Besides, she enjoyed having the house filled with people. It reminded her of her childhood when her parents lived in the house. They would host fabulous dinner parties; it was going to be good to have the house filled with laughter and friends again.

She turned on the TV so she could watch the parade while she worked on prepping the turkey. A few minutes later, Ethan came downstairs, freshly showered and shaven, wearing khakis and a button-down shirt.

"You are too handsome, Mr. Craddock." She said, walking over to hug him.

"And you, my love, are blindingly beautiful, even in your apron." He teased, bending down to kiss her.

"I'm so glad you are home today." She beamed.

Me too. I've missed too many holidays over the years."

"I'm happy Logan agreed to join us. How has he been lately?" Kay asked. She and Logan had not always seen eye to eye.

"He is more mellow these days. Blake is good for him I think." Ethan poured himself a cup of coffee and then frowned at the TV. "Is that going to be over in time for the game?"

"Yes, but if not, you have another TV in the den, and one in the cottage which I think would be a perfect man cave."

"It is a man cave since you let Mac move in there."

"I mean when he moves out, and it is just temporary." Kay defended her decision to rent her cottage to Mac.

Ethan laughed and put his arm around Kay. "I don't care how long he stays. Mac's a good guy."

"You're a prince, you know that?" Kay smiled up at him.

"Yes." He gave her a kiss and broke away. She swatted at him, laughing.

She stuffed the turkey and put it in the oven. Then began working on a sweet potato casserole. Her guests had all offered to bring dishes and dessert. Kay had made a few pies days before.

Ethan returned to the kitchen. "What can I do to help?"

"Can you organize the food and beer that you will need for the game after dinner?"

"Already, done." He smiled, proud of himself.

"Then talk to me?"

The backdoor opened and Mac called out, "Hello?"

"Mac," Ethan called back, "we're in the kitchen."

Mac appeared, carrying a dish of green beans. "I thought I'd drop this by," he offered.

"Drop it by, aren't you staying?" Kay turned to him, concerned.

"Oh yeah, I mean, I'll be back. I have to go pick up my date." He smiled at the thought of the surprise he and Sherry had planned for Kay.

Ethan looked at him with interest. Kay looked horrified.

"A date?"

"Yes, I'm sorry. I hope that is, okay?"

Kay recovered quickly, "Of course it is."

Mac smiled and nodded, "Okay, see you soon." He turned and left.

Ethan turned to Kay, "Didn't I tell you to be careful about setting people up?"

"Hush." She looked at the ceiling as if the answer was hiding up there somewhere. "I don't have time to find another potential suitor for Sherry."

"I thought you were doing this because you are convinced that Mac and Sherry are meant for each other?"

"I am, but if Mac needs a nudge to realize it, then that is what I will do."

"You need to make sure you don't burn the turkey and let Mac and Sherry take care of themselves." Ethan left to set up the den for the game later.

Kay sighed and concentrated on cooking. Today might not be working out the way she planned, but she wouldn't give up. She had seen how Sherry looked at Mac whenever he came to her office or passed by on the way to the elevator. She sighed. Well, there was nothing that could be done about today. She wondered who Mac might be bringing. He said nothing about meeting anyone and she saw no one visiting the cottage, not that she was keeping tabs on him or anything. Frankly, she had seen little of Mac since hiring him. One of the first things he had done as vice president of security was to hire men that could serve as her driver and bodyguard. Other than regular updates, they hadn't spent a lot of time together. She had been busy herself, so there had been little opportunity for her to check in with him and see how he was doing on a personal level. And this was the result. He had a girlfriend she knew nothing about.

Her mind was on Mac and Sherry when she pulled the turkey out to baste it and she burnt her hand.

"Ouch! Son of a....,"

"You, okay?" Ethan rushed into the kitchen.

"Yeah," she ran some water over her hand, "Just a minor burn from the roasting pan."

"Here let me help." He closed the oven door and began basting the turkey while she tended to her hand.

"Thank you," she said, waiting for him put the pan back in the oven.

"Next time, let me know, I'll do it for you."

"I'm not helpless," she defended.

Ethan gave her a wry smile and glanced at her hand. "I know you're not." He kissed the top of her head and disappeared back into the den.

Mac knocked on Sherry's front door and then opened it, "Hello?"

"Come in!" Sherry called from the kitchen.

Mac stepped inside. Wyatt was on the sofa with a handheld video game and the Thanksgiving Day parade on TV.

"Hey, buddy."

"Hi, Mac! Wanna play?"

"I'm going to go see if your mom needs help in the kitchen."

Wyatt gave Mac a knowing grin, "Okay."

Mac stopped at the door to admire Sherry dressed in flannel pajama pants, fuzzy slippers and a sweatshirt.

He leaned against the doorframe and crossed his arms.

"How is that you make fuzzy slippers look sexy?"

"What? Oh god I thought you were Amy. She said she was coming over to borrow some brown sugar!" Sherry said, flustered. "I wasn't expecting you this early!" She ran for the bedroom.

Mac held up his hands and stepped into the kitchen. "Don't you dare change; I like you this way." He wrapped his arms around her and kissed her.

She giggled, and he released her. "Well, I guess it is better than you know now what I look like in the morning." She said, tossing a glance towards the living room to make sure Wyatt didn't hear her.

"Well, the surprise is ruined. So, I guess there's no point in…."

Sherry swapped him with a dish towel. "You think I only have one surprise?"

"Oh god, I hope not."

The doorbell rang. She sighed. "That will be Amy."

Wyatt called from the living room, "I got it!"

"Want some coffee?" Sherry asked.

"I'll get it." Mac helped himself.

Amy joined them in the kitchen. "Morning all."

"Good morning," Mac said, holding up his coffee to her.

"Morning sweetie," Sherry greeted Amy, "I've kinda got my hands full, but the sugar is over there. Help yourself. Want some coffee?"

"Thanks."

"I'll get it for you." Mac offered her his chair and got up to pour the coffee.

Amy looked down at Sherry's slippers and then caught her eye.

Sherry rolled her eyes while Mac's back was still turned to them. "I know," she whispered.

Amy suppressed a giggle.

Mac handed her the coffee. "Thank you."

"You're welcome. I think I will go check on the Wyatt and Robbie."

"Hey Mac, are you going to watch the parade with us, or do you want to play a game?" Wyatt's voice carried into the kitchen.

When both Sherry and Amy were sure that Mac was concentrating on whatever Robbie and Wyatt were into in the living room, Amy looked to Sherry.

"Well, you are further along in this relationship than I thought if you're out here in fuzzy slippers and no makeup."

"Oh god, I forgot about no makeup!" Sherry cried.

Amy giggled into her coffee, then took a sip, "Well, he doesn't seem to mind," she said glancing towards the living room.

Sherry grinned, "No, he doesn't."

"So, what are your plans today?" Amy asked.

"The three of us are going over to Kay's house for dinner. She's invited some people from Ethan's office as well."

"Kay's house, really? Must be nice to be in tight with the boss." Amy laughed.

"It's not like that." Sherry thought about it for a minute, "Exactly."

"If you say so." Amy smiled.

"Besides, it is going to be really fun. She is trying to play matchmaker with Mac and I, not realizing we are already dating."

Sherry nearly choked on her coffee. "Why is the boss concerned about your love life?"

"Well, she is genuinely concerned for my happiness and Mac's too, but I think she feels a little guilty for dumping him for Ethan."

"Wait, what?"

"Kay and Mac dated briefly some time ago and now he lives in her guest cottage." Sherry pretended like that was old news because she knew Amy would be shocked.

"I think I'm lost."

"You are dating Kay's old boyfriend, whom she hired, and he lives in her guest cottage?"

"Yeah, that is pretty much it."

"And Ethan is okay with it?"

Sherry shrugged, "Seems to be. But the fun part is that Kay doesn't know Mac and I are dating, and we are going to spring it on her today. Mac told her at the last minute this morning he was bringing a date. I'm sure she is at this moment racking her brain who it is and how she missed it."

"You guys are mean." Amy offered.

"How is it mean? Kay has an enormous heart, and she is always helping her employees, you know that, but sometimes she gets a little carried away. And this is one of those times, so we are going to teach her a tiny little lesson."

"I hope it doesn't backfire on you, but if it does and you get fired, put in a good word for me, will you? I've been thinking about going back to work full time." Amy laughed and finished her coffee. "I'd better get going if I am going to get this dinner ready on time."

"You having family over?" Sherry asked.

"Yes, both sets of grandparents, Robbie will be in heaven with both grandmothers spoiling him today."

"Okay, well, here you go. Do you need anything else?"

"No, this should do it."

"Okay, well, just let me know." Sherry hugged Amy. "Happy Thanksgiving."

"You too, sweetie."

Sherry walked Amy to the door.

"Mom, can't Robbie stay until time for us to leave?" Wyatt stood up with Robbie.

"I'm sure Ms. Barton would prefer Robbie go home and help her get ready for their dinner."

"Ah, mom." Wyatt whined.

"Mom, do I really have to help? Couldn't I stay here and play games with Wyatt?" Robbie tried.

"Ms. Davis doesn't have time to run you home. She is cooking too, and I can't come back and get you."

"What if grandma and grandpa stopped by there and picked me up?" Robbie tried again.

"You are persistent, I'll give you that." Amy shook her head no.

Both boys looked so dejected; Sherry was tempted to change her mind.

Mac stepped closer. "What if you guys went with the program today and we all did something this weekend together?"

Wyatt turned to Mac. "Like what?"

"I don't know, ice skating. Or the new superhero movie?"

Wyatt looked at Robbie. "What do you think?"

Robbie nodded and then looked at Amy.

"I think that could work. What do you think Sherry?"

"I think so."

Mac clapped his hands together. "Okay, so Robbie, when you get home ask your dad if he can join us and maybe we can make it a guy's thing. The moms can do something fun they want to do, and we can all meet up for lunch afterwards?"

"Yeah!" Robbie and Wyatt cheered.

"Okay, good deal." Mac looked at the two boys, "Now, go help your moms."

"Okay, let's go mom." Robbie ran out the front door.

Sherry and Amy stood looking at each other.

"Do you rent him out for bedtimes and when Robbie won't eat his vegetables?" Amy laughed.

"Nope, he's my own secret weapon." Sherry laughed.

Wyatt looked impatient. "Come on, Mac. I bet there are dishes we could do."

It was Sherry's turn to marvel at the change in attitude. She turned to Amy and shrugged, "whatever works."

"You got that right. Call me later?" Amy asked.

"You know it." Sherry hugged her and watched as her friend left.

Mac and Wyatt were washing and drying the dishes that were piling up in the sink.

"I have everything in the oven. Can you keep an eye on it while I go shower and change?" She asked.

"Yes, ma'am." Mac winked at her.

"Wyatt, when you are done, can you please go get cleaned up and change?"

"Yes, ma'am." He smiled.

She nodded and disappeared into her bedroom.

An hour later, they were ready to go. Mac loaded the last of the dishes they were taking to Kay's for dinner into the trunk of his car.

Then he sent Kay a text.

"We are on our way."

"Looking forward to meeting our special someone." Kay replied.

Mac laughed and showed the text to Sherry.

"This is going to be so much fun!" she laughed.

When they arrived, Mac pulled around the block to the rear entrance of the property and parked next to the cottage.

Mac led the way, followed by Wyatt and then Sherry. He opened the back door into the house. "Kay, I'm back." He called.

Kay turned around, "Mac, why in the world are you bringing guests through the back door?"

Ethan appeared at the doorway to the kitchen, carrying his cell phone.

"Because this is the way I always come into the house." Mac laughed.

"Okay, so where is your friend?"

Ethan lifted his cell phone and started recording.

"Hi, Ms. Dandridge!" Wyatt stepped out from behind Mac.

"Wyatt?"

"Happy Thanksgiving!" Sherry appeared, holding a bag with some dishes she had prepared.

"Sherry?" Kay looked confused for a moment. "You're Mac's date?"

"Yes, I am. I was invited, wasn't I?"

"Yes, of course, but I...."

Ethan, Mac, and Sherry all started laughing.

Kay looked at each of them and then down at Wyatt. "Did you know about this too?"

"Yes, ma'am." He grinned.

Kay reached out and hugged him. "You guys are hilarious! Come in, come in."

Sherry stepped past Mac. "I have more in the car."

"I'll get them." Mac turned and disappeared.

"I can't believe you, two!" Kay hugged Sherry, then took the bag and set it on the counter.

"Why am I the last to know?"

"Oh honey, we didn't intend for it to happen that way. We were keeping it quiet at work and then when you invited us for Thanksgiving, we thought we could just have a little fun at your expense." Sherry laughed and hugged Kay.

"Well, I have to admit you got me." She looked at the two of them. "But I have to say, I knew it!"

Ethan rolled his eyes, "Here we go, I hope you two are happy with yourselves, because she is going to be insufferable now."

"What do you mean?" Mac asked coming back through the door.

"He means I knew you two would be perfect for each other!"

Ethan, not being able to take it anymore, interrupted, "Wyatt, Mac, you guys want to come hang out in the den with me?"

"Yeah, that would be great." Mac sensing this was going to turn into a conversation he didn't want to be a part of, anyway. "Come on, Wyatt."

The three of them filed out of the kitchen.

Trying to change the subject, Sherry put her hands on her hips and looked around, "Tell me what I can do to help."

The doorbell, rang. "I'll get that, you could check the oven for me."

Kay dashed to the front door, "Welcome, Blake and Logan." She smiled and hugged Blake first.

"Hi Kay, thank you for having us." Blake hugged her back.

"Logan, it's Thanksgiving. Do I get a hug?"

"Okay, but don't tell Ethan." Logan teased.

"Don't tell me what?" Ethan's deep voice interrupted the reception.

"That Logan gave me a hug." Kay giggled.

"Well, that is progress." Ethan laughed. Logan and Kay hadn't gotten along well when they first met, and Logan wasn't shy about letting Kay know what he thought about her. They had finally come around and were now quite good friends. Ethan shook Logan's hand and hugged Blake. "Come on in."

"Where should I put these?" Logan picked up two bags.

"In the kitchen will be fine."

Kay and Blake followed them into the kitchen.

"Logan Watson, Blake Morgan," Kay stepped over to stand next to Sherry. "This is Sherry Davis. She works in my office. Well, honestly, she runs the company."

Sherry blushed, "She is making that up, but it is nice to meet you."

Mac and Wyatt appeared in the doorway.

Kay smiled at them, "And this handsome young man is Wyatt, Sherry's son and Logan you remember, Mac."

Logan looked from Kay to Mac.

"Nice to see you again, man." Mac nodded.

"Yeah, same." Logan nodded. His lack of words was an obvious sign to all who knew him, he wasn't happy about seeing Mac. Kay ignored him, having been given that look too many times before.

Once the introductions were done, the men went back to the den and Kay, Sherry, and Blake finished the last-minute dinner preparations.

There was a roar from the den that nearly rattled the windows. Kay sighed, "Maybe I should just let them take their plates in there and enjoy the game."

"You're probably right." Blake laughed; "You know how they can get."

"I'll be right back." Kay marched down into the den.

Blake looked over at Sherry. "I'll bet you a dollar they are sitting at the table in five minutes."

Sherry laughed. "It wouldn't bother me if they ate down there and watched the game, because all they are going to do at the table is talk about the game."

"You're probably right."

A minute later, Kay returned. "I'll get the table set if you ladies wouldn't mind bringing the food to the table."

"On it." Blake laughed as she, and Sherry started gathering up dishes and serving spoons.

Once the table was set, Sherry went to the den. "Wyatt, can you give me a hand?"

"Sure mom."

Wyatt walked into the kitchen; his face flushed. "You feeling, okay?"

"Yeah, I'm okay."

"Why don't you go splash some water on your face and come to the table."

"Okay."

"Kay, is there a bathroom on this level?"

Kay turned, "Sure, right down this hallway." She pointed, and Wyatt followed.

"Is he okay?" Kay looked at Sherry with concern.

"Yeah, sometimes he just gets sensory overload and needs to take a break and recenter himself."

"Okay, I can have them tone it down, if I need to."

"No, no. It's okay. If it gets to be too much, he can go outside and get some air. I'll tell Mac to watch him."

A few moments later, Logan, Mac, Ethan, and Wyatt appeared at the door. The table was beautifully set with a centerpiece and candles.

Kay began giving seating instructions for everyone to sit. Ethan was at the head of the table with the turkey in front of him, Kay to his right, Wyatt was opposite Ethan with the Logan and Blake on one side of the table and Mac and Sherry on the other.

"Before we begin, Wyatt, I think you have a tradition at your house that you say before each meal. Do you mind telling the others what that is?" Kay asked.

"We say something positive that happened to us that day at work or school."

Kay nodded, "I think that is a wonderful tradition, so today I'd like for each of us to either say something they are grateful for, or something positive that has happened in their life." She turned to Ethan. "Why do you start us off?"

Ethan nodded, "Okay, I'm grateful for each of you, it is a lucky man to have such wonder friends in his life." He looked at Kay and then at Logan.

Kay was next. "I am grateful every day for Ethan and for Sherry, especially because they keep my life together. But I am also grateful for wonderful friends that take the time to share this meal with us today."

Kay looked at Sherry to keep it going.

Sherry was regretting telling Kay about this tradition in her house. It was one thing to say it in the privacy of her home with Wyatt, but now she felt a little more exposed.

"I'm grateful for my beautiful son, who brings me joy every day. I'm grateful to Kay and Ethan for opening their home to us and for meeting new friends." She smiled at Blake and Logan.

Mac cleared his throat and reached over and squeezed Sherry's hand under the table. "I'm grateful for wonderful friends, new and old." He winked at Wyatt.

Wyatt grinned, "I'm grateful for my mom for always taking care of me, for Ms. Dandridge for helping me with my school, and for Mr. McIntyre." He smiled back at Mac.

It was Logan's turn, and he looked as if he would rather do anything else but this. He glanced over at Blake and then pegged Kay with a stare.

"I'm grateful to have found Blake. I'm grateful for Ethan always having my back, for Kay for putting up with me and to new friends."

Blake smiled nervously, "I guess that just leaves me." She cleared her throat a little. "I'm grateful for this big lug," as she leaned against Logan "and for friends like Ethan and Kay and new friends."

Everyone nodded, and Ethan stood up to carve the turkey.

They toasted to their good health, and the meal began with a low din of conversation and the clinking of silverware.

When the meal was over, everyone helped clear the table and organize a line in the kitchen for loading the dishwasher and cleaning what wouldn't fit. Finally, it was all done. The men returned to the den for the afternoon games.

"Wyatt, you wanna hang out and watch football?" Mac asked.

Wyatt hesitated, "maybe in a little while."

"Okay buddy, no problem. You know how to find me, right?"

"Yes."

"Okay." Mac smiled and then looked to Sherry as if to ask if everything was alright.

Sherry came over and whispered, "You getting a headache?"

Wyatt nodded.

"Do you want to lie down or sit outside for a bit?"

"I'll just sit outside for a little while."

"Okay." Sherry nodded. "Ms. Dandridge has a wonderful wrap-around porch."

"Can I take my game?"

"If you don't think it will make your head hurt any worse, yes."

"I'll stop if it does."

"Okay. I'll be just inside if you need me."

Wyatt nodded and walked out the back door and turned right onto the porch.

"Is he okay?" Mac asked.

"Yeah, sometimes he gets a little over stimulated. Some quiet time should help him."

"Okay." Mac looked worried, but followed the others to the den, anyway.

Kay came and put her arm around Sherry. "You want some coffee and pie?"

Sherry smiled, "Yeah!"

Blake, Kay, and Sherry each with a slice of pie and a cup of coffee, sat in the living room curled up on the sofa or in chairs.

"Kay, this house is huge and so beautiful." Blake looked around the room.

"Thank you, it has been in the family for a couple of generations."

"It's just beautiful."

"Blake is an architect." Kay explained to Sherry.

"Oh, well, there is a lot of architectural history in the Garden District, that is for sure."

"Are all the houses like this?"

"Many, but not all." Kay sat her coffee down. "You want to take a walk and look at some of the other houses?"

"Oh, I'd love to." Blake jumped at the chance.

"Sherry, you want to join us?"

"Yes, I need to walk off that meal and that pie." She laughed.

"Leave the dishes. We'll get them when we get back. I'll holler at the men and let them know we're leaving."

"Do you mind if I ask Wyatt if he wants to join us?"

"Go right ahead."

Sherry walked out to the porch to find Wyatt sitting quietly.

"You feeling, okay? Do you need to go home?"

"No, I'm fine, mom. Really, it isn't as bad as it used to be."

"Kay, Blake, and I are going to go for a walk. Do you want to join us?"

"No, thanks. I'll just stay here. It is peaceful."

"Okay, I'll be back soon, and Mac is inside."

"Mom, I'll be fine."

"Okay," she smiled, and joined Kay and Blake.

CHAPTER SEVENTEEN

S herry, Kay, and Blake returned to find the men out
wondering around the yard.

"What's going on? You guys lose your football?" Kay
laughed.

Sherry got a sick feeling in the pit of her stomach. Her eyes
began searching the yard for Wyatt. Then Mac.

"Where is he?" She looked around wildly.

"Mac!" Ethan bellowed.

Mac came jogging round the side of the house. "Babe." He
went to Sherry and put his arms around her.

"Where's Wyatt? What's happened?" She looked up at him
frantically.

"Honey, we don't know."

"You don't know where he is or what happened?" She could
feel the hysteria rising in her chest.

"Both."

"Oh god!" Her knees gave out a little and Mac caught her
before she could fall.

Kay rushed over and put her arm around Sherry for support.
"Come sit down." She guided her to the steps.

Sherry looked up at Mac, "What happened?"

"I went out to check on him and he wasn't anywhere on the porch. I called out and started looking around the yard, thinking maybe he was exploring or something. Then I went back in and got the others to help me."

"How long have you been looking?" Kay asked.

"Not long, ten minutes maybe?"

"Okay, well, let's check the house and the cottage. Maybe he just needs a quiet place to lie down. I can't imagine he would wonder off and not tell anyone," Kay directed everyone.

Logan, Mac, and Ethan disappeared.

Sherry was sitting on the steps, trembling.

Blake looked at Sherry with sympathy. "Can I get you some water or something?"

"Water." Kay nodded as she sat down next to Sherry.

"Listen, it's gonna be okay. I'm sure there is a very simple explanation for this."

"My phone." Sherry looked around. "Let me call him." She waited, but Wyatt's phone only rang until it went to voice mail." She cried, "It's just that there has been so much going on in his life lately. What if he is sick somewhere alone?" She stood up, "I need to pull it together, I need to find my boy."

Blake reappeared. "Here, have a sip of this and we will all go looking for him."

Sherry took the water and drank a little. "Thank you."

Ethan returned and pulled Kay aside. "We've checked the property, he isn't here. I'm going to go in and check the cameras."

"Good idea."

"Maybe he just went for a walk alone." Kay offered.

"I'm going to call him again." Sherry pulled out her cell and tapped in the number. It rang with no answer.

Kay looked around.

"Did you hear something?" Sherry was hopeful.

"I'm not sure, do it again."

Sherry rang Wyatt's phone again, and the three ladies started walking around, listening.

"I hear something, but it is so faint I can't be sure." Kay said.

They walked around to the back and listened. Sherry kept redialing.

Logan came around the corner.

"Sherry, can I see your phone?"

"Uh sure. We were trying to ring Wyatt's phone to see if we can hear it."

"Do you have the locator turned on?" He asked, taking her phone, and tapping the screen

"No."

Kay stepped closer. "Can you track him with her phone?" She asked.

"Maybe."

Sherry looked at Kay. "What is he doing?"

"If you have the ability on your phone or an app for parental controls, you might use the GPS on his phone to find him."

"I never really thought about that, I should have thought about that." Sherry shook her head.

"It's okay, you're upset. Logan will figure it out." Kay hugged Sherry. "We're gonna find him."

The sound of sirens filled the air, and they all raced to the front of the house. Across the street on the far side of the cemetery, a fire truck and an ambulance pulled in.

They all looked at each other and had the same thought. Logan raced ahead of the three women. He sprinted through the cemetery much faster than they could have. When he reached the fire truck, he turned and waved to them to let them know everything was okay. Ethan and Mac joined Kay, Blake, and Sherry as they ran through the tombstones.

Wyatt was standing next to Logan, looking very frightened. The medics were lifting an elderly man onto the gurney.

"Wyatt, are you okay?" Sherry raced forward and grabbed him in a bear hug.

"Yes, mom I'm fine."

"What are you doing? What is going on?"

One paramedic walked over and shook Wyatt's hand. "Good job, son."

Sherry looked puzzled.

"This young man saved a life today." He patted Wyatt on the shoulder and climbed into the ambulance.

"Are you sure you are, okay?" Sherry asked again.

Wyatt blushed and looked around. "What is everyone doing here?"

"We couldn't find you and we got worried. I didn't know if you were hurt or something."

"Geeze mom, I'm not a baby."

"I know but…,"

Seeing that Wyatt was embarrassed with all the attention from Sherry, Ethan tried to defuse the situation. "What happened to the older gentleman, Wyatt?"

"Well, I was sitting on the porch, and I thought the cemetery would be nice and quiet, so I wondered over. I was looking at some of the old headstones and I saw this old man putting flowers on a grave and I thought how sad that was, and then he fell. I ran over to him. He was holding his chest, so I called 911 and the dispatcher told me what to check for and he didn't have a pulse and wasn't breathing, so I did CPR until the fire department came."

"That's why you couldn't answer me when I called." Sherry said, relieved.

"I didn't want to stop what I was doing."

Logan gave Wyatt a high-five, "good job, kid."

"Thanks."

"Well, I think you're a hero and heroes deserve a big slice of pie with whipped cream." Kay smiled at him.

Sherry put an arm around Wyatt. "I'm very proud of you."

"Thanks, mom."

The group walked back across the street. The guys returned to the game, Wyatt sat in the kitchen with Sherry and Kay, while Blake went to watch the game with Logan.

"That was really awesome that you could save that man's life, Wyatt." Kay said in between bites of her own pie.

"I didn't really think about it being awesome. I just sort of did it."

"That is what makes it even more special. You didn't think twice, you just helped someone in need." She smiled at him and at Sherry.

After he finished his pie, Wyatt asked, "Can I go watch the game with Mac now?"

"Of course." Sherry nodded.

When he was gone, she looked over at Kay, "well, never a dull moment." She smiled.

"He's a good kid."

"Yes, he is. He looks so much like his father."

"There are a lot of you in there, too."

"I like to think so."

"How has he been towards Mac?"

Sherry laughed, "He loves Mac! Sometimes I think those two have more of a relationship than Mac and I."

"I can't believe you didn't tell me." Kay laughed, washing the pie plates. "I wasn't sure how you would feel about it. I thought it might be awkward and there is just the whole dating someone you work with thing." Sherry explained.

"Okay, that was a lot."

"Yeah, I know, but I am relieved that you know and are okay with it. Because that was a lot to hold in."

"I bet, but listen, you never have to worry about me being upset about something. You can tell me anything."

"Thanks."

The guys started filtering back into the kitchen.

"Is the game over?" Kay asked.

"Yeah." Ethan said in a tone that clearly meant his team had lost."

Wyatt looked tired.

"You ready to go home?" Sherry asked him. He nodded.

Mac offered, "why don't you go come over to my place for a while? Wyatt can chill on the sofa with his game and I can entertain you for a change."

Wyatt perked up.

"Okay, sure we can do that."

Everyone said their goodbyes and Sherry and Wyatt walked out back with Mac.

The cottage had a neutral decor and Sherry guessed it was pretty much the way Kay had decorated it; she guessed Mac hadn't added too many personal touches. But it looked cozy and comfortable.

"The bedroom is back there if you want to crash for a while Wyatt. The bathroom is down the hall on the right."

Wyatt looked in the direction of the bedroom, "Thanks. I might lie down for a while."

"Yeah, man you've had a busy day, crash for as long as you like."

Wyatt went to Mac's bedroom and closed the door.

"Want something to drink?"

"No, thanks. I've had enough food and drink to last me a week."

"Have a seat." He took her hand and led her to the sofa. They sat down together, and Mac instantly pulled her close to him and put an arm around her. "This feels like the first time we've truly been alone."

"We've been alone before. Admittedly Wyatt was upstairs in his bedroom."

"I know, but this somehow feels different."

Sherry nodded. She knew what he meant at her house: he was on her turf, a house she had shared with her late husband and Wyatt's father. Here, there was no shadow of that former life. She had to admit she felt freer here, too. She leaned her head on his shoulder.

"It is comfortable here."

He kissed the top of her head. "I'm glad you think so."

"So, is this what dating is like these days?" Sherry asked.

"I do not know, but it is what dating is like for us."

She smiled.

"Did you go out on dates with Kay, or did you just have quiet time?"

"We went out." He didn't want to get too personal with the details, and he didn't want Sherry comparing herself to Kay. They were, thankfully, two very different people.

"So, no quiet time with Kay?"

"Is Kay ever quiet?"

She got the point. He didn't want to talk about it, and that was fair.

"No, I suppose you have a point."

She liked the way his chest rumbled when he chuckled.

"I think we should have a second date, where it is just two of us." She announced.

"You do?" Mac looked down at her curiously, "and what sort of date should we have?"

"I'm not sure, but something very grown up."

He kicked himself for not having thought of it before. "Okay, so are we talking fancy dinner?"

"No, we did that."

"True, although I'm not sure that was what I would call fancy. I wasn't even wearing a tie."

"I'm thinking maybe a weekend date, maybe we should go away together for a weekend."

Mac felt like his heart skipped a beat and hoped she couldn't hear how hard it was pounding.

"That sounds promising." He held her a little tighter. "Where should we go?"

"I'm thinking a cabin in the woods."

"Really? I wouldn't have pegged you for a camping type of girl."

"Oh, I'm not at all, but a cabin with a fire pit and a hot tub would be perfect."

"I'll have to see what I can do."

She smiled to herself and closed her eyes, imagining what this moment would be like if they were in front of a warm fire, alone with no one else around for miles.

She woke up around midnight at the sound of glasses clinking together.

She was alone on the couch with a pillow and a blanket. She sat up and looked around, trying to get her bearings in the unfamiliar space.

She turned to see Wyatt and Mac sitting at the dinette eating pie and drinking milk.

"Hi mom, want a snack?"

"What is going on here?" She smiled.

"Oh well, I woke up and was a little hungry, so Mac and I had a snack. And this is dessert." He grinned.

Mac leaned back. "Kay saw the light on and brought over some leftovers, including a pecan pie."

"Sure, why not?"

She looked at Wyatt. "You feeling any better?"

"Yes, I think I was just tired."

"Well, it was a full day. I'm not surprised you were tired."

"Yeah, Mac told me it was a very important thing I did today."

She glanced over at Mac, who was taking a plate out of the microwave.

"He is right. It was very important and very brave. Were you scared?"

"I was scared the man would die." Wyatt looked worried all over again.

Sherry nodded, "few people could do what you did today."

"You would have, mom."

"I would certainly have tried, but you kept your cool and you did all the right things."

"I wish I knew what his name was." Wyatt looked thoughtful.

"The important thing is, he will have a second chance at life thanks to you and I'm sure his family will be grateful for that."

Wyatt smiled.

"Here you go, my lady." Mac brought Sherry a plate.

"Good grief, this is almost as much as we ate earlier today."

"It was an enjoyable meal." Mac said.

"Yes, it was."

"Mr. Watson seems kind of grumpy." Wyatt added.

Mac laughed, "yeah he can be until you get to know him. He isn't grumpy so much as he is very serious, and he likes to protect his friends."

"But there were no bad guys around today."

"Very true, you should see him when there are bad guys." Mac smiled.

"You know him?" Sherry asked.

"I worked with him once before. He is very loyal to Ethan."

Sherry got the feeling there was a story there, but she didn't want to ask in front of Wyatt. If it had to do with Ethan, then it probably had to do with Kay. She had met Logan before as well, when Ethan had sent him to the office, and he was certainly not someone to mess with.

"I understand he's mellowed a lot since meeting Blake," she added.

"Well, the world can take a collective sigh of relief, because it would have been a matter of time before a guy like that blows his top." Mac finished the last bite of his pie.

Wyatt looked at Mac. "What do you mean?"

"Some guys are driven, determined and very focused on their jobs. They take it seriously, which is good if you're going to be a special agent, but you have to turn it off too. Or all the bad things you see as part of your job will stress you out and there will be no turning back."

"Do you ever get stressed out?" Wyatt asked.

"Hmm, not anymore. But, when I was younger, and I didn't have friends like you and your mom. All I thought about was catching bad guys and I was a little like Logan. But I wised up and decided I needed to make some changes in my life."

"I'm glad you did." Wyatt smiled.

"Me too. You guys want to spend the night here?"

"You only have one bedroom."

"True, but the sofa pulls out into a bed and in the cabinet under the TV is a game console. You can log into your account from here and play if your mom says it is okay."

Sherry rolled her eyes. "How am I supposed to say no to that? I think I've been set up."

"I'm too old to sleep with my mom." Wyatt argued.

"Yes, you are, but you and I can play video games and your mom can take my room."

Wyatt looked thoughtful. "You guys can have the bedroom, and I'll sleep out here. I really don't mind. I get it. You guys don't get a lot of time alone together."

Sherry nearly choked, and Mac laughed.

"Thank you, Wyatt. I appreciate you understanding the situation, but I don't think it would be right for your mom and I to sleep together before we are married."

"Why not?"

Sherry was still too stunned to speak, and she sat watching the exchange between her son and Mac.

"Well, some people of a certain age and generation," he nodded to Wyatt, "That are older than you were taught that it is not appropriate to sleep together or have sex outside of marriage."

"Is it because of your religion?"

Sherry finally found her voice. "Where did you learn all of this?"

"Oh mom, I'm eleven not five. There are kids at my school that have already had sex at my age."

"I hope you are not one of them!"

Wyatt rolled his eyes, and Mac thought about how much he looked like Sherry in that moment.

"No mom, I don't even have a girlfriend."

"Thank god for that." She leaned back in her chair. Thinking she was close to having a heart attack.

Mac had to hide the smile that was creeping across these lips.

"Girls, are trouble." Wyatt continued.

Mac laughed out loud, "From the mouth of babes."

Sherry shot him a sour look. "Do you care to elaborate on that?"

"What?" Wyatt looked at Sherry, "A minute ago you were happy I didn't have a girlfriend. Now you think a girlfriend is a good idea?"

"No, I am not defending the idea of you having a girlfriend, but you should not be judging people in broad general terms, based on gender."

"Okay, well, boyfriends are a pain too. It doesn't matter if it is boy/girl or same-sex relationship, dating someone just seems to be more trouble than it is worth."

"You are absolutely correct, and you don't need to worry about dating anyone until you are at least thirty." Sherry shook her head.

Mac was still laughing.

"I don't want a girlfriend, mom. I want to play soccer and video games. Robbie had a girl like him, and she got mad whenever he played video games instead of talking to her online."

"Robbie?"

"Yeah, but they broke up. He doesn't talk to her anymore."

"Did his mom know about this?"

"I don't know, but don't tell her I told you."

"I won't, I promise. Would you tell me if you had a girlfriend?"

"Yes."

"Okay." She relaxed a little.

Wyatt looked at Mac. "Did you have a lot of girlfriends before you met my mom?"

"Wyatt, that is inappropriate!" Sherry scolded.

"Why? We were talking about girlfriends and boyfriends."

"Mac is your elder and you will show him some respect."

"I'm sorry."

"You mom is right; you should be respectful of your elders. However, since this concerns you mom, I will tell you. No, I had very few girlfriends before her and I do not intend to have anymore."

Wyatt nodded.

Sherry turned to look at Mac in surprise.

Sensing he may have revealed too much, Mac looked for an out. "You wanna check out the games?"

"Yeah!" Wyatt jumped up from the table.

Mac rose and went to turn on the console and the TV.

Sherry started clearing the table.

"Hey, leave those, I'll get them."

"That is okay, it will give me something to do while you get Wyatt set up."

Mac looked from Wyatt to Sherry, his attention divided.

"Oh wow, this is the newest model!" Wyatt cried out.

"Yeah, uh well my last one was really old, so I upgraded."

"Cool."

Sherry slipped outside while Mac and Wyatt were engrossed in getting logged in and started playing. She slipped onto Kay's porch out of the way of the security lights and sat alone in the dark. She wanted to ponder what Mac had said. No more girlfriends and a romantic weekend getaway. This was getting serious. That Wyatt was fully aware of the situation and okay with it somehow made it more real. She sat in a comfortable wicker chair with beautiful green cushions, and she wondered how often Kay had time to sit out here. The thought about how fast things were moving with Mac; how happy and terrified she was all at the same time.

She wasn't an overly analytical person, so sitting there to weigh the pros and cons of the relationship wouldn't do her any good. It was about how she felt and deep down; she knew she was holding back. She wasn't being honest with herself or Mac. But she felt overwhelmed and in need of a break.

She felt like she needed more time alone with Mac to work out her feelings. He treated her and Wyatt with love and kindness, and he made her feel safe and less alone. But was that any reason to commit to a serious relationship? Was he really asking for one, but she couldn't let herself be in a causal relationship? She was afraid of what that would do to Wyatt. He had suffered too great a loss already. She didn't want him to lose anyone else important to him again at such a young age.

She got up and walked to the front of the house that overlooked the old cemetery. There were few lights there and she could look up at the stars. She wished she knew what to do. She thought about her husband and what would he want for her and Wyatt and she was confident that he would want them to be safe and happy. He was generous that way.

She heard the front door open, and she sighed. So much for alone time.

"Sherry, everything alright?"

She jumped at the sound of Ethan's voice. "Oh!"

"I'm sorry. I didn't mean to frighten you."

"No, I heard the door open. I had just assumed it would be Kay."

"She's asleep. Why aren't you?"

"I don't know."

He walked to the edge of the porch but gave her plenty of space. "I know what you mean. I can't turn my mind off sometimes."

"Tell me about it."

Ethan waited a few minutes. "You worried about Mac or Wyatt?"

She smiled to herself. "That obvious?"

"Yeah."

"I'd have to say Mac."

"Why?"

"I don't know. I have no reason to be worried. I guess I'm more worried about myself than him, really."

"That's a tough one. Mac, I could help you with, but your own feelings, well….,"

"Yeah, I know. I wish you could though."

She thought about it for a moment. She didn't know Ethan that well, mostly she knew him through Kay. But he had a way of making a person feel at ease.

Sherry turned to face him. "Can I ask you something about Mac?"

"Sure."

"How do you feel about him?"

"Well, he's not really my type." He chuckled softly. "Seriously, Mac is a great guy. He would never do anything to hurt you or Wyatt."

"Do you trust him?"

"Sure."

Sherry nodded. It was a dumb question. Mac had helped save Kay's life even after she had broken things off with him.

"Listen, Mac is a loyal, honest, maybe to a fault, and trustworthy. If he says he loves you, you can believe he does. Mac will not play games. He and Kay dated briefly, I'm sure you know that, and he accepted the fact that it would not work out between them with grace. Mac's the person who, even though things didn't work out, considers Kay a friend and Mac will do anything for his friends. He helped me save her life and I might not have been able to do it without him. And I'm glad she hired him. If I can't be there to protect her, I can't think of anyone else I'd rather have guarding her than Mac."

Sherry nodded, though in the dark she doubted Ethan could see it.

Ethan continued, "The important thing to remember is just to be honest with yourself."

"You're right."

"You both deserve the best and I think you two are exactly what each other needs."

"Thank you."

"You're welcome and for the record, we never had this conversation."

"Okay." Sherry smiled. "Ethan."

"Yes?"

"Kay is a very lucky woman."

She heard him laugh lightly.

"I know."

Sherry stood there smiling up at the sky, listening to Ethan retreat into the house and close the door. She wasn't sure how long she stayed outside, but she shivered and realized she was getting cold. She made her way back to Mac's cottage and tiptoed inside.

"You, okay?" Mac's voice came quietly out of the dark.

"Yeah, just couldn't sleep."

A small table lamp clicked on, and she blinked at the sudden light.

Mac stood up. "You aren't wearing a sweater or anything, you must be cold."

"I was wondering if you had any cocoa."

"Hmm, I don't, but I can make you some hot tea."

She nodded.

Mac put water in an electric kettle and pulled tea bags from the cabinet along with a cup.

"Should be ready in a minute."

She smiled, "Thank you."

He came to stand in front of her. He wrapped his arms around her and pulled her close. The heat from his body felt so good.

"Is everything alright?"

"Yes," and in that moment, she knew it was. She wrapped her arms around him, and they stood there, just holding each other, until the kettle clicked off.

CHAPTER EIGHTEEN

"Good morning, Sherry." Kay greeted.

"Morning, did you have a pleasant weekend?"

"I did." Kay paused at Sherry's desk. "What about you? Did you do anything fun?"

"Just the usual weekend stuff." Sherry leaned forward. "Although, I might go out of town next weekend."

Kay whispered, "Really? With Mac?"

Sherry smiled and nodded.

"Come in and tell me all about it." She said excitedly.

Sherry waited a minute for Kay to get settled, then went into her office and made them each a cup of coffee.

"Tell me everything." Kay said, leaning back in her chair.

"Well, I have little to tell yet. Mac has planned a weekend getaway in the mountains. I'm not sure exactly where or any details. We are going to leave right after work on Friday."

"Well, you'll have a couple hours' drive at a minimum. Why don't you leave early on Friday so you can get there before dark? Better yet, take Friday off."

"I didn't want to ask on such short notice."

"Sherry, you've worked here how long, and you have how many hundreds of hours of leave saved up? Go."

Sherry thought about it, and she wanted to protest, but she also wanted to go. "Okay, so how do we get Mac to take off early without him knowing I told you my private business?"

"That will be between me and Mac." She grinned.

"Okay, thank you."

"I'm gonna want details when you get back."

Sherry laughed, "If they are fit to be repeated."

"You're terrible!"

"Hey, does Wyatt know what you are doing?"

"Yeah, he knows. He is very supportive. He wants me to have a boyfriend, and he really likes Mac. So, no problems there."

"He is very mature for an eleven-year-old."

"Yeah, I guess he is."

"Mom?"

"Oh, hey honey, everything okay?"

"Yes, I've been working with some guys in security today on the monitoring equipment. They asked if I wanted to go to lunch with them. Can I go?"

"Who all is going, and will Mac be there?"

"Uh, I'm sure, but Todd, JC, and Adam are going."

"Do I know them?"

"Mom." Wyatt sighed, "They are security, they will not let anything happen to me."

Just then, Mac came up the hallway.

"Mr. McIntyre, can you please tell my mom that it is safe for me to go to lunch with Todd, JC and Adam and that nothing bad will happen to me if I am with them."

"Lunch with the three musketeers, huh?" Mac looked at him seriously.

"Yeah." Wyatt stood straight, trying to measure up to Mac.

Sherry had to smile at the way he puffed his chest out a little.

"Where are you going to lunch?" Mac asked seriously.

"I'm not sure."

"You don't seem to know a lot about this lunch." Sherry added.

"Well, I didn't know I was going to get the third degree."

Mac cleared his throat, and Wyatt glanced down at his shoes.

"Sorry mom."

Sherry was stunned. She looked from Wyatt to Mac. "If you are on your very best behavior."

Wyatt looked up, "Really?"

Sherry reached in her purse, "Here is some money."

"Wait a minute," Mac said, crossing his arms.

"You're not going to one of those places were young ladies dance in bikinis, are you?"

Wyatt blushed and laughed, "No!"

Mac chuckled, "Good."

Wyatt raced back down the hallway.

"He'll be alright, won't he?" Sherry asked.

"He'll be fine. Those guys will not let a single thing happen to him; I promise."

"Okay." Sherry said, still a little nervous about letting her son go out with three men she didn't know.

"I served with Todd, worked with JC and would trust your life to Adam. He'll be fine. But I'll go have a talk with them if it makes you feel better."

"It would."

He nodded. "Now I have to go talk to Kay. Apparently, she needs something."

Sherry looked at the picture of innocence. "Really?"

Mac frowned. "Do you know what it is about?"

"No idea." She sat down and focused on her computer.

"Hmmm." Mac strode into Kay's office and shut the door.

When he emerged, he stopped at her desk again.

"I don't suppose you had a hand in that?"

"What?"

"Apparently, I am to take Friday off."

"Really? Me too, maybe we can start our weekend early."

He gave her a knowing smile, "Yes, we can." He gave her a sexy wink that sent a thrill of excitement up her spine and strode away.

Next Todd, Adam, JC and Wyatt stopped by her desk.

"Ms. Davis?"

She looked up, thinking she would get no work done today.

"Yes?"

"We'd like to take Wyatt to lunch with us today, if that is, okay?" She looked past Todd to Wyatt, and he stood looking at her with his eyebrows raised. She knew he was begging her with his eyes to say yes again and not embarrass him.

"Where are you going for lunch?" She returned her attention back to Todd.

"We thought we walk down to Emmet's Grill. They have the best cheeseburgers."

"Okay, that will be fine."

Todd gave her a charming smile, and she imagined a lot of women fell for that smile with his dancing green eyes.

She smiled at Wyatt as he turned to leave with the small group and watched as they formed a V formation around him, one man on each side and one in the rear. She was sure her baby would be safe.

Kay came out of her office and stood staring at Sherry. "When are you going to take a lunch break?"

"I don't know. I guess when I get to a stopping point in my work. It has been constant interruptions all day. I can't seem to get anything done."

"Did you bring your lunch today?"

"Of course."

"Well, forget it. I'm going to order in something for the both of us and we will have lunch in my office."

"No offense Kay, but I looked forward to the peace and quiet I get at lunchtime."

"I promise not to talk. We will shut the door. No one will bother us and we'll set the phones to voicemail and just chill."

Sherry knew she wasn't getting out of this, and she felt compelled to say yes because Kay had generously given both her and Mac off on Friday.

"Okay, what are you ordering?"

"What are you in the mood for?"

Sherry gave her a sour look.

"Okay, you need something with chocolate, that is for sure."

"And I swear to god there no better be anything involving a turkey."

Kay laughed, "Fine, no turkey cranberry sandwiches for you." She teased and returned to her office.

Sherry sat staring at the ceiling. There was no point in getting upset about it. Most people would kill to be in her shoes. But she honestly just wanted to get as much work by Thursday as she could so she wouldn't worry about it over the weekend.

Thirty minutes later, the elevator chimed, and a food delivery person stepped off the elevator and spotted her.

"I have an order for a Ms. Dandridge."

"This way, please." She got up and lead him into Kay's office. You can put the food there on the table.

Kay got up to offer a tip.

"There was a pizza, several boxes of Chinese food, a bag of something that smelled heavenly and two small empty boxes containing chocolate cheesecake.

"What did you order?"

"I wasn't sure what you wanted."

"You could have just asked." Sherry stood there, shaking her head.

"You, my dear friend, need to lighten the hell up." Kay kicked off her pumps and shut the door.

"Take off your shoes and get comfortable." Kay went over to her cell phone, which was connected to a Bluetooth speaker, and put on some music.

"Are you serious?" Sherry asked.

"This is the perfect way to start the work week, don't you think?" She said, dancing around the table. "Honestly, I am just so sick of holiday food. I wanted anything and everything that was the opposite of holiday food."

"What kind of pizza is that?" Sherry eyed the box.

"Pepperoni with black olives and….,"

"Extra cheese," they said in unison. And laughed.

Sherry kicked off her shoes and grabbed a slice of pizza.

"There should be drinks in the fridge." Kay pointed.

Sherry got up and grabbed a diet soda for each of them.

"I wish we had wine." Kay pouted.

"We can't drink at work."

"No, that wouldn't be very professional, would it?" Kay laughed.

"No, it wouldn't."

"Great, let's do it!"

She went to the bar and poured the soda into the two glasses, then added a little rum to each one.

"Here, try one."

"I can't." '

"Yes, you can."

"No, I can't. Wyatt works here today. I can't let him see his mother drinking on the job. What kind of example would I be setting?"

"You're right." Kay went over and locked the door.

"Let's enjoy one drink before we clog our arteries with pizza, crab rangoon, and cheesecake."

Sherry picked up the glass and threw the drink back.

"Wow!" Kay watched her.

"Now, can I eat?"

"Yes."

They sat and talked and laughed for nearly two hours. Finally, Mac knocked on the door.

"Kay, are you alright?"

"You'd better open it before he breaks it down." Sherry giggled.

Kay got up and opened the door. Mac was standing there with his hands on his hips.

"Are you alright? Have you seen Sherry?"

Kay stepped aside to allow Mac into the office.

"What in the world, you two decided to have a party?"

"Well, it was impromptu and there is a ton of food. Have you eaten anything today?"

"No, I haven't, I've been working." He looked at the two of them.

"Well, here, have some pizza." Kay encouraged.

Sherry's first thought was there was something wrong, "Is Wyatt, okay?"

"Yes, he's fine, they've been back for a while."

"Okay good."

He looked at Sherry suspiciously. "Everything okay in here?"

"Of course."

He walked over to the table and snagged a slice of pizza. "Why do I get the feeling you two are up to something?"

"Nothing other than girl talk and eating way too much food." Sherry laughed. She hadn't felt this relaxed in a long time.

Mac nodded and looked at Kay. Something was definitely up. He scanned the room. Kay went to her desk and pretended to work. Mac sat down with Sherry.

"You seem pretty happy, a change from a couple hours ago."

"Oh, I'm sorry I was probably overreacting to Wyatt going out with strangers, but they stopped by my desk on the way out and I spoke with Todd."

"I see, so a chat with Todd and chocolate cheesecake is what it takes for you to relax a little and not stress?"

She giggled, well, the cheesecake helped. Mac leaned forward as if to kiss her. Sherry gasped in shock. Displays of affection at work were not something they did, but he whispered in her ear. "We are going to talk about the rum later."

She looked up at him in surprise, but he only smiled and turned to leave.

"You're a bad influence on her," he said to Kay.

"Gee, thanks!" She smiled sweetly as he left.

She got up and closed the door behind him, then turned to Sherry. They both laughed hysterically.

"I guess I better go brush my teeth and get back to work. We don't need rumors spreading around the office." Sherry said, standing up and cleaning up the food containers.

"I'll fire anyone who dares start rumors about our lunch party."

"No, you won't." Sherry laughed. "You'd never fire someone."

"Yes, I have!"

"Who?" Sherry stared her down.

"That irritating attorney, that worked here when I took over."

"Oh yeah, I'd forgotten about him, but that didn't really end well because his replacement turned out to be a traitor."

Kay nodded, "Yes and he's dead, so there you go."

Sherry laughed, "So that is the new company motto, 'get fired or get dead'?"

Kay laughed, "It has a ring to it."

"You're terrible." Sherry shook her head, still laughing.

She returned to her desk and found that she could get nearly a whole day's worth of work done. That lunch break with Kay had really helped. Maybe she had been too uptight lately.

A few minutes after five, Mac appeared again and walked past her and into Kay's office, with Todd close behind him. A few minutes later, Mac reemerged alone. "You leaving soon to go home?"

"Yes, I'm done for today. What's going on? Is everything alright?"

"Yes, everything is fine. I have a few things to wrap up here tonight, so Todd is going to give you and Wyatt a ride home when he takes Kay."

"Why?"

"Because I would feel better if you rode with Kay today."

She frowned at him. "Is this about lunch?"

"No." he smiled.

She decided she would not get upset. She smiled and started logging off her computer.

Wyatt came up the hallway. "Hey mom, did you hear we get to ride in the limo tonight?"

"I did, pretty cool, huh?"

"But what about our car?"

"Oh, it will be fine here and I'm sure we will get a ride tomorrow morning, too."

"Cool!"

Todd came out of Kay's office. "Hey Wyatt, you riding with me tonight?"

"Yeah, can I sit up front with you?"

"Sure."

Todd and Wyatt high-fived each other. Kay appeared, carrying her purse. Sherry gathered up her things and walked past Mac and smiled at Todd, "We really appreciate you giving us a ride, Todd."

Todd glanced at Mac and then smiled at Sherry. "No problem, ma'am, it will give me a chance to hang out with my buddy a little more." He smiled at Wyatt.

Once in the car's backseat, Kay put the glass up to give her and Sherry some privacy.

Sherry looked at Kay, "What the heck is going on?"

"Mac." Kay said simply.

Sherry was confused. "What do you mean, Mac?"

"He is being overprotective of you and so here we are."

"What are you talking about?" Sherry asked again

"He smelled the alcohol from lunch and decided he didn't want you to drive home. Rather than say anything about it at work, he arranged for this."

"That is ridiculous, it was one drink hours ago and I've had coffee since then. What little alcohol was in that drink is long gone out of my system by now."

"You don't have to tell me."

"Is this the sort of thing you put up with all the time?"

"Not to this extent. But Mac takes personal security very seriously, just like he took his job seriously when he was an agent and just like Ethan takes his job seriously. It is just part of being in a relationship with these Type A men."

Sherry rolled her eyes. "He actually thinks I can't hold my liquor to where I would risk putting my son in danger?"

"No, I don't think he was thinking along those lines at all."

Sherry stared out the window, "I don't like being handled."

Kay rolled her eyes, "Who are you telling? Now you know why I don't enjoy having security follow me around and drive me to work. It was bad enough when Eddie did it, but with Mac, it is ten times worse. I swear I wouldn't be surprised if he had someone watching the house at night."

"He does." She chuckled.

"What do you mean, did he tell you that?"

"No, but Kay, he lives in your backyard. He is watching the house and between him and Ethan, you are guarded twenty-four, seven."

Kay blinked. "I never thought of it that way."

"Yeah, you thought you were doing him a favor letting him stay there. I think he played you."

Realization dawned on Kay, "Son of a bitch!"

Sherry nodded knowingly. "He's crafty. That lopsided grin of his allows him to get away with a lot."

"What are we going to do about it?"

"We?"

"Yeah, he is your man. How are we going to deal with this?"

Sherry looked at her blankly. "I don't know."

"Well, we need to come up with a plan."

"To do what? Not protect you? I agree you need some protection based on past events."

Kay folded her arms. "Keyword there is, past."

"Well, I agree you need something level of protection, who's to say it won't happen again or some disgruntled employee won't try something. The company is getting larger, and we have more and more employees. I know you treat us like family, but even families have disagreements."

"I really thought you would be in my corner."

Sherry reached over and touched Kay's hand. "I am. But you can be protected without people running your life or not giving you choices."

Kay's smiled, "Exactly."

"Well, we'll work on that." Sherry agreed.

Todd stopped at Sherry's house first. Wyatt was bouncing off the walls with excitement to tell her about his day.

"Here mom, here's the money you gave me for lunch." Wyatt handed her the twenty-dollar bill she had given him earlier.

"No, you keep it, but don't spend it on silly things. Hang on to it in case you are invited to lunch again or something. Okay?"

Wyatt's eyes lit up, "Thanks!"

"Now, tell me about your day. How was lunch? Was it fun? What did you learn today?"

Wyatt plopped down on the sofa, but he was practically bouncing up and down. "First, Mac made sure I did all my homework first thing in the morning. He always does that."

Sherry smiled. "What did you do after you finished your homework?"

"Then I hung out with Todd for a little while and then we went to lunch."

"And what does 'hanging out with Todd' mean?"

"Oh, mostly he teaches me about staying healthy and getting exercise, especially now that soccer is over with for the season."

"And what about lunch?"

"Oh, the place we went to was really cool. There were all kinds of important people there in suits and stuff, and I was the only kid there. But they gave me a menu and called me sir."

"That sounds really nice."

"It was. I got a cheeseburger, but I didn't get fries because they are loaded with all kinds of harmful things, so Todd and I got broccoli instead."

Sherry smiled and thought about all the times she had argued and bribed him to eat his vegetables and one morning with Todd, he was eating broccoli instead of French fries. She wondered if she could pay Todd to get come over and get Wyatt to eat vegetables at home too.

"Then this afternoon, JC and Adam, they are techies, they showed me the remote surveillance system so they can see what was happening at the boatyards in other states! It was really cool!"

"I'm glad you are getting something out of your internship."

"Yeah, they said they can start me on some basic computer programming if that is okay with you."

"Is that something you think you will enjoy, because I don't want to waste their time."

"I think I would." Wyatt said, with a seriousness that made him seem much older than his eleven years.

"Okay."

"Can I go to my room now? I want to tell Robbie about my day."

"Sure, I'll call you for dinner."

"Okay, thanks mom!"

She sat smiling, thinking about how everything seemed to be falling into place. She went to room to change clothes and then start dinner. Hopefully, there wouldn't be a struggle over the veggies tonight. She hadn't heard from Mac, but she would make enough in case he showed up.

She was just putting dinner in the oven when there was a knock at the door.

She peered out the window and then opened the door to Mac standing on her porch.

"Hello," she smiled up at him.

"Hello."

"Come in," she stepped aside.

Mac walked in and looked around.

"Wyatt is upstairs talking to Robbie."

"Can I get you something to drink, iced tea, coffee?"

"Tea is fine." He followed her into the kitchen.

She noticed he hadn't greeted her with his usual peck on the cheek. She wondered if something was wrong or if their weekend plans were going to be cancelled.

She poured him a glass of tea; he took it and set it on the counter.

"Is there something wrong?"

He stepped in close and cupped her face. His gaze was deep and intense, and she wanted to melt into him. He kissed her deeply.

When they broke apart, she looked up at him, searching for answers.

He just continued to gaze at her and stroke her hair silently. They were standing this way when Wyatt bounced into the kitchen.

"Mom…. Oh hey, Mr. McIntyre."

"Hi Wyatt," Mac replied, dragging his gaze away from her.

"I was just going to ask what was for dinner, but it can wait."

Mac smiled, "That's okay. I'm done kissing your mom for right now."

Wyatt smiled. Sherry blushed.

Sherry recovered quickly. "It's probably going to be another thirty minutes, sweetie."

"Okay."

"Hey, you got a minute?" Mac asked.

Wyatt stood silently for a moment. "Am I in some kind of trouble?"

Mac smiled, "Of course not. I thought we'd have some guy time before dinner."

Wyatt shrugged a little, "Okay."

Sherry gave Mac a curious look, but he only squeezed her hand and guided Wyatt up to his room.

Forty-five minutes later, they were all sitting down having dinner together and Wyatt seemed to be in an even better mood, if that was even possible.

Sherry watched Mac enjoy his meal. "So, you didn't go to lunch with Wyatt and his work friends. How was your day?"

"Oh, it was pretty good. We are fully staffed at all three locations, so I feel a little better about the status of security for the company now."

"JC and Adam showed me how you can see everything from the office here," Wyatt added.

"How does that work exactly?"

Mac explained between bites, "Yes, there is the ability to monitor each location, cameras and security system from our office here, as well as in their own site. JC and Adam are incredible with networks linking everything up."

After dinner, Wyatt disappeared up to his room without asking to play video games with Mac. Sherry looked up at Wyatt's room. "Do you think he is feeling alright?"

"He's fine."

"He was very excited about his lunch with the guys at the office."

Mac smiled, "He was. Wyatt is fantastic with computers and math. If he enjoys it, he may have a promising future in that field."

"Thank you for letting him hang out with your staff. I hope he isn't interfering with their work?"

"Are you kidding? Those guys are having just as much fun as Wyatt is." Mac laughed.

They settled on the sofa and Mac sipped his after-dinner coffee. "So, are we all set for this weekend? Is Wyatt all squared away with staying at Robbie's house?"

"Yes, everything is all set. I haven't told him yet that we are leaving earlier in the day. I'm sure he won't mind. I think Amy has a full day planned for them at the science museum."

Mac nodded, "And what about you, you okay with spending a weekend away from him?"

"It will be a first, but yes. I think we are both ready." She smiled. She was more than ready for some alone with Mac. "You haven't told me much about this place we are going to other than it is a cabin in the woods, so do I need to be prepared to have to hunt for my dinner?"

Mac smiled. "No hunting, maybe a little hiking. There are some beautiful views to enjoy. But this weekend is about you relaxing and taking a breath."

She smiled into her coffee mug, "That will be a welcome change."

"Speaking of relaxing," Mac touched her arm, "Wanna tell me about lunch today?"

She had almost forgotten about that; she raised her eyebrows at him in surprise.

He frowned. "The rum and coke?"

She felt her cheeks redden, "That was just a moment of rebelliousness, and I blame Kay."

"Oh, I know it was all Kay." He agreed.

"Oh now, don't be mad at her. I'm a big girl and, well, we just got caught up in the moment. Besides, it was only once, and I think it was a way to thumb our noses at the rules for once."

"Interesting since Kay makes the rules."

"You know Kay doesn't put up with a bunch of nonsense at work and she would allow none of her employees to be under the influence on the job. It was just one small drink."

"Yeah, I know."

"Are you worried that it would become a habit?"

He considered his next words, "No, I'm not."

"Good." She nodded as if to say the discussion was over.

An hour later, Mac left. And Sherry went upstairs to check on Wyatt.

"Hey, kiddo, everything okay?"

"Yeah sure, mom."

"Listen, you know Mac and I are going to spend the weekend together this weekend, but it turns out we are going to leave earlier on Friday than originally planned. Are you okay with that?"

Wyatt put his controller down, "Yeah, mom I think it is great that you two are going to spend some time together."

"You know I will miss you and that we aren't going because we don't enjoy spending time with you."

Wyatt rolled his eyes. "Mom, I get it. You need some time with Mac. You are always working and taking me to school or practice. It's okay. I need to spend some time with Robbie and my friends this weekend without my mom." He smiled.

She wasn't sure how she felt about his declaration. It made her proud that he was maturing into a wonderful young man but sad that he could break away from her so easily, too.

"You're a great kid, you know that?"

Wyatt looked down at these shoes for a second, "You're a great mom."

"Thanks!" She hugged him.

"Mom, can I ask you something?"

"Sure, anything."

"I know you and Mac haven't had a lot of dates and stuff, but do you think you might marry him?"

Sherry looked at him shocked, "I don't know, it's a little early in the relationship, why do you ask?"

"Well, if you decide to marry him, I just want you to know that I think that would be cool."

Her heart squeezed so tight she thought she might cry.

"You would like to have a dad again, wouldn't you?"

"Yeah, I would. Is that wrong?"

"No, sweetie, it is not wrong at all."

He smiled up at her. "I want you to be happy too."

She hugged him, "You're the best son, ever."

He let her hug him and didn't squirm away. She fought back the tears, but one escaped anyway.

"Okay, a few more minutes of game time, then time for bed."

"Yes ma'am."

She went downstairs and ran her hand over the place on the sofa where Mac had been sitting. It would be nice to have a partner with someone to share her life with again. But Mac seemed happy with the relationship. She would have to wait and see how this weekend went.

Chapter Nineteen

T he rest of the week seemed to be an anomaly of the space and time continuum, it dragged on in one sense as Sherry was anxious and excited for the coming weekend, and yet, it seemed to fly by because she had so much work she wanted to get done before Friday. One of the other administrative assistants was going to cover for her while she was off on Friday. But Kay didn't have any meetings planned, and hopefully, nothing urgent would come up while she was out. She had seemed little of Mac, and she was sure he must do the same thing as she was trying to make sure everything would be handled while he was unavailable for the weekend.

Thursday night after dinner, her phone buzzed with a text from Mac.

"Pick you up in the morning around ten?"

"I'll be ready."

He sent her a thumbs up emoji. She sighed and put the phone down. She had missed him all week. The phone calls and text had been a poor substitute for his touch, and his smile.

"Wyatt, do you have everything packed for the weekend?" She asked, entering his room after dinner.

"Just about, mom." He said, shoving some underclothes into his backpack.

"Don't forget any chargers you gonna need for your game."

"I won't."

"Okay, and you have the phone number to the ranger station closest to where we will stay in case of emergency. I don't know if we will have cell service or not."

"Yes, mom." Wyatt said in a dull voice. "We've been over this like a hundred times."

"I just want you to feel comfortable."

"Mom…. I've stayed at Robbie's house overnight dozens of times."

"Yes, but only one night at a time never an entire weekend and I was always close by if you needed me."

"I'll be okay, mom. I promise."

"And you won't give Ms. Barton any trouble?"

"No, I won't because she will ground me for the entire weekend until you get back if I do."

Sherry smiled, "Yes, she will."

"And she has your permission to take away my games, if I act up."

"Yes, she does." She laughed, "But that won't be a problem because you are a good boy and won't give her any hassles."

"Exactly." He grinned at her.

"Good."

Friday morning, Amy and Robbie came to pick up Wyatt.

Amy handed Sherry a small gift bag. "Here is a little something for your weekend. Open it later." She winked.

"I'm afraid to open it at all!" Sherry laughed.

They hugged and Sherry watched as they drove away. Wyatt had seemed eager for the weekend with Robbie, and she wondered if she had been holding on to him too tightly since Chris's death.

She looked down at the bag and walked inside. She opened it as soon as the door was shut and reached inside. A silky teddy emerged in her hand. Sherry laughed out loud. There was no way she would wear that thing, and it was completely impractical for a weekend in the woods. She carried it to her bedroom and shoved in a dresser drawer. She had to dig out her bathing suit, though. Mac had suggested she bring one along. Sherry couldn't imagine the water in any of the rivers being warm enough for swimming. She hoped maybe there would be a hot spring nearby since he hadn't been forthcoming about the location of the cabin. She folded her black one-piece swimsuit and closed her weekender bag. Then went to the kitchen to make a thermos of coffee for the road trip.

She was pouring the coffee into the thermos when Mac arrived. He knocked, then stepped inside. "Hello?"

She ran excitedly to the living room. "Hello," she smiled.

"All set?"

"I was just putting some coffee in a thermos for the drive."

Mac looked at her and smiled. "Honey, it is just a three-hour drive, and there are places to stop along the way."

"Well, you've been so secretive, I wasn't sure."

He laughed, "Well, now we won't have to stop."

"I'll take your bag to the car if you're packed."

"They are in there." She nodded to the bedroom.

Mac reemerged with her weekender bag and a smaller duffle bag and her purse.

"Three bags, really?"

"Well, again not knowing what to expect."

Mac shook his head and carried it all out to the car.

Sherry grabbed the coffee and her keys and headed out the door.

Mac looked up from the trunk of the car. "Are you sure you have everything you need?"

"Yes!" she called back, locking the door, and bouncing down the steps.

"Wonderful, ready for a perfect relaxing weekend?"

"I wouldn't oversell it." She laughed.

"You doubt me?"

"Not at all."

The drive was lovely. They arrived at a rental office and general store. Sherry got out and stretched her legs before walking into the store. The smells of maple syrup and apple cinnamon assaulted her as soon as she opened the door. It was as if someone had lit every fall scented candle in the store all at once except that it wasn't a candle. It was bushel baskets of apples, bouquets of cinnamon sticks and maple flavored everything from candy to syrup. In the back of the store, there were coolers and freezers with a variety of grocery items, from milk to steaks and an aisle of necessities, such as toothpaste, headache remedies and allergy medicines.

Mac sauntered over. "Need anything?"

"No, just browsing. It's good to know it is here though."

"Yes, it is quite handy. They close early at five this time of year."

"Can't blame them. It is probably getting close to the slow season for them."

"Shall we?" Mac nodded to the door.

Sherry noticed the bags he was holding. "You did some shopping."

"We needed something for dinner and breakfast tomorrow."

"True."

They got back in the car, took a left out of the parking lot, and drove up the mountain. Sherry noticed driveways with cabin numbers listed on a sign, but the trees were too dense for her to see the cabins, which she supposed was the point of coming up here, to get away and have some privacy.

Mac slowed the car and pulled into a driveway for cabin number eight. The driveway wound its way further up the mountain. Sherry thought it would be difficult to have to drive down this way in the snow. Finally, the driveway leveled out, and the trees opened to a beautiful A-frame cabin stood before them.

Sherry gasped, "Oh it's beautiful!"

Mac smiled, "It is pretty."

He handed her the key. "Wanna check it out?"

She smiled broadly, "Yeah!" She took the key and raced for the door with Mac trailing behind.

Sherry opened the door and stood for a moment, taking it all in. The back wall was glass with a view of the valley and another line of mountains with the famous blue haze that gave the Blue Ridge Mountains their name.

"Oh Mac, this view is amazing!"

He stood behind her, watching, admiring her excitement. "Yes, it is."

She turned to face him at the sound of his seductive voice. She giggled and threw her arms around him. "Thank you, this is already the perfect weekend."

He has her a long, gentle kiss. She felt the tension leave her shoulders, and she stepped closer to him. To her surprise, he pulled back.

"Let's unpack the car and get settled, shall we?"

She smiled, "Yes, let's do that."

She checked her phone. It had one bar, so she sent Amy a quick text to let her know they had arrived safely. Then she sat the phone on the table, determined not to touch it for the rest of the weekend.

Mac put the groceries away and double checked the kitchen to make sure they were well stocked for the weekend. Then he went outside onto the deck and checked the fire pit to see if it had enough firewood, and then turned on the hot tub which he intended to use soon. He had the entire weekend planned out in his head down to the last detail as if it were a mission. And essentially it was, it was a romantic mission rather than a military one but, he intended for it to be a success.

Sherry stepped out on the deck after exploring the rest of the cabin.

"A hot tub, oh that looks so inviting!"

"Yes, it does. Wanna change and try it out?" He grinned.

"Absolutely." she rushed back inside to dig her bathing suit out of her overnight bag. After changing, she looked at herself in the mirror. She should have brought a two piece; she looked like someone's grandmother in this one-piece.

She stepped out of the bathroom and froze. She wasn't prepared for Mac in nothing but swim trunks. Her heart leapt into her throat. She knew he was fit, but to see his muscles out in the open, she was speechless.

"You are so beautiful."

Sherry hadn't heard what he had said. She was too busy staring "Huh?"

Mac chuckled and walked over to her. "I said you are beautiful."

"I feel frumpy."

Mac laughed, "I assure you; you are anything but."

Heat flared in her body as Mac touched her. For him to be so close and her with nothing but a thin piece of fabric between them was almost more than she could stand. She thought he might kiss her and suggest they skip the hot tub but instead he gave her a longer look and then shifted gears completely.

"Come on. I have an entire weekend planned, and it starts with a glass of wine in the hot tub."

She gave him a tight smile and glanced past him at the bed. She had given little thought to the sleeping arrangements, and suddenly she was nervous. Why hadn't she thought about that? It has been so long since she had been with any man; she suddenly felt even more self-conscious.

She followed him out to the deck. He had wine and two glasses waiting.

"Here, let me help you." He held her hand as she stepped into the deliciously warm water.

Sherry sunk down immediately with just her shoulders peaking above the water and closed her eyes. The scenery was beautiful but frankly the hot water and the relaxing jets could have been anywhere, and it would have felt just as good.

Mac's voice broke into her thoughts. "Would you like a glass of wine?"

She opened one eye, "Hmm, yes." He smiled and handed it to her.

Sherry took a sip, then another, and then closed her eyes again. She felt Mac enter the water, but she didn't have the sense that he was sitting close to her. She smiled to herself. Thank God he wasn't being pushy and over affectionate. Should haven't had blamed him if he was, it was their first 'grown-ups only' weekend away from everyone and everything. It would be natural to want to spend as much time close to one another as possible. But this was heaven, and she was so grateful that Mac was giving her some space. Something cold touched her nose, and she opened her eyes. Small, light snow flurries were falling. The steam from the hot tub was thick in the air like the haze of the mountains. She turned to look at the sky.

Mac looked up at the dark cloud just coming over the mountain from the west. "The weather can change fast up here."

"No kidding, do you think we will get snowed in?"

"I doubt it. These flurries are too small to accumulate. The forecast had called for a chance of rain, but it will be worth checking it again."

"No rush." She smiled, looking up at the petite flakes as they drifted down around her.

After she had finished her glass of wine, Mac suggested they go in and have dinner.

Sherry went to the bedroom to change while Mac put on a robe and checked the status of the dry firewood.

When she was done, he quickly changed and returned to shoo her out of the kitchen.

"Just relax, you will not do any cooking this weekend."

"What?"

"You are always cooking for everyone else. This weekend I will cook for you."

She was impressed, "I didn't know you knew out to cook."

He donned an apron he found hanging in the pantry. "Prepare to be amazed by my culinary skills.

She laughed, "Okay, I can't wait."

She sat at the breakfast bar and drank more wine while watching Mac move about the kitchen. There was no talk of work, or soccer games or homework, and it felt so foreign and wonderful all at the same time.

"What is on the menu tonight that smells wonderful."

"It is nearly ready."

Mac set the plates on the counter and loaded them up. "Go sit at the table and I will bring it over."

"Are you sure there isn't anything I can do to help?"

"No." He smiled.

She sat at the table.

Mac brought over the plates, "For the lady, a pan seared trout with rosemary, roasted red potatoes and caramelized onions."

"Wow, this looks amazing."

"If the lady would like, I have a nice white wine to go with the fish."

She started to say no to the wine but changed her mind, "Yes, thank you."

Mac set his plate down and brought over a fresh glass of wine. When Mac was seated, he looked across the table at her.

"Before we begin, I believe it is customary to share something positive that happened in our day today. I will let you go first."

She smiled sweetly at him.

"Today was a positive day, because I got to spend it with you, just you."

He nodded, "Today was the best day of my life so far."

She sat, a little stunned.

"Try the fish. I'm interested to know what you think."

She took a bite, "Oh this is wonderful, I never knew trout could taste like this."

Mac let out a small sigh of relief and tasted his. He nodded his approval.

After the meal was finished, he insisted she relax on the sofa with a cozy blanket while he washed the dishes.

"Would you like a fire here or outside at the fire pit?"

"Here I think."

He walked over to the fireplace and struck a match. The kindling caught up immediately.

Mac waited to make sure the logs were caught up before joining her on the sofa.

"How are you doing with this, you okay?" He asked as he slid under the blanket and pulled her body close to his.

"This is wonderful."

"Okay, just checking."

"I guess I was more ready for a getaway than I thought. I felt a little guilty at first leaving Wyatt behind and having a weekend for myself. But you know what? I think I am over it. Wyatt is old enough to handle an entire weekend without me and if I'm honest, he is probably having the time of this life right now."

"You have nothing to feel guilty about and I can assure you Wyatt is just fine."

"I know, it is just hard to let go even a little bit."

"I can't imagine. This is your weekend and if you get homesick, we will pack up the car and go, no questions asked."

She laid with her back against the side of his chest and his arm about her. She smiled, even though he couldn't see it. "I know."

The next morning, Sherry woke from a chill. She opened her eyes. She was still on the sofa, and she was cold because Mac and just gotten up. He stoked the fire and then returned.

"Hey, sorry didn't mean to wake you."

"It's okay. Is the fireplace our only heat source?"

"No, I adjusted the thermostat as well, but it might take a while with these high ceilings."

"You're right." She snuggled down into the blanket and Mac crawled in next to her, putting his arm around her and wrapping her with warmth. His body threw off so much heat that she almost didn't need the blanket, besides the fact that she was still fully dressed.

She laid there listening to the sounds of Mac's breathing and closed her eyes. It was the most relaxed she had been in years.

An hour later, they were up, and Mac was cooking breakfast. She walked out onto the deck with a mug of coffee. The flurries had been just that, and there was only the faintest hint they had even fallen the day before. She looked out across the mountain and sighed. Sherry wished she had a view this nice every morning. She looked longingly at the hot tub, its water still and cold.

"Breakfast is ready."

She returned to the warmth of the cabin.

"Are we expecting company for breakfast?"

"No, why?"

"Because this is too much food for two people."

"You underestimate my love of pancakes." He grinned.

"Fair enough."

"I thought we might go on a fun hike today, nothing too strenuous, and you'll need the energy to stay warm."

"Oh, okay." She nodded.

She ate a few pancakes with local maple syrup and bacon.

"Is that all you're going to eat, no you have to have more than that." Mac placed two more pancakes on her plate and two sausage links along with apple slices.

"Are you kidding me?"

Mac pointed to her plate with his fork after taking another bite from his second stack of pancakes.

She looked at him in awe. "I didn't think anyone ate more than Wyatt; I guess I was wrong."

Mac nodded. "Breakfast is important."

"I see that." She laughed.

After breakfast was finished, Mac still insisted that he handle the dishes alone and sent her to put on sturdy boots for the hike.

When she returned, he had his daypack on and ready to go.

Hiking wasn't exactly her idea of relaxing, but she was willing to give it a try.

There was a trail just down the road from the cabin that led into the woods. They hiked until Mac suggested a lunch break at a waterfall.

"This is so beautiful." Sherry looked around, taking it all in.

"You think so?" Mac sat down and began unpacking their lunch.

"Oh yes, the evergreens, and waterfall, the air is so clean here." She turned around to look at the entire view. "I can't imagine a place more beautiful."

Mac stood up and walked over to stand next to her. He took her hand in his. "I love the way the sunlight dances on the water, and the way your eyes dance when you are happy. You say you can't imagine a place any more beautiful than this, and I can't imagine a woman more beautiful than you."

She stared up at him for a minute, "I think that is the most romantic thing anyone has ever said to me." Her voice was a whisper.

"Thank you, but I wasn't trying to be romantic. It is the truth." He leaned over and kissed her lightly. "Now, I'm sure you must be hungry."

Sherry would have given just about anything at that moment to forget the lunch and spend more time on that kiss.

"Come sit," he motioned to her a place where someone had created a seating area out of a fallen tree and some rocks.

"I brought roast beef sandwiches and some cheese and fruit. It is a simple meal, but I hope you like it."

She sat down next to him. "It sounds perfect."

They enjoyed their lunch and the view, and as they were finishing up a deer broke from the tree line to come drink from the pool of water fed by the waterfall.

"Oh." Sherry whispered softly, so as to not scare the deer away.

Mac put his hand out to motion for her to stay still.

They sat watching for several long minutes before the deer drank his fill, lifted his head, and sniffed the air. He looked in their direction but must have deemed them non-threatening because he slowly strolled away as if he were wishing them a good day.

Sherry let out the breath she had been holding. "That was amazing!"

"It was pretty special." Mac agreed. "Shall we?" He stood up and packed up the remains of their lunch.

"Sure, but can we walk back slowly? I hate for this to end."

"We can, and we can do this again tomorrow if you like."

"Yes, that would be wonderful."

The hike back to the cabin didn't give them an opportunity to see any more wildlife larger than a chipmunk. But Sherry enjoyed the hike just the same.

They returned to the cabin before dusk.

"Why don't we enjoy the hot tub before dinner?" Mac suggested.

"I thought you'd never ask." Sherry giggled, "Race you to the bedroom!"

Mac tossed the day pack aside and ran after her down the hall.

Sherry grabbed her swimsuit from the towel rack. "I win!"

"Every time." Mac gave her a wolfish grin and put his hands on her shoulders and kissed her deeply. "You want some help changing into that?" He asked, taking the swimsuit from her hand, and tossing it onto the bed.

Sherry's mind was reeling and before she decided what she do her mouth betrayed her and said, "Yes."

"Good." Mac said, kissing her neck and unbuttoning her shirt at the same time.

She let her hands work the buttons on his flannel shirt. Her body felt like it was on fire and when he had pushed her shirt down over her shoulders and toss it in the corner, she trembled slightly with excitement.

Hours later, Sherry laid buried deep in the down pillows and blankets with Mac snoring lightly beside her. She snuggled down deeper into the bed and hugged herself. She thought that she would feel more guilty at this moment. The moment she slept with another man other than Chris. But she didn't feel guilty at all. She felt warm, loved, and cared for. She had to bite her lip to keep from giggling with joy.

She rolled over and looked out the window into the darkness. It must have been near midnight; she couldn't see much, but the world felt still. There were no lights, no sounds of neighbors or traffic here. It might be disconcerting if Mac wasn't laid out next to her with enough muscles rippling over his body to make her feel safe in his arms. He stirred and reached out for her. She inched closer, and he put a protective arm around her. She drifted back to sleep with a smile.

CHAPTER TWENTY

M ac woke first. Looking over at Sherry deep in the covers to stay warm, he smiled and kissed her forehead before silently sliding out of bed. He found some wool socks, his flannel pajama pants and a t-shirt, then padded to the living room to stoke the fire. Mac checked the thermostat in the hallway. It read sixty degrees. The fire would change that in a few minutes. As he walked into the living room and looked out the wall of windows, he stopped in his tracks. He rubbed his eyes, thinking he wasn't fully awake yet. Everything was white; the sun reflecting off the snow was blinding.

"Oh no." he walked to the windows to make sure his eyes weren't playing tricks on him. He looked around outside. There was no way they were going to go home today. He hoped Sherry wasn't too upset. He knew he would not be mad about being stuck in a cabin with her for an extra day.

The phone in the kitchen rang. He hadn't even realized the thing worked.

"Hello?"

"This is Tobias. We met when you checked in."

"Yes, of course."

"Y'all okay up there?"

"Well, I just woke up, but I think we are fine. We've got plenty of dry wood for the fireplace and we are good on food for at least another day."

"Okay, if you can use the fireplace for heat, that will leave enough propane for hot showers and cooking."

"Thanks, we can do that. Any idea how long before the roads are cleared?"

"Well, VDOT will get to the main roads pretty quickly. They were treated last night. It's coming down the mountain that will be tricky. I have a contractor who comes, but to be honest, I haven't reached him yet."

"Okay, well, no rush here. Like I said, we have enough food and heat at the moment."

"It supposed to be in the fifties tomorrow, so most of this will probably melt before my contractor gets here to clear it, anyway."

"Sounds good."

"I'll check on you folks a little later. Might want to make sure you have your cell phones charged in case we lose power. So far things are good, but it only takes one idiot to hit a pole and the entire mountain will go down."

"Good advice, thanks."

"Dial zero on the phone if you need anything."

"Will do." Mac hung up and looked around. He thought he better double check the firewood situation and bring some more in warming up in the cabin before throwing onto the fire.

"Hey, what's going on? Did I hear a phone ringing?"

Mac turned and smiled to see Sherry standing there in one of his t-shirts, a pair of shorts and fuzzy socks.

"We got a little snow last night." He nodded to the window.

Sherry dragged her eyes away from Mac and looked outside.

Her eyes widened. "Oh, my god!" She ran over to the window and pressed her hands against the glass. "It is so beautiful." She whispered, her breath fogging up on the glass.

"I'm glad you think so, because I'm afraid we cannot leave today as planned."

She turned to face him; her heart skipped a beat. There were worse things than being snowed in with a guy who tested the limits of a t-shirt the way Mac did. She smiled.

"I'm okay with that, if you are." She sauntered towards him.

Mac grinned down at her, "I'm definitely okay with it." He reached out and pulled her in for a kiss. He broke away briefly, "You're not upset?"

"Why would I be upset about spending more time with you?"

"Oh no reason, it just that usually you get a little anxious about Wyatt and…."

Sherry stared up at him. "Wyatt! I completely forgot, oh my god, I'm a terrible mother!" Mac started laughing. "You are not a terrible mother. You are a mother; you are enjoying some much deserved 'me' time. Just call Amy and see if Wyatt can stay an extra night with Robbie. I'll call Kay and tell her we won't be in the office tomorrow as planned."

Sherry bit her thumb. She felt so guilty because she was glad, she didn't have to go back to the real world today. She grabbed her cell phone from the table and called Amy.

Mac walked to the bedroom and called Kay. When he was done, he went to go check on the wood supply. Sherry was still on the phone.

By the time he had the fire burning briskly and plenty of wood brought in from outside and the dry wood rack resupplied from the lean-to near the tree line, Sherry was off the phone and making coffee.

"Everything alright with Wyatt?" He asked, rubbing his arms, and stamping his feet.

"Oh yeah, he is having a blast, and Amy said he could stay as long as necessary.

"Good, Kay said she would swing by and pick him up if Robbie was going to be in school on Monday and she and Todd could take over his education at the office."

"No, Robbie will be home from school on Monday so they can hang out at his house. But that was sweet of Kay to offer."

"I'll text her and let her know."

"Is there anything I can do to help?" She asked, looking at the fire.

"Well, wanna help me make breakfast?"

"Sure, what should we have?"

"How about eggs and bacon?" Mac headed for the kitchen.

"That sounds great. Do we have enough food?"

"We have enough for another day, after that…., how to you feel about rabbit stew?"

"I hope you're joking."

"Partially."

"Actually, tomorrow will be warm enough to melt all of this and we should be able to get down the mountain just fine."

Sherry nodded but said nothing.

"What's wrong?"

"Nothing, I'm just not in a big hurry to get back to the real world."

Mac came over to hug her. "I know what you mean, this has been wonderful."

"I hate for it to end. I know that sounds selfish, but I can't help it."

"It's not selfish to want to keep something like this alive, but I promise we can come back."

She smiled and nodded. "Now, give me something to do. Can I chop the onion for you?"

"You sure can." He slid the onion and knife over to her while he put the bacon in the iron frying pan.

"After breakfast, how about we enjoy the view of the snow from the hot tub?" Mac suggested.

"Absolutely."

"And I don't think you need that one-piece swimsuit this time." He winked at her.

She swatted at him and laughed. But he was right. There wasn't anything of her he hadn't seen last night. Still, she wasn't sure if she was ready to parade around naked in front of him.

They took their breakfast to the sofa and table in front of the fireplace.

"What should we do today?" Mac asked as he took their plates to the kitchen.

"Do?" Sherry followed him. "What do you mean, certainly you don't want to try to hike in this?"

He looked out the window and then at Sherry. Her expression was enough for him to not suggest just that.

He laughed, "Okay, come on, time for the hot tub." He took her by the hand and led her to the bedroom and handed her a robe, then left.

Sherry looked at the door and then at the robe. She took off her clothes and put on the robe he was expecting her to come out wearing her swimsuit. She planned to surprise him. Sherry walked out to the living room to see Mac already in the hot tub. He was deep in the water, so she couldn't tell if he was wearing his trunks or not. She took a deep breath and stepped outside and came to stand in front of him at the edge of the tub.

Mac sat up at attention, staring up at her. His mouth went dry.

Sherry smiled down at him and slowly let the robe slip down. She watched Mac swallow hard. Sherry tried not to let him see she felt self-conscious. She laid the robe across a chair and then stepped down into the tub.

Mac sat frozen, watching her every movement until she was submerged up to her shoulders in the water.

"You are the most beautiful woman I have ever seen." He sat still staring at her.

Sherry didn't know why she was blushing, he'd seen more of her than anyone other than Chris. She looked away.

Mac reached over and lifted a hand to touch her chin and gently turn her face back to him.

"I need to tell you something."

Her brows knitted together. She wondered what could be so serious that he had to announce it.

He held her shoulders, slowly drawing circles on her skin.

"Sherry Ann Davis, I am irrevocably and completely in love with you." He took a deep breath, "I can't imagine what life would ever be without you and I can't remember what my life was before I met you, but I know it was a dark place and I never want to go back." Mac stood up, bringing her with him.

"I love you." He repeated and then kissed her.

She stared up at him, searching his eyes for anything that would tell her he was lying to her, but she couldn't. She saw his sincerity and her heart felt like it might burst.

"I love you, James McIntyre." She smiled up at him.

"Ian"

She looked at him puzzled, "What?"

"My middle name is Ian."

"Okay then, I love you, James Ian McIntyre." She laughed, "Your parents were serious with the naming business, weren't they?"

He laughed, "Yeah, James was my father's name, Ian was my maternal grandfather's name. I never had a chance." He laughed with her.

They sunk back down in the water. Sherry sat with her back to Mac's chest and his arms wrapped around her. "Let's stay here forever." He whispered.

"Yes, let's do that." She agreed and closed her eyes.

Suddenly, the jets stopped in the tub. Mac looked up at the sky. It looked like more storm clouds were topping the mountain.

"The power must be out. Come on, we better get inside before we freeze to death." He grabbed her hand, and they ran naked into the cabin.

Sherry was already freezing. "Brrr, oh that got cold fast."

Mac steered her to the fireplace. "Stand here and put this on. He brought the blanket from the back of the sofa. "I'll be right back."

"Where are you going?"

"Just stay there."

Mac jogged to the bedroom and got dressed. He grabbed some clothes for Sherry so she would not have to leave the warmth of the fireplace.

"Here you go." He handed her the clothes."

"Thank you." She smiled as she looked at the selection. He had remembered her favorite fuzzy socks.

"The house might get a little cold because the furnace won't be able to kick on. The stove should still work because it is gas. So, we will be okay."

She smiled at him. "I'm not worried."

"You're not?" He was a little surprised since she was a city girl and had little experience in the woods or the mountains.

"No, it isn't much different from a hurricane. In fact, it is a little better because we don't have to worry about the wind or flooding."

He smiled at her. "You're such a good sport."

"Are you kidding? I had this all planned, you know. I called Tobias and had him cut the power." She laughed.

He came over laughing with her. "So, it was your plan all along to bring me here and seduce me?"

"Absolutely."

He lifted her and carried her over to the sofa. "And now you are going to take advantage of me?"

She giggled as he kissed her. "Yes."

"Good."

He kissed her over, and over, then he pulled back. "Well, that should keep you warm for a while." And he stood up.

"Wait, where are you going?"

"I need to check on a few things."

She sat up slowly, watching him in disbelief.

"What things?"

"I'm going to put the cover over the hot tub, double check the wood supply, and maybe walk down to the end of the drive to see if anyone has plowed the road yet."

"Are you in some kind of hurry to leave?" She asked from the sofa.

"No, but I would feel better knowing our options if we had to get out of here in a hurry."

She just shook her head, "Carry on then." She waved to him to go about his self-appointed tasks.

She went over to the bookcase and browsed through the selection of books. There was quite a variety of field guides, local history, several books by local authors, and several of the classics. She opted for a murder mystery by a local author and laid down on the sofa to read it. Sherry supposed it was in Mac's training or nature to want to make sure everything was safe and secure.

An hour later, Mac returned.

"Well, Tobias was right. It was only a matter of time before someone hit a power pole. There is already someone on the scene to fix it so we shouldn't be without power for long."

"I told you I wasn't worried about it. Wyatt and I went two weeks without power once after a hurricane. You get used to it." She said, putting the book on the table.

"I see."

She stood up and walked over to him unzipping his jacket, "Now if you don't need to go outside and build us any sort of secondary cabin in case this one fails, or hunt rabbit for dinner, why don't you come over here and join me on the sofa."

He chuckled at her new found bravado. "Okay."

She pulled him down to the sofa. "You sit there."

He nodded, "Okay," waiting for whatever was coming next.

"And I'll lay here with my head in your lap."

"Sounds good." Mac smiled.

Sherry sank down next to him, reaching over to grab the book and laid her head in his lap, and picked up where she left off.

Mac sat there, staring down at her. "Excuse me."

She tilted the book down. "Yes?"

"What are you doing?"

"Reading a splendid book."

"Not what I had in my mind when you invited me onto the sofa."

"Hmm, really?"

"Really." He said gruffly.

"Well, what are you going to do about it?" She playfully challenged.

"I'll show you." He slowly reached for the book and took it from her.

She watched him intently, then laughed when he opened the book and read to her.

"Oh Mac, I was only joking." She reached up for the book.

"No, ma'am." He lifted it out of her reach. "If you want to read a book, we will read a book."

And he sat reading to her until she fell asleep at the soothing sound of his voice.

"Wake up sleeping beauty,"

Sherry opened one eye. "What?"

"Are you getting hungry? I've cooked dinner."

"Dinner?" Sherry bolted upright. "Oh no, have I been asleep all afternoon?"

"Pretty much."

"Oh Mac, I'm so sorry."

"For what?" That is exactly what I wanted you to do this weekend. Relax and get some rest. Recharge your batteries." He smiled sweetly.

"Let me just freshen up a bit."

"Absolutely."

She went to the bedroom and combed her hair, and then to the bathroom to brush her teeth. When she returned, Mac had the table set with wine and candles.

"Is the power still out?"

"No, I just thought the candles were a nice touch."

She smiled. "Yes, they are."

Mac insisted on serving her.

"This smells delicious."

"I stopped by the store when I took a walk earlier. I thought roast duck with root vegetables would be a pleasant change of pace."

Sherry took a bite. "It is heavenly." She looked at him for a moment. "Wait a minute, I just realized something."

"What?"

"All this time, I've been cooking my rushed and uninspired dishes," she pointed down at the duck on her plate, "which pales in comparison to this, and you never said a word about being able to cook like this."

"I would argue that your meals are wonderful and that this isn't anything but a roast chicken but another name."

They both laughed.

"And I have a special treat for dessert." He grinned.

"Are you serious, Mac? You are too much."

"Oh, you have seen anything yet, my dear." He winked.

When they had finished, he presented her with a red velvet cupcake with vanilla frosting.

"Oh, my gosh!" She laughed, "How in the world did you manage to find a cupcake up here and in the middle of a snowstorm?"

"Don't underestimate that general store. They have many things, and you can special order just about anything they don't have on hand."

"So, they have special order cupcakes?" She admired the artistry in the decorations.

"Well, it just so happens that Tobias's wife is a wonderful baker."

"Really, and how did you know that red velvet and vanilla were my favorite?"

"Wyatt told me." He smiled.

"Oh, I see. What is the occasion? I mean, this is a very special cupcake."

"I thought it was romantic, and I wanted this weekend to be as perfect as possible." He stepped over to where she was sitting at the table and knelt on one knee.

Sherry looked at him, confused for a moment, until he pulled the red velvet box out of his pocket. She gasped.

He opened it and presented her with a beautifully cut princess diamond.

"Sherry, will you make my life complete by agreeing to be my wife?"

She looked at him, stunned. Her mouth went dry. She wanted to ask him if he was serious, but she looked around the room and realized he was very serious.

He waited patiently.

"I…. Yes!"

Mac sat staring at her for a moment, thinking he must have misheard her. "Yes?"

"Yes, James Ian McIntyre, I will marry you."

Mac started breathing again as he slipped the ring on her finger.

"It fits perfectly." She smiled in amazement.

"Do you like it?"

"It is gorgeous!" She said, admiring it with tears of joy rolling down her cheeks. She looked up at Mac and his eyes were misty as well.

"I can't believe you said yes." He smiled, "You could so much better than me, but I promise I will spend every day of the rest of my life, making sure I am the man you deserve."

Sherry cried a little, "Oh Mac, you are my soulmate, there could be no one but you."

He held her tight for a long time, just breathing in her scent and feeling her heart beat close to his.

When she stepped back, she smiled. "I'm not the only person you made happy today. Wait until we tell Wyatt."

Mac looked a little sheepish. "Listen, I hope you don't get mad, but he kinda already knows."

"What?"

"Well, Wyatt is a big part of this, and I knew it wouldn't only be asking you to commit to me, but him as well. So, I sort of asked him for his blessing before I asked you."

She looked up at him, surprised. "You did?"

"Yeah, he even helped me pick out the ring." He searched her face for any hint that he might have messed things up. "He didn't know when I was going to propose to you, though, because I wasn't exactly sure myself. But this weekend was just so perfect, I couldn't wait another minute."

She stood just staring at him in disbelief. Just when she didn't think he could be more caring or perfect, he does something as sweet as asking her son for his blessing.

"Oh, Mac!" She threw her arms around his neck and kissed him passionately.

Mac took a step back, not expecting this reaction from her, and scooped her up in his arms.

"I love you, Sherry."

"I love you."

"Let's go home."

She nodded. They packed up everything as quickly as they could and Mac skillfully guided his Dodge Hellcat through the snow and slush to the general store, where he turned in their key and grabbed them some coffee for the road. Sherry felt like she couldn't stop smiling for the entire trip. So many thoughts were rushing through her head.

"What kind of wedding should we have?" She asked, turning to Mac.

Mac kept his eyes on the road. Traffic wasn't heavy the roads weren't completely free of ice in the shady spots. "What kind would you like?"

"I don't think a large traditional wedding is necessary. I think I'd like to have a few close friends maybe, but something more intimate with us and Wyatt, of course."

"Wyatt has to be there. He is going to be my best man."

She smiled and reached over and squeezed his hand.

"Okay, so something small and private. Now the big question is when?" She bit her lip, waiting for his answer.

"I'd marry you today, but I'll assume you need a little more time to put it together."

"I just had the craziest thought." She giggled.

Mac smiled. Her joy was infectious. "What?"

"What if we got married on Christmas Eve?"

"Really, that soon?"

"Why are you getting cold feet already?"

"No, I just thought you might want some more time to plan things with your girlfriends, is all. I'm perfectly happy stopping at a justice of the peace on the way home and tying the knot." He laughed.

"I think two weeks is enough time." She sank back into her seat. "We need a venue and I wonder who we could get to officiate on such short notice?"

"I know a couple of boat captains, if it comes to that." He laughed.

But she only half heard what he said. She had a million things running through her mind. He smiled. If he knew his girl, she'd have the whole thing planned down to the last detail before they ever got home.

CHAPTER TWENTY-ONE

"**G**ood morning, I'm glad to see you made it back safe and sound." Kay greeted Sherry Tuesday morning as she walked in, followed by Todd.

"Thank you, it's good to be back." Sherry smiled.

"Well, come in and tell me all about it when you get a chance."

Sherry waited a few minutes before making coffee. She went about the task quietly while Kay was clicking away on her keyboard. Once the coffee was done, she poured them each a cup and carried one over to Kay's desk. She made sure she handed it to her with her left hand silently showing off her engagement ring.

Kay was slow to drag her eyes away from her computer screen. Sherry shifted her weight and made a small noise to get Kay's attention.

"Oh, I'm sorry, Sherry I...." Kay turned to accept the coffee and saw the ring. She squealed, "Oh my god!" She quickly took the coffee and sat it down hard on the desk, spilling a little. "What? When?"

Sherry giggled. "It's gorgeous, isn't it?" She admired the ring for the hundredth time.

Kay jumped up and came around the desk to hug her. "Sit down and tell me everything!" She walked over and closed the door. "Was there really a snowstorm?"

Sherry laughed, "Yes, of course there was really a snowstorm."

Kay sat down next to her and took her hand to look at the ring more closely.

"Oh, Sherry I am so happy for you." Kay hugged her again. "What did Wyatt say?"

"Wyatt helped him pick out the ring." Sherry couldn't stop beaming.

"Really, oh that Mac is smooth."

"Yes, he even asked for Wyatt's blessing. Wasn't that sweet?"

"He is full of surprises."

"I know. Did you know he can cook? I mean, really cook." Sherry feigned a swoon, "He refused to let me do anything all weekend, and he cooked these fabulous meals."

Kay was smiling just as much as Sherry. "No, I didn't know that. Oh, he sounds perfect!"

A thought flashed through Sherry's mind, "Kay, this isn't weird for you, is it? I didn't mean….,"

Kay held up her hand. "No, this is not weird. I am over the moon for you! For both of you. I am so glad you both found happiness." Kay squeezed Sherry's hand. "When's the big day?"

Sherry took a deep breath. "Christmas Eve."

Kay sat stunned. "You mean this Christmas Eve."

Sherry bit her lip and nodded. "Can you help me?"

"Of course, I will help you; I'd be offended if you didn't ask for my help."

"Thank you." Sherry felt tears sting her eyes, "You're the best person in the entire world!"

Kay got misty-eyed as well, "So what kind of wedding are you planning?"

"Some small and intimate, you and Ethan, Amy and her family, Wyatt is going to be best man."

"What about your parents?"

I called my mom last night. They won't be able to be here. They are going on a sailing cruise for Christmas."

"What about a venue?"

"I don't have one." Sherry looked down at her hands. "Can you help me with that?"

"You better believe it!" Let me get my journal. Kay got up to retrieve her calendar that she insisted on using, even though Sherry had set her schedule and contacts up on the computer for her.

"Okay, I'll go get my binder!" Sherry jumped up and opened the door just as Mac was getting off the elevator.

He smiled at her and walked over. "You tell her?"

Sherry nodded excitedly.

"Is she is full planning mode?"

"Yep." Sherry laughed.

"Well, I see no work with be done today."

"Hush up and tend to your half of the ceremony." She teased as she grabbed her binder from the desk.

Mac laughed and disappeared down the hall.

Sherry rejoined Kay, and they went to work at the conference table.

Wyatt came by at lunch.

"Hi mom, wanna have lunch together?"

Kay stepped out of her office on her way to somewhere.

"Hello Wyatt."

"Hello Ms. Dandridge."

"Sherry glanced at her computer screen. "Where are you going? You have a meeting at two."

"Yes, I know. I'm just going out for a bit."

Sherry looked around, "Where's Todd?"

"I don't need Todd holding my hand."

Wyatt took out his phone and texted Todd secretly, then pocketed it again.

Kay turned her attention back to Wyatt.

"What do you think about your mom and Mac?"

Wyatt smiled widely. "I think it's awesome!"

"You do?" Kay asked sweetly.

"Yeah, it will be the best Christmas ever! I'm getting a new father for Christmas."

Kay smiled and then looked at Sherry, who sat stunned. Wyatt had been happy when they got home and she told him that Mac had asked her to marry him, but he hadn't put it on these terms before.

Todd appeared, "Ms. Dandridge, do you need me to take you someplace?"

Kay sighed. "I swear you all have me bugged or something. Is there some sort of secret GPS tracker on me?" She looked down at her clothes.

"No ma'am, we are just good at our jobs."

"I need to run a few errands."

"Excellent, I'll be happy to drive you."

Kay led the way to the elevator, and Todd looked over his shoulder and gave Wyatt a wink.

Once they were gone, Sherry looked at Wyatt. "Did you text Todd?"

Wyatt grinned, "Yeah. Are you mad?"

Sherry grinned back, "No. Come around here and sit with me and we'll have lunch, and you can tell me what you have been up to this morning."

Thanks to Kay, Amy and Mac, the wedding had a venue, a justice of the peace, tuxedos for Mac, Wyatt, and Ethan. Dresses for Sherry, Kay, and Amy; They planned a reception at Kay and Ethan's with a larger crowd.

Sherry had found the perfect dress by chance. It was a simple winter white sheath. In a boutique, the owner/designer Penelope Curtis had suggested a strand of pearls and teardrop pearl earrings. She could also provide dresses for Amy and Kay.

Ms. Curtis, or Penn as she insisted Sherry call her, had a friend in the flower business and could help with the floral arrangements. The flower business turned out to be an entire garden center, but still Sherry could order a bouquet and Kay ordered flowers for her house for the reception to add to the incredibly large Christmas tree she had in the living room in front of the double windows.

The ceremony was a simple affair at Kay's house in the side yard, under a tent to keep the chill of the December out. Sherry had nearly cried at the sight of Wyatt in his tuxedo, standing next to Mac looking like mirror images of each other.

Mac nearly forgot his vows. He was so in awe of how beautiful Sherry looked in her dress with a bouquet of garden roses, pincushion flowers, larkspur, rosemary and eucalyptus in a beautiful hue of white, green, blue and violet. Her hair was swept up in a twist with a few smaller flowers instead of a veil.

Kay and Amy both cried silently throughout the ceremony. Wyatt stood beaming as Mac placed the wedding band on his mom's finger.

Once the rings had been exchanged and the kiss shared, the little wedding party made their way to Kay's living room. Candles were lit, poinsettias and greenery graced every surface possible. The Christmas tree was lit and dominated the room. The dining room was transformed into a buffet with more candles and greenery on the table.

Sherry looked around the house, joy welling up in her eyes.

"Oh Kay, this is all so beautiful."

Kay came up next to her and kissed her cheek, "Not as beautiful as you, you'll be lucky if Mac can keep his hands off you for the entire reception."

Sherry laughed, "He looks good, doesn't he?"

"Yes, he does." Kay said, glancing over at Mac and Ethan on the other side of the room.

Wyatt was looking a little lost, standing off to the side. Sherry pulled herself away from Kay, "Wyatt, honey, are you okay?"

"Yes, I'm fine."

Sherry sensed he wasn't being completely honest. "Why don't we go over here and talk for a minute."

Wyatt nodded and followed her into the next room.

"Sit down sweety," she patted the space on the cushion next to her. "Tell me what's on your mind."

"I don't know." He shrugged.

"Are you having second thoughts about me marrying Mac?"

He looked up wide-eyed, "No, I love Mac. I want him to be my new dad and I don't want you to be alone."

"Okay, then what is it."

"I'm not sure, I'm happy and everything, but a little sad too."

"Because you think that replacing your dad with Mac while exciting is also a betrayal?"

Wyatt concentrated on the floor, "Yeah." He whispered.

"I know exactly how you feel. I felt that way too for a long time."

He looked up, "You did?"

She nodded, "I did. But you know what? Loving Mac doesn't mean you love your dad any less and don't you think your dad would want you to have someone to help you grow up so you don't have to do it alone, especially all that 'guy stuff'." She smiled using the term Mac used when he and Wyatt had some alone time to talk about who knows what?

He looked up into her eyes. "Yes. So, it is okay to love them both?"

"Absolutely!"

Wyatt smiled. "Okay."

There was a soft knock at the door. Sherry and Wyatt both turned to find Mac standing there.

"Is everything alright?" He asked gently.

Sherry looked at Wyatt and raised an eyebrow.

Wyatt smiled at Sherry and then at Mac. "Yeah, everything is great!"

Mac smiled, "Good, who wants cake?"

"Me!" Wyatt jumped up.

"Okay, well let's go". Mac smiled down at Wyatt, then looked over his shoulder at Sherry.

She nodded. Everything was fine. They walked back to the dining room, with their arms around one another and Wyatt ahead of them.

The reception guests cheered the little family as they came into the room.

The End

ABOUT THE AUTHOR

Lynn Story lives in southeastern Virginia, a region that is known by several names, Tidewater, Hampton Roads, and the 757. Her Gates Point series is based on the Tidewater area and you may recognize some familiar names and places if you've ever lived in or visited the area.

Lynn enjoys writing about people and their relationships and prefers sweet stories with just a dash of heat.

She shares her coastal home with her husband and three cats. They enjoy spending time in the great outdoors, as well as book